A Bad Man Is Easy to Find

M.J. VERLAINE

A BAD MAN IS
EASY TO FIND

ST. MARTIN'S PRESS

New York

DESIGN BY JUDITH A. STAGNITTO

Library of Congress Cataloging-in-Publication Data

Verlaine, M.J.
    A bad man is easy to find / M.J. Verlaine.
      p.   cm.
    ISBN 0-312-02920-9
    I. Title.
    PS3572.E64B34   1989   89-4089
    813'.54—dc 19

First Edition

10 9 8 7 6 5 4 3 2 1

To
Jerrett and Cort

Contents

Warm thanks and deep
respect to my editor,
Michael Denneny.

A BAD MAN IS
EASY TO FIND

A BAD MAN IS EASY TO FIND

"DON'T WORRY ABOUT love," Aunt Sophie always told Ruth Ann. "Don't worry money, don't worry his family, don't worry looks, all right? But you know what you should worry? Above all, you must find a good man. A *good man*, Baby Ruth. Who will take care of you and adore the children and has insurance and doesn't drink or smack you or go around places at night. And if by chance he might also be a little humorous and maybe can dance without stepping on your knees and sometimes comes home with a flower or a bag of candy, that's nice and please God that's what I'm praying for you, darling. But always remember it's all extras, like the radio in a car. You buy a new car, you don't buy for the radio. You buy for the car. You know what I'm talking?"

"I want a husband on a big white pony," said Ruth Ann. She was five, sitting at the kitchen table making

1

doodles. "He has a hat like Peter Pan, and then he would save me from pirates."

"Take your Uncle Max," Aunt Sophie went on, hacking away on her great butcher's block table (on wheels, the most spectacular piece of furniture, by general repute, in all of Flatbush). She spent a sizable fraction of her waking hours mincing and slicing on that table, yet all her cooking came out slimy and gushy. Her meat was soft as a blintz. You'd think at least you'd get a salad out of so much chopping.

"Let's face it, your Uncle Max is not going to win the Mr. America muscles contest. And popularity? Your Uncle Max? I hate to tell you how many nice people aren't speaking to him because of remarks he passed which, God forgive me for saying such a thing, his mouth should fall off instead. But you tell me the hour of the day of the week, and I'll tell you where Max is. In the office, in the subway, in the bathroom, you should excuse the honesty. Not *in the tavern*, like some Irish, so his poor wife doesn't know to put the roast in now or two hours ago. Not *in some hotel with a chippy*, God strike me down for ever thinking such a thought. A good man, your Uncle Max. *Sound*, like a toaster that never breaks down. So maybe now and then he could be a little more cultured. So he isn't. But you won't quote me, darling."

"I want a husband who plays football," said Ruth Ann at the age of eleven, having skipped second and fourth grades and advanced into junior high school. She still made doodles, on special doodle paper Aunt Sophie kept on hand for Ruth Ann's visits. "And I might be his favorite cheerleader."

"Get all the football players out of your system now," Aunt Sophie advised. "Now is the time to be romantic and go on dates with a big handsome boy like a football player, or maybe someone from the yachting set so you could see the inside of a country club and have one of those drinks with a slice fruit on the side of the glass that the Gentiles invented because a little wine on a holiday isn't good enough for them. And you'll go to all the proms, because you're the prettiest little darling in Flatbush and who could resist you? Could I? Could your Uncle Max? Even your brother, as wild as an Indian, even he loved you so much that he was finally willing to kiss Great-Aunt Esther after you did it first to show him he wouldn't get poisoned."

"Bill Talbot can resist me."

"I don't know the name. Who is he?"

"He's the most excellent piece of merchandise in the eighth grade. And he doesn't know I'm breathing."

Aunt Sophie chopped harder. "I don't know," she said after a bit, "but at eleven it seems to me a girl should be meeting her little girlfriends to share crayons or play puppets and not be telling their aunt that a boy is a piece of merchandise."

Ruth Ann giggled.

"But so what, darling, because you're young and you're cute and you're smart, and now is when to enjoy it. Because there will Come a Time. And when the Time Comes, you must find a good man and give up All Hope of Romance. Don't I know? Am I eleven?"

"Why will a time come when I have to give up all hope of romance?"

"Because romance isn't good for women. You know who it's good for? Men. That's what the handsomeness is for, and the running around, and the taverns and hotels. That's so men can be lovers for the rest of their lives. You marry a romantic man, you'll never know where he is, because every other woman in the world will be feeding him straight lines, like Mr. Cary Grant from the movies.

You find yourself a husband like your father or your Uncle Max, so you can die together in the same bed."

"I want a husband who will read me poetry aloud," said Ruth Ann, doodling, fourteen then, and so bright that her teachers felt stingy when they gave her straight A's on her report cards. "She has the most amazing energy," Miss Fogarty wrote in the Comments space, trying to improve on the drab commendation of the letter grade. (Teachers: *Never* do this to a child.) "What does this mean?" Ruth Ann's mother had asked, feeling strict. "'Energy'? Why doesn't she say how neat you look, when Bernice Fogelberg runs around in clothes I don't know where her mother finds them, maybe they're having sales in some garbage can. Why isn't there something written here about the most amazing ironing that I do, so I could show your Aunt Sophie and she could be proud for once? *'Energy'*?"

"Aunt Sophie is proud of me without report cards," said Ruth Ann hotly.

"Good thing they don't give grades for manners and showing respect for your mother," said Ruth Ann's mother. "Because I'd hate to see your average go down."

"I'm going to Aunt Sophie's."

Aunt Sophie's was a refuge on afternoons before Ruth Ann's brother and father got home, when her mother's survey expanded and the two men took some heat off the girl. Aunt Sophie's remained a safe place even after college, when Ruth Ann moved to Manhattan and Flatbush was no longer the Whole World but a remote corner of it. Ruth Ann's friends went to the Hamptons to stave off the rolodex blues; Ruth Ann went to Aunt Sophie's and doodled.

"Maybe you should call your mother while you're here," Aunt Sophie would say when Ruth Ann arrived.

"Like the conference calls you have at the office, my Baby Ruth who is such an executive."

"I called her just before I came," Ruth Ann would reply. Indeed, she always had—so she and Aunt Sophie could have the time to themselves. Aunt Sophie knew this, and felt guilty that they were closing ranks against her own sister. Once, Ruth Ann couldn't reach her mother in time and came to Flatbush ready to lie when Aunt Sophie suggested she make the call. No sooner had Ruth Ann stepped into the apartment than Aunt Sophie, wise as three Solomons, read in Ruth Ann's face the panic and determination and the lying all ready to go. That visit Aunt Sophie said nothing about telephones.

Instead, they talked about Ruth Ann's love life, and about how she should maybe give up romance and find a good man.

"I don't think there are any," said Ruth Ann, constructing an elaborate doodle of Venice at dawn.

"Your Uncle Max, however much he may look a little like a toadstool with whooping cough, is—"

"Not anymore, I mean. The era of finding good men may be over."

"In Manhattan, of course, darling. But here in The Neighborhood there are many wonderful boys who would love a girl like you, twenty-four and so nice."

"I'm twenty-eight, Aunt Sophie."

"But you look nineteen, sweetheart, and I took an average. So. Who are you seeing?"

Ruth Ann added a gondolier to her doodle. "Don."

"No last name?" asked Aunt Sophie, inspecting a cleaver.

"His last name's Minetti."

"Italian." Aunt Sophie sighed. "What's wrong, darling? There were no Polish available?"

"He's just a lover, Aunt Sophie. I'm not going to marry him."

Aunt Sophie laid down her cleaver, steadied herself with both hands on the counter, and turned to Ruth Ann. "Sweetheart, all these years we've been having our little talks, and can I tell you something private? Just between us? When I hear you speak about love as if it was something you order on a restaurant menu, I feel my heart have a little attack, and I worry about who would cook Max's dinner when he comes home from work because I'm killed somewhere in a hospital bed."

"Aunt Sophie, I know you want me to find a good man—"

"Now we're talking!" Aunt Sophie bent over the beef, the potatoes, the cabbage and carrots, soon to be boiled to death.

"But nobody believes in good men anymore. They're not good, they're . . . I don't know. Smart, or efficient, or something. You don't know the men these days. They don't want to be good."

"Can I tell you who's good?"

"Please do."

"I love the way you talk, darling. It's college in every word. Meanwhile this lovely Mrs. Tarlow moved into the next building, and there she was in the A & P and couldn't reach the last box of her size of Brillo, so I got it for her, and we struck up a conversation, and guess what she has!"

"An unmarried son."

"No wonder you skipped two grades. Her boy Robert is a marvelous doctor who somehow got to be twenty-nine without being married, and could I remind you what we'd all save in doctor bills? He's with New York Hospital and comes home every week for Friday, and I hear he's very nice and maybe I could give Mrs. Tarlow your telephone number and he could call. Because one thing I know is Luigi Ronzoni is not coming home to *his* mother for dinner and how come I know he's not a doctor?"

"Don Minetti. And he's an elevator technician."

"I'm sorry, darling, but I forgot to bring along my dictionary of *goyishe* professions."

"He installs elevators."

"Well, no wonder you would prefer him to a doctor. Everyone wants an elevator installer in the family. Think of all the free hammers you could get."

"Aunt Sophie—"

"Maybe he's good with plumbing?"

"Aunt Sophie, *no*."

"What no?"

"No blind dates. No unmarried sons. That's Flatbush, not Manhattan. I don't have to dance with just anyone who asks." Ruth Ann began a new doodle, a map of England. She wanted to see how many places she could name.

"So where did you meet this one?"

"Why do you ask questions when you know the answers will upset you?"

"Try me."

"I met him on the street."

"You're right, darling, I'm upset."

"If you met him, you wouldn't go on like this. They can't all be Jewish."

"Their god is Jewish. So why are they Italian?"

"Come to think of it, if you met him, you *would* go on like this. You'd condescend to him, and mention things he hasn't heard of, and—"

"Who told you I would do such a thing?"

"Because that's what *his* family did when *I* went there for dinner!"

And Sophie did a little sideswiping with a grater. She was not unpleased.

Ruth Ann's friends were no more enthusiastic about Don Minetti than Aunt Sophie was, though for a number of different reasons.

"You're taking roughneck chic too far," said Boise. "And that's all I have to say." No, it wasn't. "Because when you consider all the places in which he is *out* of place, and all the ceremonies of life with which he is almost certainly *ill-equipped to deal* . . . and did everyone notice how beautifully I rendered that last bit? Because —"

"He's cute," said Teresa, Italian herself. Every so often she would ask Ruth Ann to show her Don's photograph, taken, in typical Don style, at a four-shots-for-two-quarters booth in an amusement arcade. Teresa would gaze upon the picture for a long while and say nothing; but as she handed it back she would smile.

"That's not even the issue," Ruth Ann began.

"Oh, my young friend," murmured Boise, staring at her. "That's *always* the issue."

"He's cute," Teresa repeated. "But enough is enough. Think of status." This was Teresa's credo. A librarian, she was obsessed with the procedures and hazards of the social order, especially as it obtained in the New York Public Library system. Half her conversation dealt with strategies in Developing Credibility.

Kathleen said nothing. Sometime in her teens she decided that sex, politics, and how you came out on your photographer's contact sheets were three things in which only one opinion counted: your own. She had, justly, nothing to say.

"He rescued me," said Ruth Ann.

"That calls for thank you," said Teresa. "Not devotion."

Ruth Ann and Don had met on Sixth Avenue in the Forties, when a street loony whose pants were falling down cornered Ruth Ann in the arcade under a construction site. Don, directing the installation of the elevators, happened to be leaving work just then. He pushed the crazy away, led Ruth Ann back into the sun, and asked her about twenty times if she was all right. She was crying; she tried to laugh but this ghastly sound came out instead. He was looking at her with intrigued, bewildered eyes, as if he wanted to take her in his arms and say, "There, there," but feared that anything to do with men would make her feel worse. So he took her hand and led her a few steps inside somewhere and she was actually shaking, absentminded—she forgot where the world was, momentarily—and imagined herself on the evening news, a victim, a very zapped victim assaulted by microphones.

When Ruth Ann pulled herself together, thinking of Aunt Sophie cooking and advising while she was doodling—for some reason she was very young in this thought, perhaps seven—she was sitting at a table in a coffee shop across from a nice-looking dark-haired fellow about her own age. She could not think of a thing to say; she felt as if she had been shoved onto a platform and a curtain had risen and an audience was watching her and she not only had no lines prepared—she didn't know what the play was. "Thank you" seemed underpowered, "You saved me" overemphatic. But the fellow smiled encouragingly at Ruth Ann, expectantly, even. What would Aunt Sophie say at such a moment? she wondered, and thus she found her line.

"Are you a good man?" she asked him.

He laughed. "I ain't had any complaints so far, honey."

He is probably not a good man, she thought.

Teresa says all the good men are in the west. She says that in order to survive in New York you have to be as tough as a hoodlum or a coward who runs away and lives. "Either you're part of the trouble," she says, "or you're hiding from it."

"It depends on what one means by good," Kathleen offers.

"No," Boise puts in. She is very officious when she has an opinion, which is: usually. "There is only one kind of good in men — unselfish, strong, and imaginative. What else *should* one mean? And there are some. There are. Not Jack, my rich husband. But others. Keep looking, girls." Boise is the only one of the four who has married. "Look *hard.*"

"A good man is not the whole world," says Ruth Ann. "What about a good apartment? A good job?"

"Good friends," adds Kathleen, and she is almost shy.

Teresa nodded and touched her glass to Kathleen's. Two years before, she had created a sensation in the lunchroom of the Jefferson Market Courthouse Library with a Perrier and lime, and now drank nothing else. Kathleen drank crème de cacão and milk. Boise drank Tanqueray gin. Ruth Ann drank nothing. All four of them habitually kept Perrier, lime, crème de cacão, milk, and Tanqueray gin on hand. You will see how close these four are.

"It is not a matter of good men, okay?" says Boise, for the sake of argument, and for the sake of being Boise, open to discussion from any reasonable angle. "It is a matter," said Boise, "of what turns you on. No?"

"Partly," said Kathleen. "Otherwise —"

"Fifty percent of everything," said Teresa.

"No," said Ruth Ann. "I know what you mean. But

no, you're wrong. If all it is is sex, then Don would be a good man, because he makes a festival of undressing me and he kisses me as tenderly as a jeweler getting ready to cut a diamond. And he's wonderfully furry all over." A thoughtful pause. "Can I say that out loud?"

Kathleen glanced away. Teresa shrugged. Boise looked at her. "Why not?" Boise asked.

"He's nice. He'll say 'he don't,' 'she don't.' But he's nice. *Thoughtful*, I think."

"Good."

"So?"

"Well . . ."

"But," Ruth Ann concludes, "he's not a good man. Not *Aunt Sophie* good."

"You are not in love with him," said Boise.

"No," said Ruth Ann. "I'm not."

"So you would never marry him."

"Of course not!"

"Ah," says Boise.

"Well, marry a man I don't love?" Ruth Ann cries.

Boise twirled her glass. "Wait till you're older and you know what I know."

"Marry a man I *don't love*?"

"It happens," said Boise, who knows all about it.

Ruth Ann had been smart enough to get a really neat apartment before the crush hit in the late 1970s, and her job was nearly amazing, as the assistant to a honcho in a new field that may be called "international monetary transfer." Ruth Ann qualified, uniquely, because she spoke German, Italian, Spanish, and Hebrew. She was twenty-eight and the job paid $27,000 a year and one day, in her sixth week in the office, Ruth Ann toted up her gifts and decided that she was being grossly exploited. Her boss was a hard man named Connor Heerson. He was known as The Con. Ruth Ann got along with him by staying out of his way, and did not relish asking him for a raise. She preferred to ask someone like Aunt Sophie or Kathleen.

The Con, who was Dutch once, always smiled. Among the loremasters of The Corporation, The Con was legend: captain of an Olympic water polo team at twenty, a fashion model at twenty-four, a lawyer at thirty. He had black hair and a permanent tan and a spectacular jaw. Where street king Don was all cock-of-the-walk prances, The Con would take two steps backward in aggressively amused mock confusion. But huge muscles bunched up in his suit coat when he came forward again. The Con: a grown man is called The Con, even by *Fortune;* think of it! Think of New York! Think of style and swagger, think of having the money to do all the New York things! Think of Ruth Ann, Brooklyn's Baby Ruth, taking the town. She has the looks and wit to win, but The Con is one of the hurdles she must leap.

The Con's approach was not to say "Yes?" when you entered his office. He'd just look. Early in the day, maybe he smiles. Afternoons, he just looks.

"I can't decide," Ruth Ann told him, "whether to ask very nicely for a raise or to demand one. I know what the others get, and I'm being underpaid."

"How much more do you want?"

She didn't expect it that easy. "How much more am I worth?"

He shook his head. "The system doesn't work that way, Hollander. Salaries are based on bluff, not merit. The better you bluff, the more you get."

"That's not fair to people who are straightforward."

"Like you."

"Like . . . me, yes."

He was at his desk, his big hands clasped together, his eyes aimed at her as if attempting hypnotic suggestion.

"This system," Ruth Ann went on, "encourages incompetence and discourages expertise. Furthermore . . ." She paused, then decided the hell with it. "Furthermore, I think it's exploitative."

"Of you."

Annoyed, she said nothing.

"It is exploitative," he said, "and we both know it. So why say, 'I think'?"

"Manners."

"The system was not designed to accommodate manners. Not your manners, anyway. Quick manners. Charm manners. Kind and honest manners, Hollander? No. The system rewards the adventurer, the gambler. It takes expertise for granted because that is how experts expect to be treated." He laid one hand flat on his desk, palm down, and rested his chin on the other. "Yet without the experts, the gamblers would be out of work."

"Which are you, if you don't mind my asking?"

"Both." His other hand joined the first on the desk. "That's why I'm your boss." He smiled.

"Do I get my raise or not?"

"What if you don't?"

"Mr. Heerson, I deserve more than I'm getting and I believe I'm essential to the continued success of your office. Now are you going to be fair or not?"

"I just told you, salaries are not supposed to be fair."

Ruth Ann felt ire, and she felt hurt, and she fought them both. That's how they keep the experts down, she reminded herself. They get them so busy counting their wounds they don't remember to fight.

"Gamble," he said.

She shook her head.

He extended his hands to her, palms up, lightly swaying, as if balancing one weight against another.

"No one will give you anything," he continued, "just

because you're talented and you ask nicely. You can get what you want only by threatening to become unavailable if you don't."

She forced the hurt down and impulsively decided to nurture the ire. Don't get wounded, get powerful.

"Go on, lady," he urged. "Bluff me."

If you cry now, she told herself, I will never forgive you.

"And don't cry," he added.

"I know."

"I can tell you're going to."

He offered his handkerchief. She refused it.

"I am not going to," she said, crying.

She accepted the handkerchief, black with colorful dots at the edges, and left the room.

Twenty minutes later, he found her in her office. The typewriter was humming, but she was gazing out the window. He closed her door, turned her typewriter off, sat on her desk, and said, "The trouble with you is, you're not vain enough to ask for something from a man without crying."

She turned to him. "It has nothing to do with gender."

"Would you have cried if your boss were a woman?"

"I shouldn't have cried at all."

"We'll discuss it at dinner."

"This is an office thing. I want to discuss it in the office."

"How long have you been here?"

"This is my sixth week."

He nodded. "It's time we got to know each other, Hollander. You may have been avoiding me." He got up. "Two smart, attractive people do not fear each other in this town. Anyway, it's my office." After opening the door, he made a pistol of his right hand and shot her. "Monday. Your place—I'll pick you up at eight."

Ruth Ann decided that she needed an emergency visit to Aunt Sophie's, which was fine with Aunt Sophie; emergencies made her feel young.

"So what's new with Pasquale?" she asked, deconstructing a chicken as Ruth Ann launched a grandiose doodle reflecting the shimmer of the Rockefeller Center skating rink at twilight, with those amazing stunt skaters who go backward as if they were swallows landing at Capistrano.

"Say the name," said Ruth Ann, "or I won't tell."

"So I can't make a jest, Baby Ruth? I can't show you the humor in such a pretty college girl going steady with a delivery boy?"

"An elevator technician. They make a lot of money."

"But what do you talk about?"

Ruth Ann drew her brother falling into a fashionable grande dame; all four of their hands were tangled in her muff. "You know," she said, "there may be times when I have more to say to an elevator technician than to . . . well . . ."

"I can't wait to hear this, darling. Than to who?"

"Than to whom."

"Such *college!*"

"Than to Uncle Max!"

They both laughed.

"But you're not looking for Uncle Max," Aunt Sophie went on. "Are you? No. Someone like Uncle Max, sure. A good man. But something newer."

"I'm not looking for anyone, actually. If he comes along, okay. But he'll have to find me."

"Very nice. Meanwhile my Baby Ruth is keeping company with Giuseppe the Italian elevator man and

won't hear a word about Robert Tarlow, who I just happen to have seen for myself at his mother's last Friday,
and let me tell—"

"No blind dates!"

"Who's talking blind dates? So maybe one Friday
you'll come with me by merest chance to dinner at Mrs.
Tarlow's—not that the food is so great, because I would
hate to tell you what she doesn't know from serving
onion and grieven with chopped liver—and her Robert
will be—"

"That's not a blind date?"

"What date? It's Friday dinner."

"It's a blind date," Ruth Ann cried, "with kibitzers!"

There was silence as Aunt Sophie dropped the
chicken into the boiling water in one of the most essential
acts of the Jewish woman, the Starting of the Soup.

"Never mind, darling," Aunt Sophie said, a touch of
(for once) genuine sorrow in her voice. "So never mind.
His name is Don, and you have lots to talk about, and
don't think I don't know what fun it is to break a rule and
lie in the arms of a shegetz. You see, I use the polite term
out of respect for you. Shegetz. Elevator technician. Very
nice, darling. Be. I can live with it, and you can live with it,
and your mother—may her television break down and it
takes two weeks to fix it so she misses ten episodes of
All My Children and meanwhile they changed all the actors and she doesn't know what's happening . . . your
mother can live with it. But can this elevator technician
live with it, the shegetz who has so much to say? Because
you can mix religions and you can mix backgrounds and I
don't know how many things you can mix. But can you
mix an elevator technician and a college girl?" Aunt
Sophie turned to Ruth Ann. "Can you?"

Ruth Ann sighed. "No, Aunt Sophie. Basically you
can't. Not in any real sense."

Aunt Sophie returned to her chopping board. "So can I tell Mrs. Tarlow, perhaps in a real sense?"

"Not yet. Maybe when I'm forty."

"I hope that's a joke."

Ruth Ann thought, I sure hope so, too.

There is, in New York, a roulette wheel that spins. You are the ball, and the grooves are marked "Mugging," "Apartment Handyman Sprays You with Hose," "Crazed Punk Mistakes You for an Old Friend at Park and Fifty-Fourth," "Someone Gets on Your Bus Carrying a Snake," and so on. Every day or so, the wheel spins, and, after she left Aunt Sophie's that night, Ruth Ann's ball fell into the groove reading "Your Cab Driver Is So Coked Back, Your Life Is in Danger." Ruth Ann left the car in terror at the first subway stop, assumed a gruff-and-ready body report, and force-marched herself into the subway.

Mistake.

Double mistake for a woman.

Triple mistake for a woman who is about as gruff, and as ready, as Squirrel Nutkin.

It was nearly ten o'clock. The platform was virtually deserted. A repellent black teenager erupted from behind a pillar and said something unintelligible with an air of confused menace. Ruth Ann coldly took a few steps down the platform. After a bit, the teenager came up to her again, and the few people standing nearby melted away. Not us, they chorus. We're not here.

Don't engage with him, Ruth Ann reminded herself. You stonewall them. If there's nothing to play with, they won't play. You're mute. You're deaf. You're tough.

The teenager said something, again unintelligible.

"I have a gun in my bag," said Ruth Ann fiercely, "or else."

He went away.

She was shaking.

Now, *why* do I get upset when this happens? she asked herself. I know about all this already. I've seen it in every variation. I've watched it develop and expand and take over the city. I've seen the intrusion of strangers into your privacy become the mode of New York. But I can take care of myself. I know how to resist. So why do I act like some kid sent to the principal's office?

The teenager came back, now with a friend, a white contemporary with a smile like a gash in a rotting cantaloupe. One on her left, one on her right.

She heard her train coming.

Bluff or fight, she thought. That's the city. Bluff in the office and fight everywhere else. She tightened her grip on her handbag. She must swing it as hard as she can at their heads, keep them dodging till the train gets in. Then —

But why should she be any safer on the train? They'll just follow her.

"You don't have anything against me personally," said the black kid. "Right?" His friend just . . . hung there. "Right?"

Ruth Ann stared at him decisively.

"You don't have anything against me personally," he repeated.

The train was pulling in.

The slightest move, Ruth Ann promised herself, and I'll kick his shins in, but she was lying.

The white kid drifted away, and the black breezed off in another direction, looking at Ruth Ann over his shoulder. She paused before getting on the train, to be sure they didn't sneak onto the adjacent cars. But they were haranguing passengers who had just got off, one on this side and one on the other.

Some men attack you and some protect you, she thought, as the train made off for Manhattan. And I am *not* going to weep or keen till I get home. I will master myself and play the cool New Yorker. You notice how men have all the words — *master* myself!

The subway car (containing three pairs of sweethearts, eight unattached older people, three kids swaying to the beat of the drugs in their heads, fourteen babbling psychos, and Ruth Ann) rode into town.

Saturday at brunch, Kathleen, Teresa, and Boise ganged up on Ruth Ann about Don.

"A lady must live," was Boise's summation. "But not with a clod."

"Would I trust him with my card file?" said Teresa. "That's the question I would ask about a man."

Kathleen looked innocent and thoughtful, but that in itself is critique. In Manhattan, not to defend a questionable character is to damn him: because there is no neutrality.

"Jack, my rich husband, is going to fête me for my fifty-sixth," said Boise. "As well he might. And we're going to be there, ladies. Looking *sharp*. I have the express intention of devastating all of Jack's former and current girlfriends with my jewels, house, and company. Ladies, bring the men you would take to the Inaugural Ball if Julie Andrews were the President. You know? Spiffy clean." She turned to Ruth Ann. "So no Don Minetti."

"Now's the time," Teresa agreed. "You *drop* him." Special-interest groups demanding the removal of *The Merchant of Venice* or *Huckleberry Finn* from her shelves would not have met a more stirring antagonism.

"I would like to tell you about something that happened to me a few days ago on the subway," said Ruth Ann, and she told them, quietly and simply. It was the first time she had spoken of it to anyone, and was surprised at how little hurt she sounded.

Kathleen was aghast.

Teresa was furious.

Boise lit a cigarette. "What did Don say about it?" she asked.

"I haven't told him."

"Why *not*?"

Ruth Ann stared them all down, except Kathleen, who wasn't looking. "No reason," she said.

"Of course there's a reason."

A pause.

"*Tell* him," said Boise.

"Why?"

"*Tell him.*"

"No."

"Tell him, Ruth Ann. *Tonight.*"

This is what Don said about it: "Ruth Ann, I don't really like it that you . . . you just go in there, the subway. No, Ruth Ann, no, listen. Ruth Ann. A girl like you shouldn't do that. You been a New York girl for years, and you know better, Ruth Ann. You know the drill by now. Listen. If this ever happens again, or if you even think that someone might come up to you like that, I want you to look around for the nearest man who looks like me. I'm serious. Two men'd be better even, especially if you could hear them talking about something decent. And look now, you go right up to them straight on, and you say, 'Excuse me for butting into your conversation, but a strange creep is after me and I would please ask for your protection until the train comes, or my stop, or something.' You hear me, Ruth Ann? And be nice about it but a little cold, so they don't get the wrong idea. And they won't, if you pick the right guys. No nerds. No teenage kids, like. No blacks. Nothing in a suit, right, Ruth Ann? Go to someone Italian,

Polish, Irish. You know what I mean. Do it right, my lady, and believe me, that is a sure, safe thing."

Ruth Ann was still, and she asked him, "How'd you know all this? This . . . formula?"

"It's straight, honey. It's the thing that all Italian mothers tell their daughters when they're old enough to be let out alone."

Ruth Ann gazed upon him, Don. "It works, doesn't it?" she asked, crying again. Damn, she thought. It's so easy to make me cry, you'd think no one would bother.

"So like sure it works," he said, holding her. "Come on, baby, it's not so bad. Nothing's going to happen to you now."

He *is* a good man, she was thinking. He'd make a terrific brother.

He held her for a long time. Then she spoke his name and tried to kiss him. He pulled away.

"I can't, Ruth Ann. Not now, like this."

"Can't . . . like what not now?"

He blushed. "I can't do . . . anything . . . with you. Not when you're . . . you know, Ruth Ann."

"No, I don't."

". . . ascared."

"I'm not scared."

"You were, though."

"In the subway a few days ago. Not now. And not with you. You're a nice man."

"Yeah." He drummed on a table, moved around. "It's not fair, anyway. Makes me feel like a creep or something."

"What does?"

"When you're like that, like a . . . a victim. You got to be *bold*, Ruth Ann."

She rose and joined him and shook his hand. It

seemed called for, but he was confused, and gave her a flabby response, not his regular grip.

"You're a nice man," she repeated, and thought, Four months we've been sleeping together and I hardly know him.

Dinner with The Con was jazzier than Ruth Ann had imagined it would be. What was it, exactly? she wondered the next day. What word comprehends it?

Sophisticated. It was Ruth Ann's first experience in the world of the knowledgeably debonair, of the people who take their money and style for granted. Most New Yorkers have neither, or one, or the other; and they wear them weightily, clumsily, like fancy clothes you bought from a fence. But The Con moved lightly, surely, contentedly.

Sophisticated. Ruth Ann had expected The Latest Restaurant, an idle stroll up an avenue, and a handshake at her door. What she got was dinner at a small, unknown, and superb trattoria in Chelsea, a cab ride up to The Con's apartment, and a night of lovemaking in baroque, playfully demonic styles that Ruth Ann had not dreamed existed.

"Are you a good man?" she asked, a little breathlessly, when he began, on the couch; and, as he took her drink out of her hand and placed it on the coffee table he said, "Let me show you." Presently he carried her to a chair and did the most *amazing* things, and it all happened rather quickly after that, and Ruth Ann may have blacked out on some of it, or confused one moment with another, though she distinctly remembered feeling just a bit disappointed that he was so beautifully — really so elegantly — built. Beautiful men, she had heard, can be impossible to women. She also thought, at one point, that sleeping with the boss was a cheap act, unworthy of her belief in herself, yet somewhat in keeping with the sophisticated tone of the evening. Sophisticates make their own rules.

Anyway, some hours later, snuggling up to him, Ruth Ann let out a sigh of almost unendurable satisfaction and gently began to fall asleep.

He is *definitely* not a good man, she thought.

What he was, was New York in its essence: handsome, suavely abrasive, moneyed, and selfish.

"I still want a raise," Ruth Ann would tell him, impishly (over dinner), casually (in bed), pensively (at the office). He ignored her, or he'd say, "You'll get it, Hollander. You'll get something. I'm putting my head to work about you."

That sounded promising, but that's all it was, really: promising.

"I want it now," she told him. "Whatever it is, whatever's going to happen to me, let it be now."

She did not tell Aunt Sophie that she was having an affair with her boss; in fact, she told no one, not even her brunch club. Certainly, she said nothing to Don, who still saw her once a week for an early, just-after-work dinner, and had become so tender with her, so protective and understanding, that she wondered why he was no more than straightforward . . . efficient, perhaps . . . in bed. Whereas The Con was rather remote as a person, always cocking his head quizzically at the follies of his associates, as if he were an observer collecting data. Yet in bed he was . . . well, talented. Communicative. *Involved.* It was an odd aspect of life in New York that people you hardly knew would suddenly become intimate at the oddest times.

Ruth Ann wondered whom she ought to take to Boise's party. Boise had all but banned Don, and, true, he wouldn't be comfortable at a ritzy do the way The Con would. But if she brought The Con, everyone would know they were sleeping together, and somehow Ruth Ann felt that ought to be a secret. She wasn't sure why.

So she told Boise she was coming alone to the party.

"No," Boise told her. "No, I've got *just* the boy for you. He's been staying with me because he has nowhere to go, and you'll look mad together, and frankly I don't care what you do with him because he's not my type. He's always underfoot, anyway. Come for dinner."

Ruth Ann came for dinner and met a slender, very young man with a lovely smile. He was like a twenty-year-old version of a sleepy child; for the first time in her life, Ruth Ann felt the tiniest bit . . . well, mature.

"This is Grey," Boise said, taking their hands to bring them together like a Hungarian matchmaker.

Grey didn't talk much. Every now and then, Boise petted him; he seemed to need it. He would grin and his eyes, normally heavy-lidded slits, would gaze wide open.

"Where's Jack?" Ruth Ann asked.

"Jack, my rich husband?" Boise replied. She looked around the dining room and shrugged. "Looks like he's out."

Ruth Ann laughed.

"He thinks Grey is my nephew," Boise went on.

Grey looked puzzled. "I *am* your nephew," he said.

Boise shrugged.

She made Grey take Ruth Ann home, and Ruth Ann turned firmly at the door, but Grey just kept standing there and smiling, shifting his weight from foot to foot, and finally he said, "Aunt Boise'll chop me up good if I don't come in or something," and Ruth Ann let him in.

Or something, she thought wryly. Aunt Boise ought to get together with Aunt Sophie. They could parcel out the town, divide up the territories. Aunt Sophie gets Brooklyn, Manhattan's Upper West Side, and what's left of the Bronx; Aunt Boise gets the Upper East Side and Central Park South.

Or something. Ruth Ann didn't even bother asking Grey if he was a good man. With his slight frame and uncomplicated self-confidence he was scarcely a man at all. As for good . . . well, what's good *good for*, anyway, nowadays? In a cynical city, the cynics get ahead. Am *I* good? Ruth Ann wondered, as Grey made his move with the clumsy, caring innocence that only the truly uncommitted can get away with. If Ruth Ann had known much about sex, she would have called this an old-fashioned loving, sweet, simple practice with none of your questionable contemporary variations. Yet Ruth Ann knew little about sex. Lately, she has become a woman of affairs, true. But Manhattan will do that to a Brooklyn girl.

Three men at once! Ruth Ann thought to herself a number of times over the following days. Empress Ruth Ann the Great, with her cavalier multitudes. Three men — admitting, of course, that Don was just a dinner friend now and that Grey only paid court to Ruth Ann when (she was almost certain) Boise aimed him in Ruth Ann's direction. Now Ruth Ann looked back on all those proms she had missed because only drips had asked her, all those college Saturday nights spent miserably lounging in the dorm because she couldn't even land a drip. Where were men when you needed them?

I don't need them now, she thought. She even said it aloud, but it didn't sound convincing.

Not to Boise, anyway.

"What do you mean you don't need *men*?" Boise asked Ruth Ann at brunch. "*Everyone* needs men."

"I have my career and freedom," Ruth Ann told her. "There's time. I want to get older. I'm smart but I'm not—"

"Wise," Teresa put in. She meant it kindly.

"What if you have to be born wise?" Kathleen asked.

"What if you *get* to be born *old*?" Boise countered.

"Come on," said Ruth Ann. "That's just lip." She held her hands out as her father might, to demonstrate the clarity of her observation: "You get old, you get wise. Comes with the arthritis and constipation."

"You get old," Boise warned, "you get *not enough phone calls*! Trust me, girls. The veteran's talking here."

"I don't need phone calls," said Ruth Ann. "I need a raise."

Boise said, "So sleep with the boss," and Ruth Ann's face exploded in a blush, and they all stared at her.

Kathleen looked away first.

Teresa shook her head, sympathetic and rueful.

Boise chuckled.

"Anyway," said Boise. "Who of your male harem are you taking to my party?"

"Have you a preference?" Ruth Ann asked.

"Haven't *you*?"

Ruth Ann was silent. "No," she said at length. "No, I don't believe I do."

"She and Grey look so cute together," Boise told the other two. "As if they'd been *designed*!"

"But he doesn't *know* anything," Ruth Ann complained. "He doesn't *do* anything. He never *says* anything."

"What do you want, Carl Sagan?"

"I want a good man," replied Ruth Ann, realizing with some surprise that this was true, after all. But: "I want a man who will let me be wise."

"Let's just see what happens, then," said Boise in an interesting tone.

To please her hostess, Ruth Ann did invite Grey to the party. He accepted with a grin and that thing his eyes did. "Dress to slay," Boise had ordered, and Ruth Ann did so. As she looked herself over one last time in the full-length mirror in her dressing room (her lease fondly referred to it as a "bedroom," but you'd have to have been Thumbelina to fit your bed in it), Ruth Ann wondered if she could somehow market her gift of being able to get into a totally uptown outfit *and* be on time in the same night.

Grey, of course, could not be on time in the same night, even with nothing else to do. After thirty-five minutes of browsing through *Anna Karenina* in clothes that would have made the editors of *Cosmo* suffer envy, Ruth Ann felt absurd. When the phone rang and The Con said, before she could even get out a hello, "Let's do something, Hollander," Ruth Ann told him to pour himself into his most bodacious suit and take her to a party.

"Twenty minutes," he said, and he was there in twenty. But so was Grey, shrugging. Ruth Ann decided that it was one of those New York things, and The Con could take them both. The Con was amused. "He's pretty," he said, of Grey. And off they went to the party of the month.

It's not enough that Boise has a spectacular penthouse — look, somebody has to, right? With the space, and the terrace, and the view, at night a spray of countless lights against a dust of filthy velvet. "Yeah, the Milky Way," Boise says when her guests rave. Nor is it enough that Boise has the money to plan an astonishing party and the go-to-hell philosophy enabling her to deliver one. With the live music, the dynamite food, the waiters. Yes. But this is not enough. Boise has to make discoveries. Tonight's was the wok man, a devilish-looking fellow behind a giant wok flanked by platters of beef, chicken, shrimp, vegetables, noodles, herbs, and secrets. You chose your ingredients, and in an instant the wok man cooked up your unique dish, all the while dashing off facetious non sequiturs.

"The usual sensation," Boise dryly observed, looking on. "Fifteen years ago, all you had to give them was omelets."

When Ruth Ann came in with The Con and Grey, heads turned and an Entrance was made. Boise caught Ruth Ann's eye and nodded. Teresa, who had come alone with Kathleen and Kathleen's boyfriend Harlan — with them, but alone — pantomimed clapping. She was fiercely proud of her friends.

This is the thing about New York parties: everybody's always networking, playing the room, securing deals. This is because New York is the center of the system that — as The Con warned Ruth Ann — rewards the adventurer. Idle conversations on the most incidental of topics may lead to The Break of One's Life. A cool chat may conceal abominable passions. Closest comrades ignore each other; strangers enthuse. Everything in New York is about something else — even friendship, even sex, even love.

Even Don, Ruth Ann thought, even Grey, even The Con. Or no, she realized, sitting with her chums as Boise's guests formed and re-formed in their patterns of penetration and surrender. No, they were just her three men of the moment. Her costars in this comedy of manners set in the capital city of courtship. Teresa, on one side of Ruth Ann, was discussing the novels of John le Carré with Kathleen's stalwart stockbroker boyfriend. Kathleen, on the other side, was explaining theatre-in-the-round to an opulent older man who had plopped down with his plate, winked, and said, "You appear to be artistic. I adore the arts."

My three men, Ruth Ann mused: one kind, one fascinating, one affable.

None good.

In the next room, someone struck up Gershwin at the piano and Ruth Ann's companions went off to listen. Ruth Ann stayed behind; she liked the idea of sitting by herself in a crowded party in the midst of a crowded city. She liked the way it looked. Through the shifting configurations of Boise's people, Ruth Ann saw The Con talking to Grey. The younger man seemed heavily charmed, and The Con took him by the shoulders and whispered something. Grey did his grin.

Boise sat next to Ruth Ann.

"You made a marvelous entrance," Boise told her. "Like Cinderella at the ball with two Prince Charmings."

"Prince meets prince," Ruth Ann murmured.

Boise nodded, shrugging. "So I noticed." In the next room, the pianist slid into some Sondheim, intense and romantic after the brittle, high-strung Gershwin. "Our boy Grey . . ." Boise went on, unsure of where to go next. "Our boy is a bit like water, I'm afraid. He fits the available container. And here I was hoping you'd redeem him."

"I don't want to redeem anybody."

Boise shrugged again. Silent, the two women watched The Con enchanting Grey.

"I believe," Boise finally said, "those two are planning to go home together."

"It doesn't matter."

"The *nerve* of them!"

"I want to be alone, anyway." Ruth Ann rested her head on Boise's shoulder for a moment, then slipped out of the party like . . . well, yes, like Cinderella. Like Cinderella leaving the ball.

I'm not angry, she told herself. I just feel odd.

Boise, alone, looked around the room at her spectacular party. "Who," she said aloud, "are all these disgusting people?"

Ruth Ann slept very late the next day and took a long walk. What do I need? was the theme of her walk, as she crisscrossed the neighborhoods, the *kinds* of New York, from the deep-pocket co-ops to the broken little brownstones, from the unsavory theatre district to the big backyard, Central Park.

She felt as if she had been merrily, unknowingly wasting away. Several times she thought of calling Don, the last man left in her collection; once she actually got a quarter into a phone. She didn't dial.

She wandered. What did she need? Perhaps another career, or at least another job? We all have these days, Ruth Ann knew—but what if this one is for life?

When she got home she was no clearer on where she stood than when she had set out. She had walked, literally, nowhere. So she called Aunt Sophie and said she was coming out to dinner.

"Good," Aunt Sophie replied. "Because your Uncle Max is working late all night, and *someone's* got to eat."

She was businesslike when Ruth Ann arrived, and the doodle paper was laid out. But there was something furtive in her movements. There was a Secret.

"I don't like the look on that face at all," Aunt Sophie announced as Ruth Ann sat at the table. "My Baby Ruth, so young and smart and pretty, with your whole life to start living."

Ruth Ann sighed, looking down at her doodle paper. For the first time in all her days, she had no idea what to draw. She looked up. "Oh, Aunt Sophie," Ruth Ann told her, "love is hell."

"Sure," Aunt Sophie agreed. "With the wrong people." She copped a look at the wall clock.

"I feel terminally miserable."

"Wait till after chicken soup, you won't feel miserable."

"Yes, I will," Ruth Ann moaned. "Three loves have I."

Aunt Sophie froze. "What?" she cried. "Who, when?"

"No, I mean . . . I don't have any . . . *real* loves. I have . . . three men . . ."

Aunt Sophie put her hand to her mouth, shocked silent. Not too shocked, though, Ruth Ann noticed, to steal another glance at the clock.

"Why are you—" Ruth Ann began, but Aunt Sophie guiltily turned back to her cooking.

"If this were a French farce," Ruth Ann went on, "I'd think there was a man hidden somewhere."

Just then the buzzer sounded; Aunt Sophie let out a gasp and fumbled her whisk, sending it clattering to the floor.

"Who can that be?" Ruth Ann asked.

Aunt Sophie, pressing the response button, said, "A delivery. I ordered new slipcovers."

"A delivery at seven-thirty?"

"I told them it's an emergency," Aunt Sophie feebly lied. "You want results, you got to push them."

Ruth Ann sadly shook her head. She knew what was going on. And when Aunt Sophie opened the door on a handsome, dark-haired, neatly dressed man a year or two older than Ruth Ann, smiling because he had a good life and was hoping that Ruth Ann would make it even better, Ruth Ann said, "Robert Tarlow."

He beamed.

Ruth Ann jumped to her feet. "Oh no, you don't! They told you it was an emergency, right? Quick, we've got a twenty-eight-year-old unmarried Jewish girl on our hands, someone call out the eligible professionals and get her matched up before she turns into . . . into a . . . an *independent grown-up* before our eyes! Treat her like a baby, okay? My boss won't even give me the raise I deserve because . . . because why should he? I'm not an adventurer and he knows it."

There was a pause.

"Your boss?" said Robert Tarlow, making small talk.

"My boss. His name is The Con."

"That's a name?" said Aunt Sophie.

"This is a trap," Ruth Ann went on. "The whole world is this kind of trap, and I have to stay in the world, but you're going to have to understand that I don't have to stay *here*, even for . . . obviously I mean especially . . . *especially* for a doctor on a trap of a blind date right here. Which you are. I'm sorry."

"His name is The Con?" said Aunt Sophie.

"Please don't be angry," said Robert Tarlow, coming into the room. "Your aunt invited me for dinner, that's all. No trap. Just, you know . . . a friendly night in Brooklyn. I should have brought flowers, but —"

"No. No flowers, definitely."

"My mother and your aunt are in cahoots, that's all," said Robert Tarlow, coming closer. "They think they're putting it over on us, but we're just humoring them. Right?"

"A man is called The Con?" said Aunt Sophie. "A grown man, in an office and a suit?"

"No, I'm so terribly sorry," Ruth Ann swept on, "but I can't be treated like a child, and that's what I know."

Aunt Sophie looked stricken.

"You're in the wrong," Ruth Ann told her, though she couldn't face her. "You know you are. Everyone's in the wrong lately, and not just in Brooklyn. If you knew what I knew."

"What do you know?" Robert Tarlow asked, gently.

"Please don't be so charming," Ruth Ann begged him, "when I'm working on furious."

"Okay."

Ruth Ann stood tall and threw her shoulders back and picked up her bag and moved past them into the hall. I'm absolutely outraged, she told herself, putting steel into the act. She rang for the elevator, and that's the end of being treated like a baby.

Except Robert Tarlow came into the hall with her and asked, in the nicest way possible, for her not to be angry yet. Oh, this was like a knife in Ruth Ann's heart! He suggested they sort it out peacefully. How she bridled at that. Peacefully! In this . . . this war-torn city. But after all, he said, his mother was just as determined as her Aunt Sophie, and maybe they could knock off two targets at once by giving in a little. Then the city would be peaceful.

"No," Ruth Ann told him. "The more you give them, the more they need."

"No," he told her. "The more you resist, the more they demand. You give them a little something, you get peace."

The elevator arrived.

"Please," he said. "Just stay, and it'd be so much easier for both of us."

Ruth Ann refused to look at him. "And I suppose you're a good man, aren't you?"

The elevator moved on.

"What's a good man?" he asked.

"Oh, *come on!*"

"Loyal?" he asked. "Fair? A home-loving sort? Easy on the kids and considerate about the household chores? Because that's what I am. A good man."

He was in earnest.

Ruth Ann rolled her eyes.

Aunt Sophie, who had been eavesdropping, decided that this was the Moment of Timing, and opened her door. "So," she said, "let's all come in and and eat."

Inside, Ruth Ann gathered up her doodling equipment and laid it in a drawer. "That's the end of all that from now on," she said. "I'm too sophisticated to doodle."

Aunt Sophie, deftly sliding plates and flatware into place, said, "That's my Baby Ruth from college." She seemed extraordinarily pleased with herself, though at least she wasn't grinning.

"Remember," Ruth Ann told them both very firmly—and she is polite and she has her grace under pressure, but enough is enough with getting pushed around—"don't get any ideas just because I'm still here. This is not a date."

"Be yourself," Robert Tarlow agreed.

"A little dinner," Aunt Sophie murmured, bringing on the soup. "What could happen?"

Ruth Ann suddenly felt weak, embattled enough beyond enough, but alarm bells inside her clanged her alert and she was on her feet saying no, enough is too much.

"No, I am most terribly sorry to do this to you," she told Robert Tarlow. "No, but you shouldn't have given in and I'm not going to. I just realized that." And she told Aunt Sophie, "No, I am a grown-up and this is not the last panel of a romance comic story."

Ruth Ann didn't just leave—she stormed out of Brooklyn and went right to Boise's palace in the sky and grouched and complained to her heart's content.

"What is a good man, anyway?" Boise finally asked her with a gleam in her eye. Boise felt most apt in dealing with the major philosophies of the Western world. She has been around the block.

"Robert Tarlow!" Ruth Ann almost sneered. "A

doctor! The idea, I suppose, is I need someone to take care of me!"

"You do."

Well, that stopped Ruth Ann right in the middle of her dudgeon.

"You do," Boise repeated, "because you aren't making the right choices. You have the wrong boss. You have the wrong boyfriend. You have the wrong aunt."

"Wrong for what?"

"Oh, pook," said Boise, placing a cigarette into a holder as long as a carnival hot dog. She enjoyed being colorful, unpredictable, a New York character. "Pook," Boise insisted, "because your boss exploits you. And your boyfriend is no-win dating, all sex and no truth. And your aunt makes you feel bad."

"What is truth?"

"Truth is the right man, and any woman who says otherwise is *so entirely wrong* I can't begin to *describe* it."

"Now you sound like Aunt Sophie."

Boise coughed violently and pulled her cigarette out of its holder. "I hate these things," she said, throwing the holder across the coffee table. It skittered around the edge of a book and bounced onto the carpet.

"Anyway," said Ruth Ann, "what are you supposed to do if you can't find the right man? This is the question," she noted, with a sense of relish amid the tragedy, "that is beyond the answer of the wise."

"I've got an answer," said Boise. "First, quit your job. Second, lose that Italian galoot. Third . . . what was Robert Tarlow like?"

"Nice. A nice stooge. Only a stooge does what his mother and my aunt tell him to after the age of fifteen."

"Wait till you're a mother and your son is fifteen."

"Is that what I want?"

Boise shrugged.

"Is that what you wanted?" Ruth Ann asked Boise. "To be a mother?"

"What I wanted," said Boise, "was to be Jack, my rich husband's merry widow."

"Come on, you adore him."

"Really? I wonder. How odd of you to say so."

They were moving through the apartment toward the door.

"Meanwhile," said Ruth Ann, "I have another interview tomorrow. I intend to believe in it as the beginning of the transformation of my life. New office, new people, new routine. Big salary, too. The Con runs a classy office, I'll give him that. But all of his overhead goes into the rent and the Muchas on the wall. I want to work for a man who honors his employees."

"Sounds like you're all set up for a good boss. Now what about a good man?"

"Yes, Aunt Sophie, *yes*! I'll do what I am told. Down with independence and up with the bridal brigades!"

They had been standing in Boise's front doorway, finishing up; Boise knocked on her side of the door as a judge bangs his gavel. "Ruth Ann," she said, "don't you *want* a man?"

Ruth Ann smiled ruefully, and made no remark.

I must tell you that Ruth Ann Hollander has the type of personality—bright, quick, imaginative, and very slightly exhibitionistic, the doodle girl fixing her latest masterpiece on the refrigeratior door—that does well in interviews. Whatever her personal misgivings may be about the interviewer, the job, or—who knows?—herself, she masks them under a kind of performance art of the business world, selecting the elements and themes of Ruth Ann Hollander that will play best before a given audience. And of course she has been wasting herself on

The Con's handsome, spacious, harmonious, well-versed, tactful, confident, staggeringly impressive, multinational office of dashing decor and exploited drudges. Ruth Ann is worth double her salary and a happier workplace. You know it. I know it. Ruth Ann knows it.

She had a feeling that her potential new boss knew it, too. The interview went terribly well. You can't be certain about how other people view you in a city like New York, because Ruth Ann isn't the only one who gives a performance from time to time. For all she knew, Mr. Lange simply prided himself on giving A Comfortable Interview.

On the other hand, if this was Mr. Lange's imitation of Smart, Friendly, and Sincere, he had an awfully good one. And think of this: how many men had Ruth Ann met who felt they needed to give an imitation at all? It's women who must style themselves, who try to accommodate other people's expectations, who must fit into a system designed and sustained and policed by men. An unattractive, boring woman is constantly attempting to upgrade and realign herself. An unattractive, boring man thinks he's complete as he is.

Certainly Uncle Max never tried to hold down his weight or do something with his idiotic hair or take an interest in Aunt Sophie's view of the world. The Con was a gorgeous man, no question—but it was genetics and his slithery vanity that kept him so, not a desire to please. Don respected women, you have to give him that—but out of cultural training, not any genuine intellectual deference. As for Grey . . . Grey was a child.

And Mr. Lange, while we're on the subject, was a somewhat short and very slim man, about thirty. Straight black hair. Dark blue eyes. A naturally smiling face and a serious bearing, as if to say that life is a trial but a good mood proves you're innocent. He was in shirt sleeves and tie, and Ruth Ann kept noticing the wealth of hair curling out at his wrists. She was never sure if she preferred that on men, but it seemed to suit this man somehow. She liked his hands: calmly expressive, with long fingers. Was he good-looking? Well, he wasn't handsome. He was . . . likable-looking. When he stood up to lead her down the hall and try out her programming technique at a spare terminal, she observed how incredibly trim his stomach was.

Awful. Shameful. Depressing. To have to give him a report card on his looks. This is what a women can't stand about men. This is a man's insensitivity.

Following Mr. Lange down the hall, Ruth Ann caught a quick glance at the way the wool of his pants curved against his behind, then told herself to quit it.

He sat and joked with her at the keyboard, taking his time. I'm in the running, she thought. The girl's a contender, or he would have dropped me off and left me to it. He watched her work out the technics of the test program. It was an insidiously knotty little assignment, the kind that an expert could key out and set up inside an hour but that would keep a routinely competent programmer at the board all day.

Ruth Ann did it in six minutes.

"I was going to ask if I made you nervous," Mr. Lange said, "looking over your shoulder like this. But you obviously don't believe in stage fright." He took over the board and jump-tested her program, nodding in agreement as the circuits bore out her implementation of the data. "I don't believe in it, either. Stage fright. If you have it, use it. There it is."

"There it is," Ruth Ann said.

"You'll be hearing from me in a couple of days," he told her some time later as they walked to the elevator. "I've got two more people to see, and then . . . well . . ."

They shook hands.

"Mr. Lange," she said, putting a winner's smile on it.

"Cliff," he corrected, as if they were at a party.

"Ruth Ann," she said.

"You know," he concluded, as the doors closed between them, "I really enjoyed this."

This is a good man, she thought that night, gloating in her armchair over a bag of potato chips and a half-pint of sour cream, for which she would have to pay, she knew, with a week of cottage cheese and celery lunches.

This is a *good man to work for*.

Yet she kept thinking of his hands, and his ready smile, and his light approach to things other men would make so heavy. She thought, too, of his gravity: a serious man with a sense of humor.

He is direct and considerate, she decided firmly, as if coloring in a figure in one of her doodles. She allowed herself to fantasize what he would be like with a woman, how smoothly — no, really more *sweetly* — he would ask if he could come in, with a tone assuring you how gently he can take no for an answer; how easily he would develop the body language and the touching of her hand, those fingers, and the hairs at the wrist, and she wants to undo his tie herself, dark green with red and yellow stripes; how simply and purely he would ask her if she would like to, because he is quite sensitive for a man; how lovingly he would undress her, not with The Con's theatre or Don's possessiveness or Grey's bumper-car innocence, but because he wants to communicate to her a feeling that would be sacred to them alone, that makes them strong because of what they knew of each other; or how deliciously long he would take to get to her, because they are both enjoying the approach and she feels as if they were flying in the air together; how handsome he would seem then, because love deludes the senses but likability sharp-

ens them, and this is something only women know, because men fall for looks and women fall for feelings; and
how comprehensively he would shelter her after, holding
her, her head on his chest listening to him breathe.

Oh, this is all wrong, she told herself. This is not a
date. This is my *boss* at my *job, if* I get it; and I *will.*

You know what a man would do in this position? He
would take the matter into his own hands, call the guy up
and say something like, "Look, I . . ." What do men say
when they want something out of another man? Why
does aggressiveness come so naturally to them?

Well, I wouldn't do it as if I were a man, Ruth Ann
knew. I wouldn't do it, period.

Maybe that's my problem.

Maybe I should do it.

There was a Clifford Lange in the phone book, with
an address on Bank Street, and Ruth Ann took a chance.

He's probably married and a dreadful cheat, Ruth
Ann thought as she dialed, so his wife practically lives
next to the phone and

"Hello?" said Cliff.

"Mr. Lange, it's Ruth Ann Hollander. I know it's extremely unconventional to do this — or maybe everybody
does this. But I never have. I just wanted to tell you what
a . . . really, what a pleasant time I had in your office today, and I hope this won't look too demanding of me, but
I just thought that you ought to know that I'm quite sure
I'm right for the job and I'd be glad to work for you and I
believe spirit is what counts. And attitude — I mean, a
good one. And I've got both. And . . . that's what I
wanted to say."

"Oh, I could tell that right off, Ruth Ann. I appreciate
your calling. In fact, you gave a very classy audition. I'm
sure you know that. Unqualified people are the ones who
go through life never quite knowing what's happening,

but the qualified people are very correct in what they see. Aren't we?"

He was laughing. He finds humor in what is true.

"I never thought of it that way," Ruth Ann replied. She could see him standing at the phone, perhaps scratching his forearm. He has changed into a sport shirt and jeans and he will save her from pirates. "But I guess we are."

"There it is. You'll be hearing from me quite soon."

"Thank you."

"And it's Cliff, Ruth Ann. Okay?"

"It's Cliff."

"Okay."

Then Ruth Ann called The Con. It was a short conversation. Ruth Ann gave him three days' notice and he said, "Let's talk salary, Hollander," and she said, "Three days, Heerson," and holstered the phone.

"There it is," she said aloud.

The phone rang, and she gave it her cutest hello.

"You were so honest in your approach," Cliff told her, "I felt I couldn't be less so. Besides, I don't like games. Let's not be coy—you have the job, and it's a fine one, and you'd be wise to say yes. I do have two more people to see, but their résumés don't challenge yours, so . . ."

Ruth Ann was so content, she could have danced around the room. Happy ending, Ruth Ann thought. Someone got a job!

Someone get anything else?

The phone rang yet again, this time Aunt Sophie, checking up on her beautiful Baby Ruth. Baby's all grown up now, Aunt Sophie. Baby won't be prodded, told what to do, cheated, or taken for granted, as various certain people have been doing to her thus far. Ruth Ann feels dangerous. She wants to take risks. Too much security is not good, especially if you have to take it on someone else's terms.

"That Mrs. Tarlow doesn't have to worry," Aunt Sophie assured Ruth Ann, "with that angel son of hers. Her wish is his obey."

"Well, that's his problem," Ruth Ann replied. "Because I'm going to work for a good man and sleep with the devil, just watch me."

Aunt Sophie requested further details on this terrifying turn in events, but all the elucidation Ruth Ann would fork over was "There it is" and a great deal of giggling.

She might have been eight years old again, or high on champagne, or in love.

SOMETHING
WENT WRONG

On THE FIRST WARM Friday after winter blew away, Cliff checked out of the office early and walked home, from midtown to the Village.

The apartment was empty. Alison had left another list for him on the table in the front hall, next to the mail and the little bowl of tokens and the ashtray in which Cliff liked to keep his housekeys.

Alison made her lists in pen, block letters on long, lined yellow paper, lists such as "Things To Pack for the Trip," "Things To Buy for the Party—You," and "Things To Be Straightened out With the Super."

These were acceptable lists. Cliff's chores. The dangerous lists dealt not with things but with problems: "Problems With Your Parents," "Problems About Money," "Problems in Our Marital Etiquette." That last one was a monster list, three pages. It must have taken her a week to lay it out. A week of feeling her memories for personal wounds, for injustices of Gender Ideology and instances pointing to Conjugal Meltdown and other argot of injured wifely merit that she had picked up over the last year or so. A week of "surviving," as she insistently put it. A week of dashing through the city selling apartments and blithely overtipping the takeout delivery men and working on her Confrontation Output.

This list was entitled "Continuing Problems." It was a short one:

1. You are still slamming the front door too hard when you leave in the morning, according to the woman in 8-L. She says she doesn't mind it at night, but in the morning it wakes her up.
2. The living room couch must be recovered. Better yet, replaced.
3. Colin.

Christ, he thought, as her key hit the lock; and he turned, all the more angry now because he had been so patient so long. He had the list in his hand, silent, as she came in pushing the stroller, Colin solemnly walking alongside, holding onto it.

"Glaring doesn't solve the problem," she told him, grimly merry as she so often was lately. As she put the stroller in the closet, Cliff knelt to take Colin by the shoulders.

"First day of the playground season, hey sport?" he said.

Colin nodded.

"What time is it there, buddy?"

Colin smiled. Alison had given him a Mickey Mouse wristwatch for her birthday. (Cliff got a new Mason Pearson hairbrush because, she said, his old one was going bald and looked repulsive; and she bought herself an antique map of China.) The boy never took his watch off, even in bed, and, though his readings were shaky, he enjoyed coming up with an answer.

"Two . . . four o'clock?" said Colin, studying the watch.

"Four thirty-five," said his father, stroking the boy's hair.

"Wait," said Colin. He froze, and his father froze, too. His mother went into the kitchen.

After a moment Colin said, "Four thirty-five and a half," and laughed. "Right?"

"Right!"

"Colin," Alison called from the kitchen. "Come and have your juice."

He looked beautiful now, all filled out again, a sharp little guy. He had his energy back, too, though he was not as lively as he used to be, and he was a pretty quiet kid to begin with. Not like those little cannonballs you'd see rocketing around the playground, shouting club passwords to each other, phrases peeled off the Saturday-morning television screen, as they'd fire down the slide and back up the ladder, going two at once, even three; or crazing around the place in their trunks shooting water pistols. Weekends, it was Cliff's turn to take Colin to the playground, and the father and the mothers would chat while Colin would do his networking, showing the other children some new toy he'd brought along, his little conversation pieces. Colin was the consumer advocate of the playground. This year he would have his Mickey Mouse watch.

Sometimes one of the cannonball guys would whiz by and wound a little girl with a spurt of water. You never knew how they'd take it. Some of them would say *Hey!* or something like that, and a few would cry and the mothers would have to go do some sympathizing and reproaching. There was one little blonde, a real doll, who hunched her shoulders and squealed when she got shot. She was one of Colin's friends. What was her name, now? A perfect little doll's name, too. Angela? Annette?

A few months ago she and her mother ran into Cliff as he was coming out of the candy store with the *Times*, and she asked him where Colin was.

"He's in the hospital," Cliff told her, "but he'll be back soon."

He was; and he was fine; and the doctors still didn't know what had gone wrong. He'll be fine for months, not a thing out of kilter, then suddenly he'll start losing weight and strength and the doctors put him through one test after another and toss a lot of medical-text terms around. And all they really know is how to make out the bill.

Cliff went into the kitchen, looking for and, irritated, finding the fancy hamburger joint take-out menu open next to the phone. Alison and he used to take turns preparing dinner; both of them were accomplished simple-fare cooks. Between his five-flavors meat loaf and her fried chicken they could finesse nearly a week of dinners on ingenious glamorizations of the leftovers. Cold Loaf Diable. Sour-cream chicken. She was fun then. She liked hacking around in the apartment with him, painting and switching the pictures around and sorting out disorderly closets. Now all she did was hawk co-ops to yuppies and attend to her tape messages and order from her extensive collection of take-out menus.

Colin had gone to his room. Alison was going over her printouts on a stool at the counter.

"Something went wrong at the playground today," she said. She marked off another marvelous yuppie palace, a white box with no story in it, happily ever after. "That's not a terrace," she told the printout. "That's a balcony."

"What do you mean something went wrong?"

"Just that. What I said." She looked at him. "Something went wrong."

"What went wrong?"

She circled something, checked something. "I don't know what went wrong. That's why I said 'something.' We need . . ." That look again, of rapt idiot wonder. Quickly she gathered it in: "Ah! We need to—"

"That's all?" he cut in. "Something went wrong and on to the next co-op?"

The buzzer rang.

"That's dinner," she said, getting up. "I ordered salads so we can eat anytime we want."

She went off to tend to the delivery. She even had the groceries delivered, ordering by phone. Cliff tried to discourage this. The bill is always out of line; they stick extra items in or leave something out. They cheat you like crazy because no one's stopping them, because it's more time and trouble to correct their bills, because if you go somewhere else you'll get the same treatment.

"So what?" she said. "It saves time. You can always make more money, but you can't make more time."

They had plenty of money. They used to have plenty of time, too. Now they seemed to have different kinds of time, his and hers, a civil war in the family state. It's hard to want peace with so much in play. The winner gets to own all the time lying around.

Alison came back with two whopping bags of ready-made nonsense food and started loading the stuff into the fridge.

"Alison," he said, "why did you put Colin on a list with that jerk across the hall and the couch in the living room? 'Continuing Problems'? Is that how you regard our son?"

She inspected saran-wrapped plastic bowls. "One tuna, one chicken, one avocado." She fingered tiny containers. "Dressing," as if remarking that their presence fills a gap, answers a question. "Oyster crackers. Napkins."

He reached over and took the napkins from her and threw them into the air. It was the most violent protest he had committed in the last year; instantly, he felt he should have moved earlier. He had allowed her to fill the rooms of their mansion of love with mystery and acceptance — of anything, no matter what — to infiltrate his time with glum solitudes that wore a smile as jarring as an Eastern beggar's prayer bell, to haunt him by not being there.

"Now, *that*," she said, "is negative input. I will transcend it. You can have the avocado, if you prefer. Colin likes tuna. I don't care. Chicken . . . or whatever . . . because salads are becoming vulgar to me . . ."

Cliff grabbed the phone extension, ripped it out of the wall, and hurled it across the room to bounce off the oven door. He grabbed her printouts, wondered what to do with them, dropped them, retrieved them, shoved them at her. "What happened at the playground?" he said.

She paused, turned to the fridge, took out the apple juice, got a glass from the cupboard, poured the juice into the glass, put the container back in the fridge. Sipped the juice. Faced him.

"If I hear a Buddhist homily out of you," he began, dangerously mad.

She waved this diversion away. "What happened," she said, "is hard to describe. What I mostly remember is how I felt about it as it struck me. But I know that some things have to be experienced to be understood. Your treatment of the telephone just now, for instance, is an act of aggression against my emotional contours that may or may not make a picture when I report it to the yoga lady." A sip of juice. "She may not be able to see it. I mean, of course she could *see* it, but could she—"

He grabbed her glass of juice and threw it against the fridge, where it shattered. He tore the fridge open and threw the take-out salads onto the floor, against the walls, and along the counter. There was a silence now.

Then he said, "What happened to our little boy at the playground?"

"You cannot hurt others with violence," she said. "You can only hurt your—"

He struck her. He struck her again. Not hard. A gesture.

"That's what you can hurt," he said. "Like you're hurting me. Because I don't know why. Because this is what you're doing. Because you take the time to torment me. Now you tell me what happened in the playground or we'll do this war right now and I'll win because my patience is fresh out. The next thing that comes out of your mouth is an answer to my question or a provocation, which I will treat in the traditional manner. And you will be sorry." He was so mad he was shaking. "Talk, lady."

She said, "When Colin and I came into the playground . . . it got very quiet. We were alone. They left us alone."

Still shaking. "And what did you do?"

"We went home."

"Why did they leave you alone?"

"I don't know."

"Why didn't you tell me that in the first place instead of tantalizing me with this 'something went wrong'?"

"We don't live on the data," she explained, "we live on the feelings. And I wasn't sure how I—"

"Why would you call that boy a problem? Put him on

that damn list like a . . . like some agenda for the griev-
ance committee?"

"He is a problem. If his feelings will be hurt when I
take him to the playground, that is a problem."

"*They* are a problem. He isn't. The problem is outside."

"He is a problem because he is ill. Illness is a problem. We have to do something about it. You have been
putting off facing up to the karma of his—"

"*The boy is not a problem!*"

She moved away from him, surveyed the wreckage of
the salads.

And "*You* are a problem," he went on. "There it is."

She pulled some paper towels off the roll next to the
sink, still on her time.

"Maybe attention is a problem," he said. "Not
enough attention."

She sadly shook her head. "He gets all the attention
he needs. We do everything we can, both of us." Her *both*
was Betsy Ross's scissors shredding the flag. "It's medical
now. We have to feel that. We have to explore our feelings." She paused, clearly on the verge of some punctua-
tional revelation. Here it comes, he told himself. "That's
all I dare say," she concluded, "except that your castra-
tion-fear aggression is bound to destroy what is left of our
compact."

They stood posture to posture for a bit. Then she bent
to clean up the mess he had made of her takeout.

"Save me the avocado," he said, leaving the kitchen.

In the doorway of Colin's room, Cliff watched his son
sitting at his little desk, listening to a Muppets tape. Occasionally he took a sip of something from a ceramic mug
with his name on it. Alison had sent away for it, in answer
to an ad in the *Times:* "Your name on a mug for $6.95."
Last Christmas, that was.

"What time is it, Col?" Cliff said, coming into the room.

Colin turned around. He covered the watchface with his hand, to prove his expertise in time. "Eight-thirty?" he guessed.

"How could it be eight-thirty? That's past your bed-time."

"You know what?"

Cliff sat on the bed. "What?"

Colin switched off the tape. "Instead of starting kin-dergarten next year, why don't I be in a movie with the Muppets and Pee-wee Herman?"

"Well, we'll see what we can do about that, sport."

How can doctors treat a kid like this and not find a solution? Where do they get the steel? Mooching around in those white coats. These cute little faces looking up at them and all they say is, "We'll have to test." He looked so drained the last time, too, as if some dreadful beast of myth had been sucking up his insides. Yet he never com-plained. He went through it all the way you go through school or have your teeth cleaned.

"I know what part I want to play, too," said Colin. "In the movie."

The strangest thing about it all was that neither Cliff nor Alison had as much as spoken to a doctor on their own behalfs since they were married. They were healthy people.

"What part do you want to play?"

"I want to be the man that comes in at the end and saves everybody who's in trouble." He took a sip from his mug. "What if I did that?"

"You'd be a hit, sport."

"Then if I went to the playground, they'd all want to be my friend, wouldn't they?"

"They . . . yes, they really would."

The absurd thing about marriage, Cliff thought, was that you were expected to lie down every night next to someone you sometimes got along with and sometimes didn't, the antagonistic feelings colliding through force of culture. Through sheer politeness. Cowardice, too, maybe. Lack of Confrontational Output. Cliff couldn't understand people who said they didn't like kids, or couldn't get along with them. Kids are easy to like. *Grown-ups* are hard.

"How about a game of Chinese checkers, Col? We can listen to your music while we play."

Smiling, Colin went to his toy chest and pulled out the game. Cliff rose and went over to the cassette machine. "What have we here?" he said. "It's somebody's mug, all helpless and trusting. I think I'll steal a sip while no one's looking."

Colin was laughing, and Cliff switched on the tape.

Later, Alison put the boy to bed. Cliff had gone out for a walk. After the sunny spring of the afternoon, the cool evening depressed him, because only he, in this family and even the whole neighborhood and probably the world, had the correct time. He supposed he ought to have someone to talk to, and thought immediately of Ruth Ann, his coworker and mistress or girlfriend or whatever the hell metropolitan etiquette termed that now. His date? They're all kids again, dating. He saw himself loading Ruth Ann up with his troubles, the man obliviously spending the good time of the woman who humors him because a front of friendship redeems the humiliating hunger for sex. Well, I'm not that selfish, he thought. And I'm not oblivious.

He went home.

He looked in on Colin, visited there, sat on the child's bed and watched him breathe.

Christ, if I did something bad, I'm sorry. I repent. I'll

make up for it. I've been patient, haven't I? Even gallant.
I've forgiven atrocious acts of sabotage upon my well-
being. I've been gentle too long; that's why I got rough.
We all mark the limits somewhere. Then it's Confrontation Output time.

He put a hand on Colin's brow, not knowing what he
was feeling for.

He remembered driving over to visit his best friend
from high school, Charlie Duane, one summer during college. Charlie had developed a brain tumor and was suddenly dying, and nothing could be done; and Cliff recalled
Charlie's father saying, as he led Cliff to Charlie's room,
"This little boy is very, very ill." As if Charlie were still
four years old. As if our parents freeze us, visually and
emotionally, in the clarity of our innocence and the reckless, loving intensity of our need.

Alison was reading in bed. She nodded as Cliff
passed, on his way to the bathroom.

In the living room, he stretched out on the problem
couch with a vodka and lime and reflected. Some people
have to have something working all the time — the radio,
the stereo, a magazine, puzzle cubes. Cliff found it helpful,
sometimes, just to lie back and think about things. This
was a space of time, all his now. If something went
wrong, something must be set right. Problems are in the
eye of the beholder. The part you want to play is the part
you ought to play.

After a while he made another drink and put on
some music, schmaltzy orchestral arrangements of old
show tunes. "Easy listening," they called this, back before
there was Perrier or yuppies. Easy reading. Easy living, in
a no-fault morality of smash-and-grab feelings. It got very
quiet; they left us alone. What does that mean? *They left
us alone.*

Cliff checked Colin again, stood at his door and made sure he . . . what? Was not left alone. Was still being permitted to live under some riddle of survival. Solve me: and you'll have time and easy feeling and the part you want to play, one problem less.

Eventually Cliff got blitzed, and he dug a sleeping bag out of the closet and spent the night watching over Colin.

Saturday was Alison's big day to show apartments and Cliff's day to take charge of the family and its holdings, such as making Colin's lunch, taking him out, and answering the phone. Lunch, Cliff decided, would be BLTs, with separate platters of toast, bacon, lettuce, and sliced tomato, and a little bowl of mayonnaise. Colin sat at the counter watching his father put the show together. He had startling concentration for a four-year-old, sipping milk out of the mug with his name on it and commenting now and again on the preparations. There was nothing Cliff enjoyed in life as much as answering Colin's questions, nothing. Nothing.

Colin and his mug. He wouldn't drink anything except out of that mug. Even the juice in the box with the straw that devious manufacturers lavished upon a gadget-loving land had to be poured into Colin's mug before he would taste it. As if he would fade from the world if he could no longer grasp his name in his hand, witness a proof of his time.

"What do you want to do today, Col?" Cliff asked as they ate.

"Aren't we going to the playground? Isn't it warm today, too?"

"Yes, it's warm."

"This is good toast." Colin made his BLTs open-face, and ate them by hand, piece by piece. "I didn't get a chance to show them my watch yesterday."

Cliff nodded. After a while he said, "Why not, Col?"

Colin shrugged the way kids do, hiking his shoulders as high as they go, holding them, then dropping them so heavily you can almost hear the tendons bounce.

"You want some more milk?"

"I think I better have juice now."

Cliff took the mug to the sink to wash it.

"Could I bring my cassette player to the playground?"

"Let's travel light today, Col. I'll tell you what. How about trying something new? Instead of going to the playground, we'll take a long walk all through the city." He pulled a paper towel off the roll and began to dry the mug. "What do you say?"

Colin looked like a kid in some movie when they take away his dog. "Can't I go to the playground?"

Unknowingly overtaxing the ceramic, Cliff snapped the handle off and dropped the mug to the floor, where it smashed into shards and chips.

"Oh Jesus, Col, I'm sorry. I'm really sorry." Cliff quickly knelt to pick up the pieces, then realized how useless this was. The mug was totaled. "Hey," he cried, jumping up to distract Colin like a circus clown trying to dizzy an audience of orphans. "Let's go right out and get a new mug, okay?"

"Oh, I know it was time for a new one, anyway," said Colin, radiant in his cheery fatalism. "Where do you get a mug that you really like?"

"Don't worry, we'll find you one. How about we try it without the stroller this time, sport? You're a little big for a stroller."

"I don't use it much," said Colin. "Only when I get tired. You know."

Cliff nodded. "I know."

Colin nodded, too.

Cliff put a hand on Colin's head. "It's okay, Col," he said. "It's not your fault."

They went to a cards-and-souvenirs shop on Sixth Avenue, the kind of place that used to claim to deal in "notions." There Colin, to his delight, found a Mickey Mouse mug to match his watch. Even the box it came in thrilled him, because it bore artwork precisely like that printed on the mug itself. He refused to deface his treasure with a brown bag, and wouldn't rest till they found a bench and sat down so he could take out his mug and admire it.

"We better go to the playground," said Colin, "and show them my mug." He checked his watch. "I guess it's just about time for that," he said. "Right?" He looked at his father. "Right?"

"Whatchu got there?" cried a bag lady, plopping down next to Colin. "What's that cup?"

Colin silently showed her.

"That your drinking cup?" she said. She cackled. "I got one. My special cup, untouched by human mouths. Got to be careful these days."

"Of what?" said Cliff.

"The tremors of time," said the bag lady with great determination. "We're on a journey to a greater god, where they all talk with their hands. And the ones that don't get invited have to die."

"Come on, Col," said Cliff; and he took the boy to the playground.

It was the first warm Saturday of the year, and the place was in full session. Colin smiled as he walked down the concrete ramp, holding his mug and Cliff's hand. The mothers were alert. The kids shouted and pranced. The playground blazed with youth and energy. No one had

anything in mind but the moment. This is the way many
people live nowadays.

There was the little blond doll, Colin's friend. She ran
up to him, and her mother called out, "Marietta!" Her tone
was light. Cliff's eyes met hers as Colin started to show
Marietta his watch. So that's her name, Cliff thought, as her
mother called her again and she answered the summons.

"Come on, Col," said Cliff, moving deeper into the
playground. He felt the mothers' eyes on him; but I'm just
a man with his little boy. We bought him a mug. He
wants to show everybody his watch. Simple pleasures.

"David!" cried David's mother, when Colin was
about to show David his mug; and her tone was not light.
When David went away Colin tightened his grip on his
father's hand.

Cliff sat Colin on a bench. They watched the children
breezing by. Colin called out to one of them, and he replied, "No, I'm not allowed to talk to you."

Marietta's mother saw this, and turned away. Cliff
went up to her, and she put a hand on his shoulder and
said, "I'm sorry."

"What's going on?" he asked her.

She shook her head. "I can't help it," she said. "I
can't —"

"What's wrong with my son?"

"Perhaps you should tell me."

"What's that supposed to mean?"

"Clifford. You know what it means. That poor little
boy shrinks into a wraith, then comes back to life, then he
shrinks again. What's wrong with him? What does he
have? People are afraid of that."

Cliff shook his head. "Nobody knows what he has.
It's one of those . . . conditions. He . . . he just fades
sometimes. Is that a reason to ostracize him?"

"I know how you feel, because —"

"You do not know how I feel!"

She stood right up to him. "Oh yes, I do. I very certainly do. I happen to be a parent, too. I am very aware of . . . of the world a child lives in. But what you have is very scary to the rest of us. You have to understand that. There are *illnesses* flying around now, and no one knows who's going to get them or where they come from. We don't know who's safe. My husband told me not to take any chances with our daughter. Do you want to argue with him?"

She turned to look at the central playing area, where Marietta was being mock-threatened by three cannonballers playing detective.

"Let's see some identification," said one of them. Marietta put her hand to her mouth, giggling.

"You may be under arrest," said her assailant.

"She was a disorderly passenger on the subway cars."

"Colin," said Cliff, "is not contagious. I'm not ill, am I? My wife is not ill. It's just a syndrome, locked inside him. It doesn't come out. It's not a —"

"You don't know what it is," Marietta's mother said quietly. "Certainly I don't."

"Should we take her in, boys?"

"Think of the position I'm in. All of us. Think of it that way."

"Yeah, a vacation up the river should keep her out of trouble."

"I have to do what is right for my child."

Marietta, still giggling, ran away from the cannonballers and found herself at Colin's bench. He was holding his mug, out of the box and all ready to show. Wide-eyed, her hand on her mouth again, Marietta admired Colin's new prize. The cannonballers, unwilling to give up their game of cops and robbers, surrounded her, pistols at the ready; and three mothers sharply called out three names. The boys retreated. One of the adults added in, "Marietta, go to your mother right now!"

Marietta, bewildered, slowly walked away. The playground was still. A moment in the absolute present, time for the taking. Everyone was looking at Colin. He got off his bench, went to the water fountain, carefully filled his mug, and went back to the bench. He did not look around. He sat and sipped his water. He wanted to show them how his mug worked, what you can do with the things you have.

Cliff went over and sat with him, an arm around his shoulders.

The kids began to play again, yelling and laughing.

Colin put down his mug and studied his watch. His father took him in his arms and held him, and Colin started to cry. After a bit, he was quiet and went to sleep; and they stayed like that, together, for quite some time.

THE NUDE
SCENE

WHEN KATHLEEN WAS seven, she asked her mother, "When I grow up, what will I be?"

"Whatever you want to be," her mother replied.

"Hmm," said Kathleen, her hand on her chin.

"How about a nurse?"

Kathleen shrugged.

"A teacher?"

"I don't like teachers. They're always mean to the kids."

"Well, what do *you* think you should be?"

"I know, I know," Kathleen smiled. "I want to be a spook."

Kathleen grew up tall, slim, and pretty. Her parents keened when she departed Nebraska for New York, but they knew that she was a little too good for Nebraska

somehow. Too intent, too honest, too swift. When you ad-
dressed her, she answered the second your voice gave
out—if she hadn't already broken in on you—while everyone Kathleen knew took five or six seconds to reply to
anything, and that was on a clear day. New Yorkers move
fast. Kathleen expected to fit in very easily.

The modeling agencies could not use her; not eclectic
enough, they said. But casting directors who "developed"
television commercials loved her at sight, for they knew
she was sincere. How sincere was she? She was so sincere
the women on the covers of *Vogue* wished they had what
she had.

For her first few months in Manhattan, Kathleen
roomed with a cousin who lived in a high-rise on the Upper East Side. (Nebraska is wide open, but the families are
tight.) Then a studio fell vacant in the cousin's building
and her cousin's boyfriend bribed the super on Kathleen's
behalf and she got it. Two months later the building co-
oped, and Kathleen bought her studio on the windfall
from a detergent commercial in which she asked the boy
next door for the secret of his spectacularly bright wash,
was immediately asked out, and then joined by a spark-
ling hunk who said, "Finished, sweetheart?" as the boy
next door looked foolish and Kathleen's father, off in
Nebraska, growled, "Who's *that*?"

"Fred," Kathleen's mother cautioned him. "It's only a
play."

But it wasn't. It was only a commercial, and Kathleen
wanted to act for real, in theatres, playing people who
didn't spend their entire lives being sincere in laundry
rooms. Kathleen dreamed of trying Chekhov, Shaw,
O'Casey, even Philip Barry. She would read aloud from
her roles of choice in the cozy room she had staked out as
her Making It turf, a back apartment, not sunny enough
but overlooking a great mimosa tree—and how she would

pace and turn, heave into a chair for the curtain, and thoroughly emote! Kathleen was untaught, and not, perhaps, one of the great naturals. But at least she knew that she must somehow relate her feelings to those of the characters she portrayed. She knew that since Stanislavsky, since The Method, since Meryl Streep, the best theatre was the truest theatre; or no, the best theatre was truth, a penetrating spontaneity. An actor must have a passion for honesty.

Kathleen's cousin said no, in New York you really ought to have a passion for support systems. They had been reading aloud from the Gwendolen-Cecily teatime duel scene from *The Importance of Being Earnest*, and Kathleen chided her cousin for treating the tea things as if they were merely props in a play.

"That's what they are," said the cousin, wondering when her boyfriend would call.

"No," said Kathleen gently. "These are the tea things, and this is tea."

Kathleen's cousin put her book down. Enough of this reading from plays. She wanted to enlarge upon her favorite subject, Survival in New York. "It goes like this," she said. "Good friends, great apartment, great job, summer escape place, cab money, deep-pocket plastic, emergency gentleman willing to escort on short notice, and ambition for the future so it's worth surviving in the first place. Now." She went through this résumé, in more or less the same words, every three or four weeks to everyone she knew, including her boyfriend, who listened on the condition that she rub his stomach while she spoke.

"Almost no one gets all these down," the cousin went on. "Like they have neat friends, okay?—but a dingy apartment. Or the right job and an apartment with a terrace but no ambition. Nothing to live for."

"I'm living for art," said Kathleen. It would have

sounded pompous if she weren't so sincere. "For the right
to play Saint Joan, the Lady Millamant, Blanche DuBois.
Eventually Amanda Wingfield in *The Glass Menagerie.*"

"Yes. Okay. Uh-huh. But you've got to have your
minimum four support elements down, Kathleen, if you
plan to survive here. Four, at least. Great friends, great
job, great apartment, and lots of cab money, fine. Great
apartment, lots of plastic credit, a dependable emergency
gentleman, ambition, fine. But not less than —"

"How come no love?"

"Huh?"

"Your support things don't have love in them. Romance. A lover."

"Lovers turn up by themselves. You'll see."

"Oh, good," said Kathleen, thinking that it couldn't
be that easy.

The phone rang. Kathleen's cousin answered with
her usual "Okay," and, three seconds after, managed to
frown and grin at once. It was obviously her boyfriend.
"No," she said. "Don't change your clothes and don't
bring beer. Just come, you turkey. And come *now!*" As she
hung up, she explained, "He likes it when I give him
heck."

"What if a lover doesn't just turn up?" said Kathleen.
"I mean . . . don't you think love belongs on your list?"

"No, it just happens, like the weather. I've been here
for six years and I know."

Kathleen's cousin may have meant that a woman as
pretty and sweet (not to mention sincere) as Kathleen gets
snapped up because Mr. Right is right there waiting, and
he's smart and quick. Kathleen was snapped up by a
Boston WASP named Harlan Fahnestock, and no Har or
anything: one called him Harlan or else, though it
sounded to Kathleen like the little boy who would get
wild at a Four-H social.

Harlan Fahnestock was an investment analyst, and Kathleen's cousin was right: he did just turn up, at a party given by the casting director who kept hiring Kathleen to play America's sweetheart in television commercials. In Kathleen's business, one does not spurn parties given by casting directors; one arrives with something interesting and spends the time networking. But Kathleen came alone, and the casting director, who really liked her, took her up to this tall, terribly handsome, and somewhat stiff man in a wonderful dark suit set off by a tie so red, so prudently, handsomely, stiffly red—but so *red*—that Kathleen could scarcely keep her eyes off it. She spent the party talking to this man and not networking. She wondered what sort of man would wear such a tie—surely not the sort of man who would remind you of the Lutheran pastor back in Nebraska. Yet this man did. She was a bit surprised when he asked if he could take her home, and tried to pass it off with some deft Manhattan joke. "A kiss in the dark," she said, "on my stoop."

"I mean all the way home."

Kathleen looked at him. No, at his tie.

"You're an enchanting girl," he went on. "And men are going to take you to bed. You'll be safer with me than with the rest of them."

Startled, Kathleen reached for some more Manhattan wit. "Well, you know, I'm part spook."

"I'll bring you gently to earth."

Now Kathleen was shocked.

"I don't need to be safe," she said.

"I think you do."

He was right, and he did take her home and she felt safe, probably for the first time since she had left Nebraska. He was not an ecstatic lover, but strong and smooth and thoughtful. Dimly, as she fell asleep in his arms, Kathleen wondered what the Lutheran pastor was like in bed. Just before dropping off, she murmured, "He has nine children."

"That's news," said Harlan, who was about ten years older than Kathleen, and there was silence in the apartment, and they dreamed.

Kathleen was not a gifted actress, to tell the truth; she simply had a vision of herself in fascinating clothes speaking beautiful English. Like many others who float into the theatrical profession and, maybe, in a few years, out of it, she had an engaging personality that can, in limited arenas, hold the eye. But in an evening of heavyweight drama, Kathleen would flounder. Harlan caught this at once, and Kathleen knew he had, yet she didn't mind: for part of becoming an actress is proving oneself, astonishing one's friends so that they must trade in their unquestioning loyalty for an informed admiration. Kathleen did not expect to flounder forever, and didn't want flattery: she wanted loyalty, and from Harlan most of all. Frankly, she did not think all that much of *his* profession, come to that; and *he* knew, and he didn't mind, because he didn't think too much of it, either. But then he didn't believe in working out of a passion for honesty. Harlan did not have passions — he had beliefs. One was that men of family and culture and education went into a respectable and profitable line of work. He might, he told Kathleen one evening when they were talking of things, just as easily have become a lawyer.

"Why didn't you?" she asked.

"Because being a lawyer is like doing homework for the rest of your life."

"Being an actress," said Kathleen, "is like being on recess for life. Because it's like a game, but you take it *very* seriously while you're doing it."

They looked at each other, each glad not to have to do what the other did.

"You must respect my profession," Kathleen said, "even if I am part spook."

"I do respect your profession. I think it's very exciting to sleep with an actress night after night. Even if she is part spook."

Kathleen blushed. "The theatre is sacred to me."

"I know it is."

She looked away. "And I'm not an actress because it makes me fun to sleep with."

"I'm sorry, Kathleen." She looked at him now. "That was insensitive of me. I really meant that you're a very stimulating woman." He held out his right arm very slightly, and beckoned her with the tiniest motion of the upper two fingers, stiff and casual at once.

He's such a New Yorker, Kathleen thought, coming to him; and she was pleased.

Her cousin, however, thought him Bostonian, and not exciting enough.

"He gets a little quiet when strangers are around," Kathleen explained.

"He looks like he'd feel naked without a tie."

"What's so awful about that?" Kathleen replied, thinking that her cousin's boyfriend wouldn't look formal in a coffin. "He happens to be an amazingly nice man."

"Oh," said her cousin. "Nice," she echoed, in a tone implying that nice stood somewhere between acne and chronic drooling on the popularity chart. "That proves he's no New Yorker. Wait till he loses his temper and slaps you. Then he'll be a New Yorker."

Kathleen's eyes widened. "He would never slap me!"

"Listen, Kathleen, the man who doesn't lose his temper isn't a man."

"Does your boyfriend slap you?"

Kathleen's cousin looked dangerous. "Maybe he would if I let him. In fact—"

"I think I'm doing pretty well," Kathleen cut in, changing this absurd subject. "In less than one year in New York, I have a lively career, a cute little place of my own, and a handsome boyfriend."

"Do you love him?"

"Of course I love him," said Kathleen, wondering what love is, exactly.

"Anyway, you do not have your four things yet. Your support elements. I mean, that *tiny* apartment and—"

"I have ambition. Isn't that one of them?"

"Well, yes," said her cousin, grudgingly. "But it's the least important."

"I still don't see why love isn't one of the things."

"I keep telling you, you get that just by being here. New York is Love City. It's like the extra square of fabric they supply with a tailored—"

"I wish I could get acting jobs, at least. To feed my ambition."

Acting jobs—real ones—were hard to come by. Commercials, which paid much, much better in the first place, were easy to land and easy to handle, once you got your first one. Moreover, they were made, for the most part, by an entirely friendly group of people. What little Kathleen had seen of the theatre, however, suggested that the passion for honesty was compromised by other passions, especially those for attention, sympathy, and not getting badly needed psychiatric help. Kathleen's first (and last) day in an acting class treated her to more name-calling, screaming, and weeping than she had heard in ten years. (Recess for life, she reminded herself, as she left.) And auditions were like a Soviet show trial: everyone seemed determined to find you guilty of something, yet you knew you had done nothing wrong.

Getting into one thespian union made it relatively easy to slide into another, and Kathleen's commercial work entitled her to show up at Equity interviews and avoid the nonunion cattle calls. But for what? One day she read for the part of a lesbian nun rapist, not one of the classic roles Kathleen had bound her hopes upon. But perhaps all actresses had a responsibility to refresh the repertory with contemporary work, even if this meant pronouncing four-letter words Kathleen herself never used. Well, art is truth and some people do talk like that. She wondered if Meryl Streep would play a lesbian nun rapist — wondered, even, what a lesbian nun rapist *was*. A lesbian who rapes nuns? A lesbian nun who rapes?

But all right. Work is scarce; or do you want to play America's Sweetheart to death? So Kathleen plunged in. She knew that she had read abominably, yet the director sat grinning at her for quite some time.

They do that to make you nervous, Kathleen thought.

"You're very promising," he said.

"Thank you."

Then nothing, and he's grinning away.

"You know that, don't you?" he said at last.

Kathleen smiled politely. She wasn't sure what she knew, which is the correct way to handle Manhattan after spending the previous twenty years in Nebraska.

"Promising. Leads on Broadway, I'm talking. Hollywood, promising talk shows, *Entertainment Tonight*. Promising. All you need, see?, is the first break to get inside. *Inside*, lady. That's all you need, but that's very important. Because without that first job, you can't get anywhere. Can you?"

Kathleen waited.

"So promising," he said. "And so pretty. So very cute and pretty. Now, I can't think of anything that would please me more than to cast you in this play." He waited, as if she had a line due.

"Would you like me to read another scene?" Kathleen asked, hoping that was the line.

"No, I'd like you to come over here and let me taste your pretty mouth."

Three beats. Then she said, "I'll forget I heard that."

"Do you want the part or don't you?"

She very gently set the script down on the chair she had sat in, crossed the room, and went out the door without wasting another moment of her life.

She went to Harlan's apartment, a sizable den in Chelsea only a few blocks from where she had auditioned. Harlan wasn't home yet; Fräulein Halbeck, his maid and cook, was still at work. Mondays, Fräulein cleaned. Wednesdays, Fräulein washed. Thursdays, Fräulein cleaned and shopped. All three days, Fräulein cooked dinner as well. And whenever Kathleen was there, Fräulein would glare at her as if Kathleen were East Berlin. Fräulein was of Social Security age, but the kind who dies on her feet. She seldom spoke; even the sight of Kathleen weeping in Harlan's leather armchair didn't inspire comment, though Fräulein's eyes dropped many a remark. She bustled between the kitchen and the bedroom, the closets and the bathroom, checking the sauerbraten, changing the bed linen, shredding the cabbage, straightening the pictures, and resenting Kathleen.

This, Kathleen thought, shaking herself in shame, is not how a New York woman behaves. Maybe I don't have enough support elements, but I shouldn't fly into tears just because the theatre is filled with people like that.

Fräulein mashed the potatoes ruthlessly

Anyway, I don't want Harlan to see me crying. He'll be home any minute. I'll be reading a book. Would Saint

Joan cry if a man tried to seduce her? Would *Siobhán McKenna*? I need to be tough and I will be tough.

Fräulein inspected the meat as if she believed it were trying to burn on the sly. No. She smiled; just right.

Years from now, Kathleen thought, I'll be laughing about it. Bad experiences make you strong.

The oven door slammed, Harlan came in, and Kathleen burst into tears, all at the same time.

He saw her, put his attaché down, took off his jacket, came over to her, pulled her right up out of the armchair with both hands and held her. He may bear a little boy's name but he's quite a man. They were so used to each other by then that only after considering it later did she realize that he had said, "I won't let you go till you tell me what's wrong" without actually speaking it.

"*Sie weint der ganze Tag!*" Fräulein snapped, surveying them. It sounded unfriendly, and they ignored her.

One of the notable things about New York is that while it is filled with love it is also filled with careers, and Kathleen did get a part at last, in a surprisingly uninflamed off-Broadway comedy about six alumni of an orphanage spending Christmas together after a twenty-year separation.

"It's such a neat script," Kathleen told Harlan. "All these great confrontations, and a little flirting, and it's sad underneath because—"

"Orphans?" said Harlan in a tone suitable for "leprotic child molesters?"

Kathleen put the script down with an air, and she stayed calm, but she was annoyed. "What's wrong with orphans?"

"How can you play an orphan? You have parents who keep in touch so regularly that if I didn't hear their ring by dinnertime Friday night, I'd tell the phone company to send a repairman. Your mother sends cakes through the mail as if there were no bakeries east of the Mississippi and your father calls me 'young fellow.' Sweetheart, no one is less of an orphan than you."

In her passion for honesty, Kathleen said, "Acting is observation. Acting is technique."

"No doubt."

"*No!*"

Her force made him stare.

"No," she repeated. "Not 'no doubt.' It *is.* Acting invents reality. You don't have to be an orphan to play an orphan, you just imagine how an orphan feels. Acting is sensitivity. Which you could use a little more of."

"Oh hell, Kathleen. It's not that important."

"Yes," said Kathleen. "Yes, it is. It is." She is not a spook. She is a truth, a feeling of how the facts appear. A rendering, a distillation. An actress. The nerve of him.

"Do you want to marry?" she suddenly asked him, not the usual Kathleen, a gutsier Manhattan girl now. A Making It Kathleen. "Well, *do* you?" she went on, glad that she could startle him.

But Harlan, cool as always, startled her. "Of course," he said.

"I mean, do you—"

"—want to marry you? Yes. Is that what you wanted to hear?"

"What about children?"

"It's usual."

Kathleen had always seen herself with a little boy and girl, about three years apart. The boy, she thought, should be the older, and on Christmas he could wear a little red tie. Kathleen would be a good mother. She was patient, like her own mother; and enthusiastic and reliable.

"You don't have children because it's usual," she told Harlan. "You have them because you want them. Because, if you don't mind my saying so, you *deserve* them, out of your mutual respect and love." She was furious.

"Kathleen, people don't live on a sense of entitlement. They live on a sense of what is usual."

"Well, *I* am not usual!"

"You're building nothing into a big fight."

Oh, it most certainly is not nothing, Kathleen thought, but she was too angry to speak just then. How beautifully two people can be together, how nicely they fit—then a tiny difference of opinion shudders into a vast gaping pit, and helplessly they tumble in.

"If you don't respect me," said Kathleen at length, dangerously reasonable, "you shouldn't want to marry me."

"Respect is what, Kathleen?" said Harlan. "Do you want respect, real respect? Or do you want theatre?"

Kathleen didn't quite understand that, but it sounded fierce, and she rallied to reply, but he just reached for her and held her, because he had had enough fight and this is his solution.

And the trouble is, Kathleen feels so happily nested in Harlan's arms.

Lovers will quarrel. Then, the first thing they ask is, Can I get along without that one? If the answer is yes, they weren't lovers: they were dating. If the answer is no, they'd better make up.

Harlan apologized and Kathleen thought, I'm getting tough with the wrong people. But I have this passion for honesty.

Kathleen's colleagues had comparable passion. Some of her fellow actors were so Method they behaved at all times exactly as their characters would, and since one was playing a loud idiot and another a pushy cad, the customary postrehearsal beer-and-burger sessions were rugged. And they would treat the stage as if it were a room and there were no audience to play to: they would turn their backs to the seats or mumble so dully even Kathleen, onstage with them, couldn't make out their words. But art, Kathleen reminded herself, is contrary. A challenge. One scene in particular defeated her, one in which she seduces one of the orphans into seducing her. There was no rough language, and a blackout spared them the fervent details, but the scene just was not coming, till finally Marco, the pushy cad, said, "Maybe we should take off our clothes."

Kathleen said, "I . . . what?"

"Because you're being so uptight about it. Yeah."

"It's not in the text," cried the playwright, jumping up.

"Yeah, well. Maybe it should be," observed Marco.

"It's a valid point," said the director.

Kathleen said, "I really don't want to — "

"Because they're going to do it," Marco went on. "So what's the big secret? Right? Bodies? Come *on*!"

"If I had wanted them to strip," the playwright began, "I — "

"Big deal!"

"Maybe if we just rehearse it in the nude," said the director. "A look-see." He patted the playwright. "Just to try it out."

Kathleen said, "I don't believe I'd be — "

"If they'd play the text," said the playwright. "I mean, really, if they'd use their stupid actor noggins and read the words and — "

"Maybe this text lacks a little something," said Marco. "This text, I don't know." He let his script slide to the floor. "Oh look, I dropped the precious brilliant *text*!"

"*You* gave the worst audition of anybody!" the playwright screamed. "I warned them you were nothing!"

"Why don't we just," the director began as the actor stormed out the street door. "So, uh, if we could," the director went on as the playwright stormed out the front door. "Well," the director told Kathleen.

"I don't want to take my clothes off," Kathleen said quietly.

The actor and the playwright eventually drifted back and the director went on to other matters. But the next day, when they reached the same scene, the actor again suggested they play it without clothes. This time the playwright agreed they could try it nude for the purposes of rehearsal. Apparently he and the director had gone out for beer and hamburgers, too.

Kathleen still said no, and the director said they could hold off for a day and would Kathleen go out for a drink with him after rehearsal?

He started in with how nicely she was coming along; and what a poignant quality she brought to the character; and how theatre is a process and you have to experiment and nothing's ever finished, ever; and so why won't she just rehearse the scene with Marco as they have so very patiently asked her to?

Kathleen said no in every way English works. She said she loved the play and (most of) the cast and was very stimulated by the opportunity but she just didn't see how taking off her clothes would improve the scene's presentation. She insisted, "We have to find the way to *act* it."

"Acting," the director told her, "is the most honest thing there is. You're up there naked, showing the public who you are, begging them to respect your feelings. Or am I wrong?"

He waited. Kathleen, who agreed with him, would nonetheless make no reply.

"I'm not wrong," he pursued. "You're naked, vulnerable. You become someone else, someone who vomits his guts out. Yet who does the vomiting? *You*. You're the one who's there, not the character. *You*. You, naked—so what's the difference if you're dressed or not? What are clothes? A *mask*! A mask, and theatre is truth." He extended his hands as if displaying an unarguable fact. "The truth." He nodded. *"Truth."*

Kathleen was silent. The director, sensing that she wouldn't give in, accepted a temporary stalemate and adjourned. "Thank God it's Friday," he sighed as they parted; and Kathleen went straight to Harlan's—thank God it *was* Friday because Fräulein Halbeck wouldn't be there—and she called her agent and said, more or less, "Help."

He said, "You have to do what they're doing."

"Whoever is doing nudity now?" cried Kathleen, betrayed.

"Sounds very avant-garde. Could make the show hot."

I don't want to be hot, thought Kathleen, hanging up. Worse yet, Harlan made no comment about her latest adventure in the naked city of theatre. He nodded pensively, raised his eyebrows comically, and clicked his tongue. But he said nothing.

"What should I do?" Kathleen asked.

"What you want to do."

"No, I mean . . . how do I deflect this nude thing? They're kind of ganging up on me."

He cut slices of lime for the Perrier without as much as loosening his tie.

"Harlan," said Kathleen.

"Right here."

"I have to disarm them."

He handed her a glass. "I won't tell you what to do, Kathleen. If you're old enough to love, you're old enough to make your own decisions."

"Don't tell me. Advise me."

"On one condition: what I suggest, you must do. Must, Kathleen."

"Why?"

He took the armchair. "People pay me a considerable commission for my advice."

"On investments."

"They take it or they find someone else to advise them. If my advice is worth hearing, it's worth taking."

"On *investments*, though."

"Investments," said Harlan, with a wink, "are life. Money is life. Do you think theatre is the only truth?"

Kathleen sat opposite him. She felt very embattled and wanted something more sympathetic from the man she slept with.

"Acting is an investment," Harlan observed. "You gamble with your time, and your emotions, and—most important of all, I expect—a certain amount of hope for success that other professions pay back more securely. More quickly. What if you didn't have those lucrative commercials? You'd be typing or waiting table. Maybe for years. Years and years, Kathleen. It's not an investment I could recommend."

"Are you advising me to give up my life's ambition? The only support element I have?"

"I'm not advising you unless you're committed to my advice, I told you." He smiled. "And what is a support element?"

Kathleen outlined her cousin's list.

"What about love?" asked Harlan, a slim and reasonable man, a little tired just now.

"Well," said Kathleen, "it depends who is making up the list."

Harlan nodded.

"It's just that it's so unfair," Kathleen went on. "They

know we don't need to do it. They *know* that. Maybe there are people who enjoy taking off their clothes, but I'm not one of them."

"Isn't that the point?" He seemed more than tired. Exhausted. "For men like this director, there's no winning in stripping a willing victim. You can't debauch a whore — you debauch an innocent."

"Is that . . ." she said, ". . . what I am?" She meant to say, ". . . what they're doing?"

"I'm going to take a nap. Come lie down with me."

"No." She put her feet up on the couch. "I have to think."

He pulled her up. "You can think next to me."

Thank God it was Friday because there'd be no rehearsal, for two days of thinking time. But then, Kathleen realized, there was nothing to think about. She didn't want to do a nude scene and she wasn't going to.

Kathleen imagined what her father would say if he knew. He had a slogan that ran, "Nothing good ever happens in a place like New York City. Never did. Never will."

Kathleen's cousin had plenty of opinions on the matter, all so irately directed at the world of men that she ordered her boyfriend out of the apartment. The indecency! The hypocrisy! And what did Harlan have to say?

"Harlan won't say anything unless I . . . let him tell me what to do."

Kathleen's cousin was speechless.

Kathleen gave a sad shrug. "He doesn't want to waste his advice."

"That *animal!*" her cousin said at last. Words were failing her, and she could only make noises, like the breathy oohs of officious aunts in Edwardian novels.

"He did say one thing," Kathleen ventured. "He

thinks that the men in charge of the play are trying to . . .
well . . ."

"*Ooh!*" her cousin observed.

". . . debauch me."

The cousin was silent for a bit. "What does that
mean?"

"Corrupt me. Sensualize me against my will."

Now the cousin was so disgusted she couldn't even
say *ooh*.

"Tomorrow is Monday," said Kathleen. "It'll start all
over again. Unless they give up."

"You're new in town, so let me tell you a secret about
men and sex: they never give up."

"Everybody gives up somewhere along the line."

"What if you had to choose," her cousin asked, "between doing what they want and getting fired?"

"But it's not a choice yet. I need a way to get them to
back off before it comes to that."

Her cousin, with an odd look, said, "Let Harlan tell
you what to do. Those Boston people don't have guts but
they're smart."

"Harlan has guts."

"No, he has ties."

Kathleen was too thoughtful to take the joke. "Do
you think I should let my lover tell me what to do?"

"No," said her cousin. "But I'm dying to hear what
he'll say."

Monday came, but the director concentrated on the
third act and the nude scene was not mentioned. Tuesday
morning, however, she arrived to find that the cast had
been given a late call. Besides her, there was only Marco,
standing alone on stage, grinning. And he said, "Okay,
let's strip." He said, "So we're going to go for it."

Kathleen just stood there.

"Hey," Marco called out to the director. "I told you!"

"Go gently," said the director.

The playwright shook his head and snorted.

"Kathleen—" the director began.

"No," she said.

"I *told* you, man!"

"Look, we've been very patient, but—"

"No."

"They grow up chicken in Iowa," Marco exulted.

"Excuse me," said Kathleen, and she left, and took a long walk and reminded herself to be tough, but all she could think of was the way the three men were looking at her when she walked into the theatre. The three goons.

Kathleen went home and practiced Saint Joan and let the phone ring. She wondered if all theatre was going to be like this play. Then she called Harlan at his office.

"It's important," she told him. "I'd like to speak to you. But now. Would that be possible? Right now?"

He took a few seconds to read her tone, then said, "Meet me at my place in an hour."

She got there first. When he opened the door, he stood in the entranceway regarding her, and she thought he might be annoyed; but he crossed the room to her so fast, she thought he must be a New Yorker after all. Boston is more heavily paced. And he held her with a New York grip, demanding and possessive.

"That damn play," he said.

He released her but held her by the waist, and he smiled, and said, "Now you smile."

"I'd better not."

"Come on."

She smiled, precariously.

"What an actress," he noted. "Once more, with feel-ing."

They went out to lunch. At last, over the coffee,

Kathleen told him what had happened, and asked him what to do. So he gave his advice that she would have to take.

"Quit the play," he said. "Those people you're working with are creeps using theatre as a front."

"I think they want to be honest. I guess those two characters *would* be undressed if they were alone in a bedroom together. I mean —"

"They're not alone in a bedroom. Are they? They're on a stage in front of an audience of strangers. What do you want, Kathleen? If theatre were *really* honest, everyone in plays would be saying um and uh and repeating themselves a lot. And if you were Saint Joan you'd be burned alive and the play would close on opening night."

Kathleen said nothing, and they walked back to Harlan's apartment in thoughtful silence. It was the first day of natural spring, not the season's first calendar date but the day when New York's strangely unfriendly spring sun unveils the arms, navels, and legs of teenagers, laborers, and bums. Chic New Yorkers prefer fall, even winter. New Yorkers look good in coats.

The cross street was empty, but Sixth Avenue was crowded. Two workers, shirtless, cordoned off behind red tape, tore up the street for one of the utilities as shoppers and strollers ambled around them. An old woman, carefully waiting for the green light, started across the road leaning on a cane. Out of nowhere, a teenager roared up recklessly against the traffic flow on a bicycle and crashed into the woman, who crumpled with a feeble scream and lay on the asphalt, her limbs splayed. One leg was shaking.

Kathleen gasped and turned to Harlan; he had leaped over to a telephone booth and calmly pulled out a man who stood there calling him horrible names as Harlan dialed.

All around Kathleen, people froze in shock. One of

the workmen was kneeling over the old woman, stroking her forehead as he murmured something. The only one in motion was the teenager, who shook himself and re-mounted his bicycle without as much as a backward glance. He would have ridden off if the second workman hadn't grabbed him by his shirt collar, lifted him off his bicycle, and yanked his arm so violently it cracked. Kath-leen saw him kick the teenager into the gutter—he was shouting something, or both of them were; she saw ev-erything but she couldn't hear—and still no one moved. The old woman was there, and the teenager, and Kath-leen, shaking.

"Dj'ou call the medics?" the second workman asked Harlan as he crossed back from the telephone booth.

Harlan nodded.

"Good man."

Harlan took Kathleen's arm and steered her on.

"We should . . . shouldn't we call the police?" Kath-leen asked.

"I called nine-one-one for an ambulance."

"But that man broke that boy's arm."

"Too bad he didn't break his legs, too," said Harlan. "Then he'll think twice before he goes slashing through the streets running down pedestrians."

They said no more till they got inside Harlan's apart-ment. As he rummaged through his mail, Kathleen said, "I'm amazed at how calm you are. After what we just saw."

"I'm angry about what we saw. But it's not going to change my life." He shook his head at her sorrowing face. "You want to know about the honesty of theatre? What did we just see? That was *honesty*. An old woman was probably crippled for life by a street urchin who couldn't care less about her, or you, or me. Do you want honesty or do you want theatre, Kathleen? Think about it."

He was indeed angry. Reminding herself that she had agreed to take his advice, she called her agent to tell him she was quitting the play. For some reason, her agent didn't like no for an answer. Leave it to him, and they'll work it out, and so on for quite some time, till Harlan strode over and took the phone from Kathleen, not over-gently.

"Will you hang on a minute, please?" he said into the receiver. He held it against his chest. "It's only a play," he told Kathleen. "And you're not a spook. And love is a support element. I think an important one." He picked up the receiver and said, "This is Harlan Fahnestock, Kathleen's lover. She's quitting the show. Tell them I said so."

And he hung up.

TERESA
FORGIVES
HERSELF

THERE WAS A MAN AT the corner of Sixth Avenue and Bleecker Street at noontime, holding up handmade cardboard signs numbered from one to ten as women passed by, the numbers being his rating of their looks. He, a featureless, potbellied construction worker who labored at a nearby site, was barely a one, but this in no way diminished his enthusiasm. He smirked as he judged.

Teresa ignored him. She had been avoiding such men all her life. But the seventh or eighth time she passed, safe on the other side of Sixth Avenue, she stopped to watch. A question had hit her: does he juggle ten signs? He didn't. After a few minutes, she had seen all his signs, a ten, a nine, a seven, a five, and a two. For a moment, Teresa wondered what would happen if she passed him, if she allowed him to rate her. For a moment only, for she knew she never would.

Teresa was not pretty. Not good-looking. Not sexy.
Not "exotic." Not anything in the category called Lovably
Featured. She was not a horror. Intelligent and honest,
she had concluded, after years of sifting the euphemisms
of her friends and reading the impatient critiques of
strangers, that she was acceptable. Good enough to get by
in a host of situations, good enough even to command
some little authority, some respect, if she remembered to
keep a pleasing calm about her. But not sharp enough to
entice, to promise, to win. Rough men left her alone, and
that can be useful. But so did the nice ones.

What kind of life did she deserve? Teresa designed
charts to guide her thoughts. There was something reassuring in the setting down of names and terms, the making of distinctions, the scheduling of a program. It was like
planning a little library of your existence. What kind of
family did she deserve? What job, friends, living space?
And, yes, what kind of romantic life? For surely everybody
falls in love sometime; far less attractive women than
Teresa could be seen patrolling every block of the town
with men in tow. Teresa was tidy, thoughtful, and so thor-
ough in her charts that, once made, they were seldom re-
drawn. Teresa was perceptive. That is often the result of
being somewhat less than good-looking: you find something else to maneuver by.

Teresa knew what job she deserved: she had long
planned to be, and duly became, a librarian. This was fair,
she knew. She read a great deal—another result of looking like Teresa—and found herself constantly urging her
favorite stories upon her friends, lending books and, when
necessary, issuing reprimands to those delinquent in returning them. She *was* a librarian, then, had been all
along. Why not make it official? Perhaps she should have
become a writer, for she had that sensitivity that forever
regroups inwardly, in pain, then pushes out, in relief,

seeking to reorder the world along more just lines. But she lacked the writer's ability to believe pretty lies. And she was a gifted librarian. No one in all the Jefferson branch knew the decimal cataloguing system as she did. Hearing of a book, even of an idea for a book, she could immediately locate it on the shelf by number. At times she assigned numbers to chance comments: on the subway once she overheard a grade-school teacher distressing a colleague over the quality of an American history textbook she had to teach from. Teresa murmured, "Nine seventy-three point zero seven," and the woman turned to stare. "Wouldn't that be nine seventy-three point zero four?" she asked Teresa, slightly amused. "United States, historiography?"

"Zero seven," Teresa told her. "United States, historiography, study and teaching."

The woman said nothing, but her face read, *"Jeepers!"*

What kind of family did Teresa deserve? She had not done badly. John Irving might have plotted the characters, she thought: everyone well-intentioned but somewhat unintelligible. Her parents tried to accept her at her own valuation—she could see them listening carefully to what she said, but then they would look at each other as if signaling, "Did you understand that?" Neither did. They were Old Country, born in New York but raised in a kind of Naples West on Mulberry Street. English was their first language, but they smiled in Italian. Teresa's older brother was distant, her younger brother congenial; both took her for granted as a fixture of the house, like television or the bowl of Planter's peanuts Teresa's mother maintained on the dining room table. (She considered it a hostly extravagance.) Teresa wondered if this was the living space she deserved. She had saved up and gone to look at apartments, but what was affordable was unlivable, what was livable was in Washington Heights or Brooklyn, and everything else was a co-op.

She asked her older brother if he had any connections in the rental trade.

"Yeah, sure," he said. He took a long look at her. "What do you want to move for, huh?" he asked. They never mentioned it again.

So she lived with her parents, twenty, twenty-one, twenty-two, undated, unmarried, unloved. What romance did she deserve? Was she to wait or seek? Some nights, in her room, she would go halfway through a chapter without truly reading; instead, she had been thinking how foolish it was to let another day pass without trying to put herself in the path of someone who would meet her and become enchanted. Or was it a wasteful lunacy to think of enchanting a man? She could rise and wash and dress and go out. It was in her power. That's why the torment is pure: you *know*, every moment, that the alternative is in reach. Love is free. It beckons. It says, If you wait too long, you will lose access. I am not on permanent hold, it says.

There were days when Teresa was content and days when she was restless, obligated to use the city. On one of the restless days, Teresa forced herself to accompany some girls from the library to a bar in the East Sixties, and the barmaid brought her a glass of sherry and said, "From the blue tie," pointing out a man sitting at the bar. He seemed nice enough; why wasn't he looking at her? Was she supposed to approach him? Maybe that was it: "Thank you for the drink" is the first line, to forestall those obscene come-ons men were expected to hand out, to establish a social rapport. That had to be it. Teresa knew nothing of bar protocol, but she was well-mannered enough to know that when someone gives you something you say thanks.

So she waved at her library chums, pointed at her sherry, made a "wish me luck" grimace, and went up to the man in the blue tie and said, "I'd like to thank you for the sherry."

He turned to her with an odd look, something between surprise and irritation. Then he heaved about on his stool and put his back to her.

Teresa was stunned, but collected her wits and let them steer her back to where she had been standing. What could she have done wrong?

"Hey, real sorry," said the barmaid, coming up. "That joker says he meant someone else."

Teresa nodded. The barmaid ambled off. Teresa thought. She looked around her, averting her eyes from the man in the blue tie. She put on a preoccupied smile, as if passing a few minutes before departing for an impressive engagement elsewhere in the neighborhood. She considered nodding her head to the music, then thought she'd better not. She looked over at her coworkers, avidly talking to what appeared to be twins. She surveyed the general run of people in the bar, and decided that she wasn't *that* much worse than the other women—and, while we're at it, the men weren't exactly Hollywood material. Some were noticeably overweight, or had terrible posture, or greasy smiles—and at least one that Teresa knew of, in a blue tie, was atrociously thoughtless. All right, the barmaid had made a mistake. Would it have been so difficult for him to play along, give his innocent victim a few minutes of conversation so she wouldn't . . . she didn't have to . . .

"Hey," said an unshaven man in a wrinkled shirt. "My big friend would love to get to know you."

Teresa blinked at him.

"Know where he is? Look down."

"Here." Teresa handed him her drink. "I haven't touched it. Please give it to someone nice."

The bar was seventy blocks from her home, and Teresa walked all the way.

What kind of friends did she deserve, at least? One must have friends. In novels, Teresa noticed, the protagonist never seemed to lack for people to talk to, be understood by. But in New York thousands were utterly alone. Where did one make friends, really? Teresa drew up one of her charts. The categories were Childhood, the Neighborhood, Work, and Chance. She filled in the names of her friends where they belonged, and decided to distinguish them further by a rating code, from one to ten in ascending order of closeness. Like that man on Sixth Avenue, she thought, with a start of disapproval. But then he was rating women on their looks, a helpless vulnerability; while she was rating both sexes on degree of intimacy, entirely a matter of free will. We can't choose how we're born but we can choose how we behave.

We can choose our friends, too; why had Teresa not chosen more? Her rating code yielded only two tens, and they were virtually honorary by now, both companions from grammar school who had gradually lost touch with Teresa after marriage. There was an eight in the Work category, Andrea Walters, Teresa's lunch partner when she went out; usually Teresa took a brown bag into the rec room. But eight was generous for Andrea, sensitive and moody, impossibly protective of her shelf of specialty, Feminism, American, history and polemics. The next highest score, on the whole chart, was a six—her father, one of the few men who made the list at all.

This is not a good showing, Teresa thought. I wonder if I'm lonely.

She considered whether or not to put Kathleen on the chart. They were not friends exactly, yet across the library counter Teresa felt a flow of some warmth as they

chatted. Teresa greatly envied Kathleen her looks, of a radiant prettiness, clean and bright. She envied Kathleen
because she knew that being pretty was how Kathleen
got her boyfriend, and probably how she got him to come
to the library with her. Few couples came there; when
you have romance, you are your own story. Libraries are
the refuge of the lonely. But there they were, this couple,
usually on Saturday afternoons; she would take out something in the 790s or an 812 — drama; playscripts — and he'd
get an Ed McBain or a Larry McMurtry. People who saw
Teresa every week of their lives never passed a word to
her. But Kathleen had begun saying hello, then threw in a
word or two about something or other, and finally they
introduced themselves and actually had conversations, especially when Teresa was on desk duty in the main room.
Kathleen and Teresa were forever comparing literature to
plays — Teresa thought of it as "their" topic — because
Teresa felt that nothing could replace the richness of a
novel and Kathleen felt that the vivacity of performance
brought composition to life. They used such words, too;
talking to Kathleen made Teresa feel intelligent. She knew
she was, of course. But it was invigorating to use it, stir it
about.

Yes, Kathleen definitely belonged on the chart. But
where? Teresa had met her at work, but that category was
really for colleagues. Teresa wrote Kathleen in under
Chance — just as well, as there was no other name there.
What rating? Nines and tens were people so close you
could write a book about them. Even an eight seemed to
need some purely social connection, not conversation
across a counter. Teresa wondered how Kathleen would
take it if she suggested they have lunch some day. Kathleen was terribly nice, but reserved, too. She might be
taken aback by a personal appeal in a professional situa-
tion.

Then this happened. Teresa came into the living room to say good night to her parents, more or less watching television as they always did—they'd run it, at least, and sit facing it, certainly, but did they pay attention to it through their running analysis of the day's events? No matter; it made them happy. Teresa had no interest in television, except Channel 13, when it screened adaptations of novels. But this night with her parents she was fascinated by a commercial in which a pretty young woman challenged her husband to tell the difference between instant and brewed coffee.

"I know her," said Teresa.

"And this brand is less costly than the other," the woman in the commercial was saying.

"The kind of wife gives her husband instant coffee," Teresa's mother philosophized, "would put ketchup on spaghetti and say, 'This is dinner.'"

"That's Kathleen," said Teresa.

Her parents looked at her.

"I know her. From the library."

"Tell her espresso after dinner," said Teresa's mother. "And not to worry about cost."

"Maybe a little gelato," said Teresa's father.

"Maybe," Teresa's mother agreed.

Overwhelmed by the coincidence, of the life in the art, Teresa sat with her parents, staring at the screen. Kathleen is on television, she kept thinking. Kathleen is an actress, a public quantity. Could she be famous? Teresa knew little of pop celebrity. Her parents were delighted that she was spending the evening with them for once, but Teresa didn't really want to talk with them. She wanted to see Kathleen again. On television.

In the library a few days later, Kathleen laughed it off. "It's a living," she said.

But Teresa remembered seeing a witty and flamboyant man interviewed on Channel 13, and he had said, "People will forgive you anything if they have seen you on television."

"It's magical," Teresa told Kathleen. "It entitles you somehow."

"To what?"

Teresa did not know, not yet; and they went on to discuss what sort of play one might make of *Vanity Fair*. But Teresa could not shake the idea that Kathleen's television appearance made her special, even though intelligent people did not think highly of television, especially commercials. But then it did not generally matter what intelligent people thought, did it? It mattered what *everyone* thought, preferred, did.

So it happened that when a local news station programmed a feature on the Jefferson Market Library and proposed to audition those of the staff interested in taking part, Teresa leaped forth. Perhaps she wanted to be forgiven for not having been born a Kathleen; perhaps she wanted a chance at the magic herself, the entitlement.

Kathleen coached her in video deportment. "Don't say 'What?' It slows up the action and a thousand viewers will switch channels. Always look right at them, into the camera. And smile."

"That's all?" It seemed skimpy advice for such a major adventure.

"It just zips by, you'll see," said Kathleen. "Suddenly they're taking back their microphones and turning off the lights, and you'll beg them for more."

Smile. Doesn't everyone smile when people are looking? Teresa wondered how often she smiled, looked right at them, said "What?" She practiced in her room, slipping down the hall to her parents at their television to check on the way the pros carried it off and returning to her room for more practice. At her interview, she picked the television person in the center of everything, looked right at her, and didn't say "What?" Teresa was chosen, and stood on the library steps with a camera aimed at her and about twenty people hanging around deciding things.

Teresa was on television. She would be phoning the names on her list to warn them to tune in and watch her become entitled. Passersby slowed to examine her, even the Sixth Avenue traffic. Some Con Ed workers, shirtless in the heat, were staring as if they'd never seen a television camera before. The television people decided to take a panorama of the building, and raked the scene with their magic, and, thus encouraged to take part, the Con Ed workers began to pose and yell silly jokes. One of them, a dark-haired Italian of about twenty-six, was extraordinarily muscular; when a girl went by, he agitated his chest muscles and grinned at her.

"And of course it's a very historic site," Teresa was saying. She looked right at them and smiled.

The television people were avid and precise about what they decided. They were impatient with mishaps. But Teresa didn't let them fluster her. I'm on television, she thought; or no: I'm going to be on television, later, when they air the feature. Still, I'm already the center of attention. Already forgiven. The Con Ed worker with the amazing body was still looking at her, and she calmly marveled at him as he showed off and joked with his gang. Teresa wondered if he was joking about her. He seemed to be pointing her out, and the other Con Ed workers were looking at her, too. Astonished at her lack of tact, she refused to move her eyes away from the man, and he went on seeing her, their two faces blank, just looking. She wondered what he was like, wondered how many women of Teresa's age and background knew men like that, and where they had met them.

He isn't handsome, she thought. But with men that doesn't seem to matter. Not to them.

The television crew moved into the building, following Teresa as she revealed points of note in the collection. Kathleen was right; it zipped by, leaving Teresa stimulated and deflated. She wanted to do it all over, and then another program. Perhaps she should do one on single young women who don't know how to meet men. She thought again of the Con Ed worker, dwelling, some might say shamefully, on the heavy contours of his torso, the fullness of his thighs, the way his hair was clipped at the back of his neck. Maybe it's not improper for me to think of men as sex objects, she thought. Maybe it's not immoral. But maybe it is culturally hopeless. Why torment yourself with reckless wishes?

For the rest of the afternoon, Teresa enjoyed house celebrity, accepting the homage of the admiring and snubs from the envious. For an hour or two she tasted life as known to Barbara Walters or Connie Chung. Even the outside world was paying court: Teresa was summoned to the front desk, where someone had apparently asked for "the TV lady."

It was the Con Ed worker.

Go for it is what Teresa told herself as they spoke. She tried to seem pleasantly, not forwardly, flattered. She thought: be like Kathleen.

Perhaps she succeeded, because he asked her if she would go on a "coffee date" with him. The term was new to her. He could wait till she got off work, or come back. There were some nice places, he said. They could go to? He hoped she wasn't offended that he was coming on so strong and, like, he wasn't dressed up. But it's just a chance thing, he said, you know?

Teresa said that would be very nice, and her day was

nearly over. He was waiting for her when she came out, at
the curb, looking up the steps at the library doors as if he
wanted to see her make an entrance into his world. They
settled in at an outdoor table at the V-shaped place on
Seventh Avenue, and Teresa ordered an *au lait* because
that's what a woman of the world would ask for.

"Make it two," he said.

How easily he handled himself. Don't men ever get
nervous?

She fielded his questions about her life, glamorizing
herself slightly, and asked him the same questions. His
name was Polo. He had never, he said several times, been
on television. They were an odd match with the same
background: same nationality, similar neighborhood and
family—yet he was vital, massive, a specimen; and she
was sensitive and unfashionable. By rules of personality,
they deserved different things, she thought. Why had he
wanted to meet her? She sneaked a look at the chest
muscles swelling his T-shirt, and he caught her and
grinned.

"This friend of mine," he said. "I like do a favor for
him sometimes, so he lets me use his place, you know?
He's always traveling, for his job. Since I don't have a
place of my own."

"Everything is so expensive," Teresa noted, trying to
imply that she had found a bargain somewhere.

"So anyway he's out of town now. I have it all to
myself. It's real neat. Up on the East Side, you know.
Swank, real swank."

Teresa, unpracticed but intelligent, waited.

He smiled and shrugged.

"I was just thinking," he went on after a moment.
"I'd like to take you there." He took her hand very gently,
counted her fingers, smiled again. "I could be really nice
to you."

Teresa wondered if Kathleen's handsome Ivy League boyfriend had, their first time, put it like that, with his vested suits and Ed McBains. How would Kathleen handle it? Teresa had no doubt how *she* was going to handle it. She put her other hand on his as if men invited her to apartments every day of the week, and, woman of the world, said, "Let's go."

Was it because I was on television? she wondered. He saw the camera and thought . . . what?

He lowered the blinds, his face serious and calm. It was a small studio, uncluttered, clean. More space than furniture. There was a doorman out front.

"Let's get comfortable," he said.

She followed his lead, wearing his expression. Serious. Consenting adults. Like other Catholic girls of her generation, Teresa had made her few experiments in odd places with furtive, fumbling boys of her high school. Later, she felt less guilty than disappointed. Not that she had expected the romantic sweep of a soap-opera actor: but it wasn't fun. It was forced and gloomy and insistent, like writing a book report on a novel you hated.

"This is going to be fun," however, Polo told her.

Teresa certainly hoped so.

In the semidarkness, the television lady became passive and let the man from the audience take over. But she looked right at him and smiled, and he smiled back, a bit crookedly, and he tripped while taking off his pants, and his laugh was so easy it asked her to laugh along. When they kissed, she touched him boldly, and he was very considerate with her, yet very direct, and she kept thinking, He isn't handsome.

He said, "This is really good."

"Of course," she replied, that woman of the world.

He knows something about looks, she thought. He knows how he wants to be seen.

One thing—maybe the only thing—that you can't pick up from books is how to make love, but Polo was so expert he didn't need much help. "Hold on tight, now," he urged her. Teresa was so glad to. She was having the sort of fling that pretty girls take for granted. As his head bent over her, she felt his hair, his ears, his neck. She wondered if later she would miss him, become obsessed and morose. Or maybe they would turn into sweet-hearts—but he was enough like her brothers to make that implausible. She deserved better than her brothers. She wanted a very sweet man in a suit, a just man who read books and watched Channel 13.

This is my fling, Teresa reminded herself as Polo was really nice to her and she was swept away.

Much later, in full darkness—it must have been nearly ten or so—they lay next to each other and talked. Teresa did most of the talking; Polo's most intent remark was, "Hey, if I was a smoker I'd be smoking now." He laughed, and suddenly Teresa said, "Why did you ask me up here?"

"You *know* why, lady."

"Tell me, anyway." Because she didn't.

He shrugged, lying under her, and her body trembled. His finger drew a valentine on her back. "Because my hobby is, I collect tens."

After they had dressed, he said nothing about seeing her again, did not ask for a phone number. But he kissed her for a long time at the door and she took a cab home and sat in her room thinking and dreaming. She knew it was cheating, but she entered Polo on her chart under the Chance category—it's just a chance thing, you know. She rated him a ten, which was only fair.

And the next morning, walking to work, Teresa held

her ground and walked up Sixth Avenue on the east side, intending to march right past the man with the numbered signs. He wasn't there. Probably his job had ended and he had gone off to some other site.

Teresa walked on, disappointed. Surprised that she was disappointed.

She was smiling.

ON THE SIDEWALKS OF NEW YORK

THE CACKLE LADY SAID she never had no ID card, and Mamie just went, "Huh!" Some candy went by, and the two women watched them. Then Mamie went on, "You got one."

"I *don't*."

"Let me *say*, because *everyone* got ID card. You maybe not carry one. Sure. You ain't see it, hear tell of such. Sure. You never *received* ID card. But yes, you got one. Everyone gots one. They making them up in an office somewhere. FBI making them up. I got ID card. You got ID card. The President got ID card. The President's turtle —"

"I never liked turtles."

"You know why they gots ID cards?" Mamie continued. "Because of crime. And they got to arrest the perpetrator. So then they go around this big room full of ID cards, and they pick one, and that's the perpetrator. So they can arrest him?"

"Turtles are mean," says the Cackle Lady. "They move around as slow as ice-cream wrappers in the gutters, say April, May. Way down where no one sees them. Then they sneak up to you and *snap!* — off goes your leg."

"That's what ID cards is for, to arrest you." Mamie shook her head. "They come and that's it, you run hard. You got to run."

The Cackle Lady was going through her bags, checking to be sure everything was there. One bag was for food, one for clothes, one for souvenirs, and one for anything else. When her bags got too full, she hid them in places known only to her, but sometimes, when she came by to retrieve a thing or two, they were gone. Candy was stealing them, she was sure. You can't trust candy. They say to everyone in their office they're going out for lunch, fancy as can be, sitting down at a table and saying, Oh, do you have tea today? to a waitress. What they really do is poke into the Cackle Lady's hiding places and run off with her bags.

The Cackle Lady took out the remains of several hamburger sandwiches, which she habitually speared out of the garbage and restyled into one. She kept plenty of napkins handy to protect her hands from mystery sauce. As the Cackle Lady ate, Mamie looked on balefully.

"Don't *like* that stuff," said Mamie. "They put things in it to hypnotize you. Then you have to come back and have another."

"Fine with me," said the Cackle Lady. "I always want another anyway."

They sat in silence as waves of candy passed them, some averting their eyes from the two women and some staring at them. One candy man in a suit shook his head in disgust as he went by, so the Cackle Lady cackled at him.

Mamie moved on, because there was something she had to do. Time, like the city, is a sequence of places in which certain things happen, a rhythm of coming and going, errands and accidents. You move from one moment to another just as you move from place to place; and after a while all places are the same and an accident is as useful as an errand and anything you say is as good as anything else you say, and maybe saying nothing is better. You move on.

So the Cackle Lady continued to eat and the candy continued to pass and Mamie picked up her stuff and moved on. She was looking for something she had lost some years before.

Every day, in the good weather, she went off to look. She had a vague idea of where it ought to be, but vague ideas are of no use in a city with so much time and place in it. One street might look like another for years; suddenly the town shifts and, for block after block, everything is different. Sixth Avenue, now: Mamie remembers how it looked before the office buildings came, and all the vendors and musicians and strolling candy. Sixth Avenue was dark, once, under the El, all brownstones and suspicious-looking people hightailing out of sight when you told them off. That was before ID cards, back when Mamie and Dade were living with a dog named Follow.

They lived down by the West Side Highway near a tunnel place. It was not a good life, but when Dade made a hit somehow they could go out, and Mamie would buy Follow a hot dog, which was his favorite thing to eat. It was not a good life, because Dade only wanted to lie around drinking Thunderbird, or sing, or get mad. When Dade got mad, Follow would stay close to Mamie watching Dade, and when Dade made a move that dog would growl, long and slow, so mean. And Mamie would pet him and say, "That's right, Follow."

Follow was a stray dog, and everybody knows that is the best kind of dog because when you take in strays they treat you like God. Follow would not part from Mamie, so they used to take long walks together. That was a good piece of Mamie's life. And Follow was smart. He always knew when Mamie had a bit of spare change from the phones, because when they passed a hot dog place and Mamie had change, Follow would stop and look up at her and bark. And Mamie would say, "You want a downtown?" Because that's what Mamie's mother had called them, "downtowns." But when Mamie didn't have change, Follow would pass those hot dog places right by. He was proud as well as smart.

Finally Dade got drunk one night and whacked Mamie and Follow bit him, so Dade threw Follow out the window. From the top floor, that was, where they were living. Then Dade turned around looking at Mamie and she ran for the door, but he caught her in the stairs and kept on whacking her, and he kicked her, too. She didn't say nothing. Later on she woke up and went to find Follow. She looked at him there in the back alley for a long time and then she went away. She just hunched up her shoulders and started walking. Some folks sit there for hours or maybe they pace a little bitty. Mamie walks. She has walked all over, in every part of the city, for a long, long time now. Long time. Once she came on a place where they were making a movie, and they put her in it in the background, doing her walk, and they gave her some money but somebody took it off her while she was sleeping in the park by the library. Whoever it was touched her, too, but she pretended to snore and shake and he went away.

Nowadays she will walk to her old tunnel place and

think about where to head next from there. The tunnel is just about the only thing she remembers from her old days that is still where you can get to it. Then she goes looking. If it's not one street, it'll be another. She'll find what she's looking for some day now. She knows it's a good sign if she spots a stray dog. You can't miss a stray, because they move around kind of quick and businesslike, as if they weren't really thrown-away dogs, but snuck off from their friends for a spell. Even after being alone for weeks, a dog keeps hunting around at people to see if they are the ones, because dogs may know about downtowns and spare change, but not about time. It's funny, though, that when you try to pet a stray it jumps away and its head goes down.

You know what the Cackle Lady said? She was out by the clinic and she saw Dade, joking around with some friends, and then his face got funny and he threw up. But the Cackle Lady also says she saw Michael Jackson in the clinic, and Rosemary Clooney and President Truman. The Cackle Lady said President Truman gave her a cigar and Mamie said, "Let's see it," but the Cackle Lady said she already ate it. Mamie just went *"Huh"* to answer, but she knows that a President is candy and candy do not go to clinics *at* all. Dade, maybe, but not Presidents. Maybe the Cackle Lady did see Dade, but Mamie doesn't care. And once she decides she doesn't care, she won't care about *anything,* even the nitrogen bomb or aliens. She has cared about things, just like anyone, but there comes the time to hunch up your shoulders and do your walk. And if any alien tries to mess with her, she is not going to pretend to snore and just hope it goes away, not anymore.

Sure, she used to think things would come out right if you don't make a lot of noise, but now she knows that isn't true. So if you're tired of walking and want to take a nice ride, you can get on a bus and holler at everyone that you want bus fare and you can do pretty good. The drivers don't care any more than Mamie does. The Cackle Lady won't get on a bus. She says if you don't get off in time, they ride clear up to Alaska and won't let you get back. But the Cackle Lady also says she saw Marilyn Monroe on a bus once, crying, naked.

This is the problem, that you can't believe people. They got too much *energy*. You just mention the name of someone, or a place, or an idea, and they say, "Oh, I know him," or "I been there," or "I know all about that case." Everybody is like the Cackle Lady, telling you about what they saw. Half of it they don't remember right and the other half they just making up. And that can ruin the place all over as sure as a wrecking truck. Mamie is trying to remember very exact about how it was, and she doesn't want anyone running her off with crazy stories *at* all.

Dade was like that, stories and everything. That's what pointed him out to Mamie at first. He had a way about so. A way of some kind. He could be nice when he thought it was time to be nice. But it took a lot out of him. And eventually he'd come around to resenting you. Back in the old days, when they first met, Dade spent all night in the bar on the corner of the street where Mamie was living. Sometimes she was there, too, with Follow. That dog didn't like Dade right off.

Dade said, "Sure do admire the way you step into a place, girl. Like you was a nice close friend of the owner. Dade notice a thing like that."

Follow growled.

"Sweet dog," says Dade.

"He don't like you," says Mamie.

"Oh, he still sweet."

Mamie didn't like Dade, either, but she let him talk at her, do his nice thing. She knew what was coming, and when it comes she says *no* so loud Follow barks. It wasn't the right time for Dade that night, Mamie was thinking, whoever he be. But they kept meeting at the bar. The table would fill with Mamie's friends, or Dade's, and they all got friendly. So Mamie got friendly with Dade, though Follow told her no.

Mrs. Lotto didn't like Dade, too. And that was something to make a body wonder, because Mrs. Lotto said you got to like everybody. The good ones, she said, they can't help being liked. The bad ones — well, it's not their fault entirely. Someone was mean to them before they was big enough to help it, and that makes them bad. You have to lean down close to the pain, Mrs. Lotto said, to understand it.

She didn't say it in those words, because she talked fancy. She had more name, too, Mrs. Somethinglotto. But Mamie never got it all the first time so she called her Mrs. Lotto. It was a wonder they didn't get a ID card out on her and take her away somewhere, because Mrs. Lotto was always out doing things that the candy people don't like. She never passed a cripple or blind man without giving them a nickel. No matter how poor she is, she said, they poorer. That's okay. But then she talk to them, ask if they lonely, and if they was she invite them to dinner. Sometimes they wouldn't come, but sometimes they did come and then they wouldn't leave. Mamie would wait till Mrs. Lotto gone somewhere and go next door and throw that garbage out. When Mrs. Lotto get back, Mamie tell her they got a call to go somewhere else.

That night Dade threw Follow out the window, Mamie was thinking maybe to speak to Mrs. Lotto about the pain of Follow, and maybe Mrs. Lotto would help her lean down and understand it. Mamie didn't know why, but she was afraid to see Mrs. Lotto. She figured maybe to come back another time to Mrs. Lotto, but another time the pain of Follow was still there, always too strong and

stinging for anybody to be ready to understand it. Now it's
all these years, and the time is good, but Mamie can't find
the place. She's looking all over, been looking for years,
but the streets is gone, the people gone. You look at a
building and you say, I was there once, but you stand outside and watch that building and see only candy coming
in and out, and you *know* you was never there, because
sure as the Cackle Lady going to cackle there was never
no candy where *you* was, looking at you or looking away,
the two things candy do best. Candy people. One day
they came and got a ID card on the West Side Highway,
even. Come back the next day. Gone.

Mamie sat on a child's swing in a little stone park
near a new high-rise. Wind tore at her, the hard weather
coming, eager. Mamie's tired. Can't do her walk, can't find
what she lost, can't do nothing. The Cackle Lady says, if
you wait long enough, candy takes everything from you.
They need it all, more than we do. They use it for things.
The Chrysler Building is made out of saved tin foil, she
says. But Mamie's seen plenty of candy crying in the street
cause they lost something themselves. Mostly they lose
money, or friends. But they don't lose a whole place.

There's candy people now, right here in the children's
playground, giving her those looks that pretend they ain't
looking, trying to figure out about Mamie. But she'll never
tell. Mamie don't enjoy to talk at candy. Just looks.

Man says, "Would you like half of my sandwich?"

Mamie takes it.

He sits on the next swing. "I'm waiting for some very
dear people. What's your excuse?"

Mamie shakes her head.

"No excuse?"

Mamie gives nothing.

"And half my sandwich and all?"

Mamie looks at it.

"Aren't you going to eat it? It's good. I'd eat it, only I'm not hungry."

Mamie puts it in her bag. Later, she'll trade it to the Cackle Lady for something. And she is very casual as she says, "I'm looking for Mrs. Lotto." She can be conversational, you know. "She was here once. Somewhere around here."

"When once?"

"Before."

"Long before."

Mamie says nothing.

"Right?"

"Before *you*, anyway."

He laughs, and Mamie shrugs. If he asks for her ID card, Mamie going to do her walk and *move along*.

"It's a great day," he sighs. "The city is so peaceful here. Midtown is crammed with people, all of them frantic to get to tomorrow. So hungry for things, hungry for . . . for the money of things. They never pause. All that power to hit on, that . . . Confrontational Input. That's their energy. Selling. Trading. Buying. Instead of feelings, they develop material needs. I think that's why I've been fighting with everybody lately. I feel superior to them all. Almost all."

"You possibly did something loco," said Mamie. "All candy be loco. They changeable. You can't be sure of any."

He swung a bit, then slowly came to a stop.

"That's why I'm looking for Mrs. Lotto. Seems she can help a body when the pain is deep."

"I'm sorry you're feeling pain."

"Who ain't?"

He nodded. "There it is."

Mamie got up. "I got to talk to Mrs. Lotto." She hefted her bags and walked around the swings several times. "I got to find that person." She dropped her bags, took a few steps, came back to them, and sat on the ground, hugging herself.

"Have you tried looking her up in the phone book?"

"I don't remember what the front of her is called," said Mamie. "Now, how could I look her up in the directory?"

"Do you remember her address?"

"I don't remember to *find* the building, now how can I *name* it, then?" She was almost wailing. "Maybe it's not there! Not to *be there!*" She clasped her hands, her head shaking, so rueful. What mistakes a body can make, letting a place run out of its time, so they come and take it away. That's how they do. Letting it go. Don't this candy see that?

"Where was it?" the young man asked.

"You have a argument, okay," Mamie went on. "If you come back soon, everything still be there. But what about you wait too long, and you *can't* come back? Somebody look at your clock, say, 'That one's time be up,' and they send out the authorities, shuffle everything here and there. Turn around by and by, you got *nothing*. Everything gone from you. Nothing left but the tunnel. Good for *nothing!*"

The man nodded. "Ma'am, that is really lost," he said.

A young woman and a little boy approached them from the street, both eating ice-cream cones.

"I got you one, anyway," the woman told the man. She gave him a vanilla cone.

The boy was looking at Mamie.

"Hey, Col," said the man, "why don't you show us your watch?"

The little boy asked Mamie, "Do you want to know what time it is now?"

Mamie grumbled some at this. She don't need no time anyhow. All the time is gone.

"What time is it, sport?"

Colin stretched out his arm, so Mamie could read his watch. That's candy, always got plenty of time for anything they do. Candy and time is like a marriage. Hold it, they say. I want Thursday again, I need more night, I could use me another breakfast. Everywhere they go, there's time.

"Come on," said the man to the woman. "Sport." As the three started off, the two candies wrapping the little boy in looks, the man turned to Mamie.

"You take care of yourself," he said.

Mamie didn't even look at him.

"I hope you find what you're looking for."

Mamie shook her head.

"Well, sometimes . . . sometimes things that seem far out of reach are just around the corner. I have to hope so."

Watching them go, Mamie muttered, "That boy don't know about it *at* all. Candy always believe everything around a corner to you."

Mamie thought of the corners she had turned, all the nothing she had found there. A part of her began to realize that she wasn't going to find Mrs. Lotto, but the part of her that needed to was stronger, and hushed the other part.

Time to do her walk. But Mamie's so tired. Maybe the Cackle Lady saw Dade and maybe she didn't. But one thing is sure, that *somebody* saw him. Because everybody's somewhere, and just because Mamie don't see them don't mean *at* all.

Mrs. Lotto's somewhere, too. If Mamie could find her, Mamie would feel much better, because Mrs. Lotto knew things and also she knew Mamie, and could tell Mamie about Mamie things even Mamie didn't know.

So Mamie got to find Mrs. Lotto, even if everything that make sense suggest she can't, because Mrs. Lotto's got to be somewhere in all that time of the city that keeps on going past you. You can get tired all you want to, and you can fall down and cry about it, and you can even die, slap down there in front of everyone, all covered with snow and ice and screaming to them for help. Nothing's going to change. You dead, everyone else eating ice cream. No one dead's going to change the city, no matter how proud and smart you be, or how many clocks you choose to look at.

Stray dogs, that's all it is. Except for Mrs. Lotto. Stray dogs barking at each other, say Take me home, Give me a downtown.

Mamie's so tired.

That candy child and his clock. Follow was quicker, and where is he now? Gone up in the time. Some say the city is buildings and some say it is pain. Mamie says it is time, because that is the only thing that never stops going against you. There's always more buildings, more pain. There is always less time.

The wind rises, circles around Mamie, bites her as she turns against it, crying, "Stop you!" Snatching at her bags, hiding from the time. She doesn't like the look of this winter *at* all.

New York Woman

JESUS, CUT ME SOME slack here, will you?

Get the picture: Don has spent something like two hundred bucks on her for one night, what with tickets to *Cats* for starters and dinner at this Village joint she read about in *New York* magazine that like, if she couldn't tell her friends about it so they could wobble all the way home with envy, the whole evening is nothing.

Honey, whatever you say. I'm a good guy. I can ride the circuit. I'm with you. You want *Cats,* and I mean sharp seats down front there, you got it. You want a fancy joint in Greenwich Village, I give you this fancy joint with sugar in my heart. All I want is a nice time in return, a little heavy metal and making nice at the far end of the evening's adventure. I show you respect, you show me respect, and that is a decent thing between a man and a woman.

So *Cats* is like . . . fun, if you like a theatre show where nothing happens and everyone's an animal. And a hundred smackers seems like a lot to pay for just one play. You could nab a big-time hotel room for that. And the restaurant is okay, even if it's the kind with a menu in some foreign language so you have to ask the waiter what everything is and feel like a dope, which they probably do that deliberately in the first place to make you grateful they're letting you in at all.

So okay. Don's a good sport, anyone'll tell you. But there's a certain moment on any date when you know whether you got a straight-up lady or some pure bimbo on your hands. A certain moment, and the whole evening's spread out before you like a building's cut up on a blueprint.

I'm coming back from the men's room, right. And there she is, carrying on a conversation with the two hotshots that were sitting next to us. And it suddenly hits me that this fancy honey with her *Cats* and her Greenwich Village restaurant and her menus and waiters *can't exist for like two seconds without she's involved with some guy.* Any guy. Whoever's handy. Like she can't wait quietly for you to come back, no, she's got to be playing off some male man — and not because she's on the make or anything, because as a matter of record here she's pretty fucking tight with it. She's the virgin of Queens, in fact. So what I'm talking about is not flirting. It's just like she can't *relate,* see? to anything except a man is there and she's playing to him. You know it? She can't just sit there and wait for me to come back and then it's more Don. No. She's got to find some *other* guy and do it with *him* till I get into the picture again.

Which can be pretty damn annoying to the man who spent two hundred bucks on her that night, hey? And the lady is such a dumbo in the first place that when she asks the hotshots next to us if they come here a lot, and they say sure, they live just down the street, and like they're roommates, and they got those va-voom leather jackets hanging on their chairs . . . well, it's pretty damn obvious they're gay, isn't it?

I mean, what more do you want, the phone number of the guy who does their flower arrangements?

But Don's date is asking them where their girlfriends are tonight. What is she, a marriage broker? And finally they've had enough of this and they want to get back to their own stuff. And believe me, they can see that Don has had it with this four-way conversation, because he always shows you just how he's feeling right on his face and that's it. But she's still going away at them, flapping her mouth off like Don's not even there.

That's the moment: pure bimbo. So it's a wrap, kiddos one and all, and when I drop her off at her place, I give her, "Thanks for a swell time, hey?" with this tone in my voice that makes sure she knows it wasn't so swell. And I'm walking. Then at the elevator I turn with a slick smile there and she's staring at me in the doorway, real confused. I'm supposed to feel bad, see? Because it's this rule about you shouldn't be mean to the ladies, no matter what. Like no hitting on them, no crude remarks, no showing them their place. But enough is enough, thanks for the scam, and I'm out of here, you copy? It's a good lesson for her, let her learn it.

DON: Don't jump on your guy's program.

Let's go to work. Don is complaining to Ralphie about his hard-luck dates, because he can't seem to find one lady who's right for him. Not that Don has any trouble getting into the loving zone. That is not the problem

here. The problem here is crazy ladies. They've all got
something wrong somewhere.

Like this one tonight, who's got to tackle every man
she sees.

Or the bimbo from Forest Hills who thought she was
so ace because of her la-di-da job in some show-biz
agent's office on Fifty-seventh Street. She kept calling
Don "the Martin Scorsese type," and what the hell is that
supposed to mean? Are you saying you like me or you
saying you junk me?

Or the one in Bay Ridge who would write Don these
sexy haikus after their dates. Look, I like to know that my
girl appreciates what I can do for her when we mambo,
because I'm not the kind of a guy who takes his pleasure
without listening to the rhythm of the lady. No, when
Don gets to the heavy metal he is one of your considerate
guys. Besides, the hotter your lady, the better the fuck, so
making sure that she is right in there on top of the fun is
good for everybody, right? You know, Miss Bay Ridge
Haiku there would cry out sometimes right in the middle
of it, like Don was hurting her. He knew he wasn't. But
still he would reach out to stroke her neck, and kiss her so
sweet, and man, she loved it. She really loved it. Because
that is a very hot and loving thing.

Then one time he called, and she said she can't see
him anymore because his life lacks a theme. I mean, come
on, a *theme*?

DON: What am I, a goon? Because that's the
feeling I get from these ladies, you know.
Now, am I a goon or what?

Ralphie tells Don, "Your trouble is, all you've been
dating is B and T. Like those girls you pick up in Cre-

scendo's. Those and Bridge and Tunnel babies from the boroughs. What you need is a girl with swing, dig? A Manhattan broad."

"Swing?" says Don.

"Swing. Smarts. Style. Girls with style is what. You hang around Crescendo's, all you're gonna get is those borough rags. Think they're hot stuff. So what are they? *Nothing.* Tight-butt princesses. I've done Crescendo's, haven't I? Do I know?"

The Crescendo is this dress-up disco bar I frequent, as you might say. I ran into Ralphie-boy there one night and now he refers to it like we went to high school together or something. Crescendo's, he calls it. The asshole can't even get the name right.

So I told him, "I don't get all my girls at the Crescendo, okay?"

He says, "You ought to try the Manhattan bars. Up on Second Avenue. Benchley's. Zig Zag. The Dizzy Duck. Or how about those ads in the *Greenwich Village Voice?* Some very hot things in there, bo."

Don't you love the way he finds to talk? *Bo?*

"Hot things," Ralphie-boy goes on, his eyes kind of fading out on you like he's dreaming, "for the man who knows how."

"Yeah," I says, "I don't need no blind dates."

"Can't hurt to try."

"*Ads,* for the love of Christ."

"They got a lot of swing in those ads. And you won't get stuck with no Brooklyn princess in the *Greenwich Village Voice,* anyway."

Ads, he gives me.

LEWIS MUMFORD: Any fair picture of New York must confess the underlying sordidness of a large part of its preoccupations and activities.

THOMAS WOLFE: Nowhere in the world can a young man feel greater hope and expectancy than here. The promise of glorious fulfillment, of love, wealth, fame — or unimaginable joy — is always impending in the air.

Ads in a paper. This is a dumb idea, like everything that comes out of Ralphie. But Don bought a *Voice* and read through the personal ads, just to see what swing might be. It was hard to get used to the idea of a girl putting an ad out for a date. What kind of girl would do that? Don was about to throw the paper down in disgust when he spotted one ad unlike the others:

DON'S AD: Woman offers course in metropolitan style. Men: are you failing to meet the women you want? Free-lance photographer of great sophistication will teach you to be romantic and suave. Wolves beware. This is strictly business.

"Wolves beware" — Don liked that. Maybe he ought to clip the ad for Ralphie, hey? That guy could use a little suave, maybe. "Men: are you failing to meet the women you want?" Hell, who isn't? Look, if Don gets stuck with a rag from time to time, imagine what ... on the other hand, why is a sharp guy like Don having such a hard time meeting the women he wants?

Don is looking at himself in the mirror. He turns, hands in pockets, struts, grins.

Frowns.

He *is* sharp, right? Right?

I mean, he's polite with his dates, waits for them to sit down or holds the door, all that stuff. He may not be a Hollywood pretty boy, but he's real solid looking and he takes care of himself, never been in better shape.

He changes out of his work clothes, because . . . just to . . . for the hell of it, okay? Gets on the dark brown slacks and the tweed sports jacket, shirt open at the neck. How's that?

On second thought, he gets on a navy blue tie. Gives the whole thing a sort of college look. A college guy with big shoulders and pirate's eyes. That's what that blonde from the Slope told him, pirate's eyes—and she meant it as a compliment, because she was holding his hand when she said it, right across the table from him the first time they went out. She sure wasn't no dog, either, and they had a great night together. Then Don must have done something wrong, or said some dumbass thing without thinking, because she got real cold on him all of a sudden, and from then on whenever he called she was busy and couldn't talk.

"Free-lance photographer of great sophistication." She probably looks like somebody's leftover aunt. Wolves beware is right. Beware of the dog.

Don tries loosening his tie and smiling like a Manhattan playboy type. He decides he looks lopsided. Cancel that one. He looks fine the way he is. And who needs a "course in metropolitan style"? A leopard don't change his spots, right? Kind of daring of her to put her phone number right there in the ad. That's real temptation. That really is.

Don picked up the *Voice* and read the ad again. Just

for the fun of it, he imagined calling the number and saying . . . well, so what do you say right there? "I want to
take your course so I can get sporty and meet fancy
ladies"?

Don shrugged out of his jacket and laughed out loud.
He got up and like paced the room, thinking it out. Back
at the mirror, he told himself, "Look, you're pretty damn
sporty like so, huh? And if the ladies can't dig it, that's
their problem!"

Right?

Right.

So he put his jacket back on and straightened his tie
and called the number in the *Voice* ad.

What you are, he told himself, on his way to their
first meeting, is a first-prize dope. Because in the first
place she's asking fifty bucks an hour, plus he has to
freight the expenses. And in the second place, who says
she knows anything? And in the third place, the whole
thing is like extremely dumbo in the first place. But hell.
Hell, a man owes himself an adventure every so often.
What else did he have to do, anyway? Kill another evening at The Crescendo?

She had a nice voice on the phone. And she spoke
real careful, like a doctor.

"You must be wondering what my credentials are,"
she told him.

"Sure," he said. What the hell.

"I am a New York woman," she said. "I have a small
but very high-tech flat in an extremely gentrified neighborhood. My friends are in theatre, music, publishing.
One of them is a highly regarded performance artist. My
dress is fashionable, but not slavish. Every other Sunday,
perhaps a madcap hat. When I'm in a bright mood, I
throw a party with live music. A string trio, friends of

mine. When I'm feeling desperate, I sample something in the housewares department at Bloomingdale's, even if it's only a refrigerator magnet, and I brighten immediately. I take my breakfast each morning in a café downstairs at a table by the window. They know me there, and I watch the city tumble past. I am a photographer. I see things as they are and as they might be. The visual. The cultural. The verbal. This is style. I do not care about the emotional, because the reason we have style is to hide our emotions and keep everything light and smooth and crisp. I am a New York woman."

There was a pause.

"Sounds like you got a lot of swing," said Don at last.

"What?"

"Swing. Style."

"*Swing.* I must remember that."

"Yeah, swing."

"I must emphasize," she went on, "that my course in metropolitan style is strictly business. Yes, I do *not* get involved with my clients in any way. *Ever.* It's only fair. You'll forgive me being so intense about it, but I don't want there to be any misunderstanding."

"Sure, honey."

"Not honey. My name is Brenda."

Flustered, Don said, "That's a nice name."

"Thank you."

She told him to meet her for dinner in a restaurant on Columbus Avenue in the Seventies. He was thinking, as he walked in, that if they spent two hours it would run him a hundred smackers *plus* the food tab. But Don wouldn't turn back now—he liked to see things through. Besides, this real cute brunette was giving him the once-over, and Don figured as long as he had to wait for his *Voice* lady, the New York Woman, he might as well make this little sweetheart's acquaintance, and he ambled over to her table. But before he could snap her a line, she said, "Don?"

Startled, he began to stutter. "No, I . . . uh —"

"I'm so sorry," she said, smiling, calm as eggs at breakfast. "You see, I'm waiting to meet someone I've never met, and I —"

"I mean, *yes*, I am. I'm Don. Like . . . you're Brenda?" He sat opposite her, startled again when she held out her hand. What, does he kiss it? Then he remembered that some women shake hands with men. That's real swing.

"Hey," he said. "How did you know it was me?"

"Your looks match your voice."

He watched her, trying to see if that was some put-down.

"You dress very nicely," she said. Definitely not a put-down.

He shrugged. "I just wanted to make a nice impression."

"Making an impression," Brenda told him, "is really what style derives from. Impressing people whose respect you need. Some think style is a talent, something you're born with. Yet is it?"

She smiled. She seemed to be waiting for me to answer.

I sort of shook my head.

"I'm sure it isn't," she said. "That's why I give this course in metropolitan style. These lessons. New York lessons."

I just looked at her.

"I expect it's a matter of dropping the wrong habits and picking up the right ones," she's going. I'm focusing on her light blue eyes there. "It's being observant," she tells me. "Sensitive. Considerate. That's all it is, I think. Really."

She smiled again and I smiled, too. I know the drill.

"Why don't we order, and then I'll give you an idea of how the lessons run. And if you're still interested, I'll share with you some . . . some critical notes tonight, some things you might want to think about. And of course—"

"I'm interested," said Don, cool about it, thoughtful. He's giving her the nice-guy smile, makes him look bashful while he's thinking about slowfucking her, way at the end of an all-night session after she's blown his head off and the two of them are so into it that time just moves aside for them and it's like they're in the center of a room spinning around them, fast and slow at the same time.

Keep looking at her eyes, boyo. Hold on to the soft smile and don't start peering down where it all happens, because this one isn't going to like that. You can tell just by the glasses, brown horn-rims with the real round lenses that cute girls wear so they won't look too cute. It makes them even cuter. It makes you want to shove the table over and scoop them up in your arms, all of them, a hundred a night, I don't care.

"I'm really interested," Don told her.

"Then we ought to order."

She took out a pocket spiral notebook, bound in black leather, complete with a little metal pencil.

"And remember," she said, giving him this real strong look through those cute little round glasses. "My course in metropolitan style is absolutely on the level. Sheer business. I never become intimate with my clients. It only unleashes dangerous emotions."

Her whole spiel was loopy, and that was the loopiest item yet, but lady, *okay*, whatever you *say*.

"What do I call you?" Don asked.

"You can call me Brenda."

"And what do you call me, hey?"

"What would you prefer?"

"Anything but late for dinner."

He laughed. She silently wrote a little something in her pad thing.

"Call me Don," he said. "And no dumb jokes, right?"

She finished writing and looked up, with that funny serious look, something like in her eyes maybe, Don wasn't sure. Really *nice*, though.

"Don," she said, "please always keep in mind that you are paying for my time so that I can . . . advise you, just so, yes, on how to upgrade the impression you make. I owe it to you to earn my fee. And the only way I can is to talk to you about your behavior. Now, sometimes it may seem to you as if I'm picking on you or . . . well, being petty. Yes? Please don't take it personally. I just want to do my job. All right?"

He smiled.

"Why don't you order a bottle of wine for us?" she asked, studying her menu.

Boyo, Don thought to himself, you're in this one right up to the goddamn part in your hair.

Of course he fumbled the wine. Ordering wasn't too bad — he just pointed at a French name and said, "Let's have that one." But when the waiter pulled the cork and poured a bit into Don's glass and stood there doing nothing, Don said, "That's all I get?"

"Why don't you taste it," Brenda said, "and see if it's all right?"

Don waited, sizing it up, what's going on here, huh? Finally he took a sip and muttered, "It's okay."

After the waiter left, Don leaned toward Brenda and said, "If that guy pulls one more stunt on me, I'm gonna cream his face for him."

Brenda explained about tasting the wine.

"Oh," said Don.

And he made dumb jokes, and called her "honey"

again, and he asked her how she got into this racket anyway, which she said it was rather a personal matter — and
each time he blundered, she was right there with the old
pad, till he started to make a joke of it, like "Right, let's
get a note on that one, hey," and "Can we order dessert
or do you want to break out another box of pads first?"
She laughed right along with him, too. He got another
note for putting too much sugar in his coffee, but he was
having such a good time, he didn't care how many notes
he got. It took her a good half hour to tell him all the
things he did wrong, and to explain about what he should
have done instead. But in a strange way he enjoyed hearing about his faults, and listened carefully. Some of what
she told him sounded as loopy as everything else she said.
But hell, anything a pretty lady has to say is nice to hear —
and there's our boyo Don taking his dinner in a real Manhattan swing joint. He's not complaining.

In fact, he's entranced.

Even when Brenda starts in on how New York is a
city of history. When she says, "Great men and women of
the past follow our progress." When she says, "We must
live up to their example."

MARK TWAIN: In Boston they ask, How
much does he know? In New York, How
much is he worth?

CHRISTOPHER MORLEY: New York, the
nation's thyroid gland.

ROBERT BENCHLEY: My first dissipation in
New York was a church supper, so identical
with the church suppers I had known in New

England that it was impossible to imagine
that on this same island was the Gomorrah I
had heard and been warned so much about.

DON: I don't know about no church suppers.
But I guarantee you, you stand on any corner
of the place, pull out your tony and a twenty-
dollar bill, and the girls will form a line
around the block.

Brenda and Don made a date for a second meeting
and parted outside the restaurant, shaking hands again.
She had a real soft grip, and Don almost like put his other
hand around it or something. Heading for home, he tried
to figure out why he had had such a good time getting
told like what a slob he was. At first he thought it was
because Brenda was such a classy lady. But since she
wasn't a real date that couldn't be it. Then he thought it
was because she was so careful about his feelings when
she gave him her notes, because God'll tell you the people
Don knew weren't careful about anybody's feelings except
their own. Then he thought it was because, for the first
time, he had spent an evening being the center of attention.

And that was it. That really was it.

Because every other time he went out, *he* had to do
all the work. Like, was she having a good time? Did she
like him, or was she just getting away from her folks for a
night? Was it time to put an arm around her, or should he
wait fifteen minutes more? This time with Brenda, for
once, everything in the date was about *him*. And he
wasn't even paying all that much, you know, when you
figured how much he was getting out of it.

Don met Brenda once a week, and she covered him

with notes like she was a paperhanger and he was a wall. "You sap," he'd tell himself, taking the subway into Manhattan, laughing out loud. "You bum sap."

She made him stock in Mozart and Brahms for his stereo, fancy-dancey movies for his VCR.

She gave him a list of hip culture words to memorize, like "street theatre" and "minimalism."

So like when the clerk in Don's video store there said, "Can I help you, sir?" Don replied, "What's hot in film noir this week?" and every girl in the place stared at Don like he was Mister Smarts.

I could have had any one of them, but that Brenda, you know, she gets me all fired up about *A Passage to India*, so I lay in a copy. I ask her over to my place to see it. She won't come. Lets you down gentle, sure. Got to be careful not to unleash any of those dangerous emotions, hey. What's the lady afraid of? Thinks old Don here's going to spring a little bedroom theatre on her, right? A passage to Brenda. Like I can't put on a New York kind of social night for once? After all she's showed me how?

She taught him to order scotch instead of beer, and to ask for it by the brand—"Cutty on the rocks with a twist," which sounded like a porn movie to Don.

She got him to stop wearing clothes with the manufacturer's label showing. Don had always thought designer logos were a hip thing, but look, the lady knows. He's paying her to know.

She took him to Lord and Taylor and made him buy more dress-up clothes, striped shirts and a navy blue blazer that crosses over itself. Brenda said he looked like a prince in it.

"Some prince," says Don. "Runs elevators for a living."

"Every man looks his best," she told him, "in jacket and tie."

"What if a guy wants to show off his build, hey?"

"Don, do you want to impress women or win a physical culture contest? And if you don't stop saying 'hey' all the time—"

"I copy."

She shook her head and made a note.

He gave her a serious face and shook his finger at her horn-rim glasses.

"If you don't be good," he began, but she laughed, and he laughed, too.

That's the kind of fun we were having.

She even let me come along on a photo shoot in Central Park, and I joked about how this was just about our first date, even if it wasn't dinner and a show. She didn't say anything to that. She was getting real involved with light readings and camera angles. She was real fast, too. Sharp. I like people who know what they're doing.

"You a good photographer?" I asked her.

And she said, just like that, "Yes."

"You're a good style teacher, too."

"All the really metropolitan people have two specialties. At least two if not more. That's why the city moves along at such a pace—everyone has so much to do."

She was lining up a shot of some kids fighting in a playground, and Don thought, Lady, I could eat you with a spoon.

"Tonight," she announced, "I have to cover a party at The Limelight. Snapping away at the town dandies. It's not my favorite work, but I believe I do it very well, and it pays. There are worse things to do to get along, and I'll not play waitress to anyone!"

She was pretty fierce about it, too.

"Hey, I can respect that," Don told her.

She let him come back to her apartment for tea. It

was his first time in there, and he told himself, Boyo, you
better be a real metropolitan guy now and behave yourself.

Don played it cool. He complimented her real generous on her photography, which was all over the walls
there, though the pictures were about as loopy as you
could imagine. A teenage druggie yakking his guts into
the gutter. A ravaged breakfast tray. Potholes. A line of
bums against a wall, except one of them's some fancy guy
in a top hat. The wierdest one was a little dog wearing a
rubber elephant's head, surrounded by razzing kids.

I guess Brenda could see I was just doing my best to
make nice, because she said, "When I'm paid for my
work, I have to please others. But when I work for myself,
I please only myself. Maybe that's not a good thing, I
don't know. That's how it has developed so far. I have to
show what is real, what is there in our feelings. I am trying to capture the mixture of New York life, because I am
a New York woman. In my art, I encircle what is dangerous and unhealthy in our lives. I contain it. My art is a
shriving."

She stops dead right there and of course I'm standing
around like a dope who doesn't know what to say after.
But she was very surprising all the time, just nothing like
the girls Don had known. Like now she's quiet, then suddenly she's making speeches about the city of history or
the mixture. I mean, who the hell knows what you're supposed to say after to that stuff?

Then she grabs a photo out of a pile of them leaning
against the wall and holds it up and asks Don, "What do
you think when you see this?"

Looks like the back of a slum building. Big letters in
paint against the bricks: "No one is insane. Kill all mur-
derers."

Don stares at it. He says, "I don't . . . how do I know what I think? It's . . . art, right?"

"What does it tell you?"

"You took it, lady. You tell me."

Don turned to Brenda, maybe to smile at her, I don't know, but she held the photograph in front of her.

"You tell me, Don," she says. "Each view is different to each pair of eyes. Art defers to its audience. *You* tell *me.*"

"Well, just put that thing down, okay?"

She lowered the picture, and Don examined it.

"You tell me," Brenda repeated, almost in a whisper, like she was trying to figure it out herself, even though she's the one who made it.

"I tell you . . . well, it's maybe like . . . something like about what you're not supposed to believe. What do you say? Like it gives you the opposite of what it really means? Because the joker who painted that message sounds like he's insane himself. Say I'm right?"

Brenda set the picture back in its pile, leaning against the wall.

"I don't know," she said. But she sure did sound convinced about something.

I don't know either, but if this was dating, it was like TV without a picture tube. We saw each other all the time, but only for like dinner and talking, or a walk in the afternoon, then tea at Brenda's, then I go home. Any other lady like so, and I would have given her the brush right off. But there was still that terrific high she gives you, that idea that she knows nothing at all in the world but me, and how I feel, and what I say, at least while we're together. She's a screwy lady, the way she talks sometimes, but she's the goods. I thought about her all the time, never wanted to put the move on a girl so bad. But I had a good idea she'd run me off if I did.

So that made me sore.

And *that* made me nervous, being sore.

It's probably how I came to blow my temper at her that day on Fifth Avenue. It was a little thing, too. Anyway, it started little.

They were out on one of their walks, on one of those bright, wonderful days New York can pull out of a hat when it cares to. As they passed the Forty-second Street library, they came abreast of a young man playing classical guitar, his case opened to catch bills and change. The library's usual complement of afternoon loungers, loners, and drifters filled out the scene, but a small crowd stood carefully listening as the young man announced his next selection; he added that he was available to play for parties. Brenda stopped to hear him and Don shifted his feet impatiently till they moved on.

"What a way to live," Don sneered. "Playing for handouts on the street like a wack-out. How'd you like to date that clown, huh?"

You always knew when you did the wrong thing. She would get quiet and he could sense her body stiffen beside him.

"What'd I say now?"

"You were intolerant," she told him. She sounded heavy about it, too, as if she had noticed this flaw in him many times before and was waiting for a real classic offense before she struck.

"You were intolerant in New York," she went on. "Our city of mixtures and stimulation. That boy is sharing his music with us. What right do you—"

"He's sharing his open palm, is what."

"What is he taking from you, Don?"

She turned to him, furious.

"What?" she insisted.

"Well, don't I—"

"Why do you criticize him? He's earning money at his art, that's all! And I hear you denigrate him!"

"He's available for *parties*, you heard him. Is that art?"

"*I'm* available for parties, too, because I *have* to be to live! Does that—"

"I didn't mean you."

"His music is New York! His guitar is the mixture!"

"His music is a crock of shit, lady!"

"*Where* is your *tolerance*?"

"Where's *yours*," he countered, "for me? Can't I talk free with an opinion, too?" Jumping all over my program. Can't even ask you over for a VCR night. How does that make me feel, huh? You ever think about that?

She sure was thinking something, the way she was staring at him. A couple of people nearby were staring, too. Talk about your street theatre. A little minimalism in the tantrum and you'd have a real high-class New York scene there.

Don said, "Hey," as gently as he could in the circumstances, but she backed away from him. She said "No." She shook her head. "No," she says, pushing me away, and now I'm trying to apologize, it's all over, I don't care about the guitar guy, I mean, who the hell cares, but she's giving me the no and the shaking.

"Look, I'm sorry." How many times do I got to say it?

"I'm sorry, too," she said. "Because you've made excellent progress, really. So many men find it difficult to take criticism, especially from a woman. You've actually been comfortable with it."

They started walking again, but they were walking different. Separate, like.

"You took the course seriously," she went on. "My course in style."

Is that *took* as in past tense? Graduation City? End of the lessons?

"I can't go on taking your money, Don. You've done what you set out to do. You're a metropolitan man now. I'm proud of you."

She wasn't looking at him, though.

"I expect," she said, carefully, "it would be appropriate for you to . . . for us to finish the course before . . . to end it now, Don. I really would."

Don thought fast.

"Tell you what," he said, keeping his tone breezy. "Let's have one last lesson, okay? For the road, like, to celebrate."

She's shaking her head again.

"Something real metropolitan. Listen. I'll see you home. We'll get one of those funny little champagne bottles and drink on it."

They had stopped walking. Maybe that's how it had been all along with her, Don thought. That's a date with Brenda — smoothing around for hours in this great kind of *deep*, this feeling there, and then standing still, real gloomy and, like, you didn't know what was going to happen next. Like one of Brenda's photos, maybe. A mysterious picture of something.

"Come on," he urged her, keeping his smile nice and easy like some movie guy. He winked at her.

"Well," she got in — but Don was a whirlwind, and he said, "Sure," taking her arm, and "Come on."

It worked. Brenda's place was smaller and even more weirdo than Don had remembered, but then that was true of most Manhattan apartments. The living room had something new, a big brown wooden thing that opened at the top and turned out to be an old-time record player. Brenda put an old-time record in it, turned this crank at the side, and out came crazy old music like Mouseketeer Ballroom or something.

"It's a Victrola," said Brenda, all puffed up about it.

"That's swift," said Don, making his impression and giving the right picture. He knows about style now here. He opened the champagne like a pro and proposed this toast: "To metropolitan style."

A few moments later, as Brenda took the record off, Don said quietly, "So who's the new guy?"

"What do you mean?"

"Yeah." Don took a swallow of champagne. "The new guy you got taking my lessons."

She looked at him, bewildered, and he gave her a flash of the pirate's eyes.

"By the way," Don went on, "thanks a lot," his voice noticeably louder, "for taking my money and then dumping me for—"

"Don! You know that's not—"

"Yeah? Oh *yeah*?" He rose. "What do I know, huh?, except you got a pretty neat racket going here, don't you, hey? At least the other bimbos I dated let me spend a night for my—"

"I think you had better leave. Now!"

"Look who's insulted, will you?" He was towering over her, but she calmly stood her ground, staring at him, nose to nose. Nose to jaw, anyway.

MARK TWAIN: They do not treat women with as much deference in New York as we of the provinces think they ought.

HELEN LAWRENSON: There is something about city life which has a peculiarly corroding influence on the male nervous system.

MARK TWAIN: Who the fuck is Helen Lawrenson?

HELEN LAWRENSON: Women seem to
hold together better than men. But it isn't
going to do women much good if all the men
collapse. And who the fuck is Mark Twain?

DON: Who the fuck is anybody around here?

"I thought you were a nice man," Brenda said at last.
"This is the manifestation of a beast."

"That so?" He pulled off his jacket and his tie. He
was smiling. "Well, the beast is loose in your apartment,
lady."

"Get out of here," she told him.

He moved toward her. He's still smiling.

"I'm not afraid of you," she said. "You are a mistake. I
dispense with you!"

"The beast is loose," he repeated quietly. "This is
crunch time, lady. You going to scream?"

Without a word, she ran into the bedroom, slammed
the door, and locked it. Don shrugged and easily shoul-
dered the door open, but the flashbulb blinded him and
he backed away, shielding his eyes and shouting *Hey!* as
Brenda charged on him, snapping his picture, again,
again, again.

"You're going on my wall," she told him as she took
and clicked and froze him in art. "You're going to be my
trophy."

"Look, will you—"

"I'm calling this series B and T Lout Rutting in Midtown."

"Now, just hold it!" He snatched the camera from her. "Joke's over."

"This is no joke, my fine man!"

"Mine was," he said, trying to catch his breath. "I just wanted to teach *you* something for a change. You don't drop a guy by taking him to your apartment, don't you know that, a metropolitan girl like you? You do it on the phone, or write a letter. What are you giving these lessons for, anyway?" He dropped the camera on the couch. "Letting strange men call you up. Lady, it's dangerous stuff."

"I always interview the clients before—"

"You never know what a guy is thinking. Especially if he's got a little style, right? Style is how we hide our emotions. Didn't you say that to me?"

She reached for the camera, but he put his hand on it. No, lady. No more camera now.

"Come here to me. Come on. We'll settle it quiet here. Just us." He had her by the waist. "What kind of girl puts ads in a newspaper? What are you like, New York woman? Are we going to find out?"

He was kissing her, real soft, little-boy style, kissing her between the phrases, humming as he kissed. It didn't matter what he said, graffiti on a wall.

"How did it end with the other guys before me, huh?"

"There weren't any," she breathed out, looking up at him, her hands on his shoulders, his arms, feeling the muscles. "That ad was in the *Voice* for almost a year before—"

"Hey, come on, now. Come on."

She held on to him and he held her back. This is a good moment.

"Come on," he said, starting to undress her. "So what are you crying now? Sure." Taking off her glasses to peer at her like some college inspector or something.

"This is very awkward," she murmured, very comfortable where she was and not about to move. "I always—"

"Shh," Don told her. He likes to do the talking. "Just relax. Don is me and I am Don and we are going to be very, very smooth to Brenda here."

Standing with her in the center of her living room in the fading sunlight, he was all around her, his body pressed against hers, petting her, smooching her up, whispering in her ear, discovering her, framing the pair of them in her window. She stirred, as if to close the blinds.

"Let them watch," he ordered. "We can be their picture on the wall. What is it telling them, huh?"

He had her between his thighs. Her back arched as he sucked on her breasts, with a slow, steady pull; and when she gasped he laughed and stroked her neck just below the ear.

"Oh, lady," he said, "you don't know everything."

THREE *PEOPLES,*
TWO *VOGUES,* AND
A *VANITY FAIR*

Ir is a truth univer-
sally acknowledged that everyone in Manhattan Who Matters came from Somewhere Else. This is because the only
way to get Mattered is to be Connected and only an out-
sider would realize that one has to Connect. Most think
they're already Connected just by being there, knowing
where the deli is and having cousins in all the boroughs.
This is not being Connected: this is being alive. Being Connected means you can get into this season's hot disco, for
free, with five guests, on the night Liza Minnelli's expected.

New York is a tight city. When Peter Dillinger—an
exceptional New York native—looked for his first apartment, he didn't even try the Important neighborhoods: the
Village, the Upper West Side, the East Fifties. Important, he
reminded himself, scurrying over to the far east high
Eighties, Tribeca, Hell's Kitchen. Important. It's what you

try to be, Important. It's not what you do, it's how you look, Important. It's not how you feel, it's what you control. *Important.* Connected. Going uptown, making it happen.

But New York is a suspicious city, hard to get into even if you were born here. Peter found himself a place far west on Forty-fifth Street. *How* far west?

So far west that if he took about twelve steps to the left while chewing Sen-sen and wearing polyester, he'd be a cracking plant in New Jersey.

He also found the right clothes (from the magazines), spiffed up his accent (from television), and smarted out a promising job (in a talent factory, the kind that deals for artists and writers as well as actors). Somehow the money never evened off. He was always in debt, always having to sweat out a swank shirt till it went on sale, always broke before payday, always late with the rent. But as Deborah the secretary from Staten Island put it, "So? Welcome to New York."

Yet it is an unwelcoming city, not only abrasive but savage. Once, running an envelope from the office to a client, Peter was crossing the huge intersection at Twenty-third Street where the Flatiron Building stands, when two men broke into a fight. This was a weekday in spring at about one o'clock, High Lunch Hour, thousands of people passing, hanging out, watching, going into trances. It was the usual New York episode: someone knocks into someone else, someone calls someone rotten names, someone snarls, "Oh yeah?" and gives a push, and someone charges and takes a swing and knocks someone flat on the sidewalk in front of the entire world.

This particular fight was not an even match. The assailant was a big roughneck, the prey stocky but short and, stylistically, all glasses and tie. He looked stunned to have been hit, as if lying on one's back on the pavement only happened to figures on the evening news. A third man came over to help him up, and now the big guy with the fist shouted, "That's buster for _you_, punk!" and he socked the third man, too. The guy with the glasses and tie scrambled away, leaving the fighter hulking over the innocent third party—Peter, as it happens—who was down on the sidewalk and stunned himself.

"Get _up!_" said the bad guy, heaving and fisting, ragged and unshaven, a goon who lives on trouble. "Get on _up_, because there's some _more_ buster, now."

Peter stared at him.

"Buster _up!_" the man shouted, kicking Peter's foot.

What most impresses you about a scene like this (you realize later) is that a whole load of people are standing around watching, most of them strictly construing the right and wrong of the case, the big bully versus the smaller, nicer fellow. They know what's fair.

(Everyone knows what's fair. Not everyone is fair; but everyone knows what his actions are worth. Everyone is responsible for his choices. Everyone is guilty of his life.)

But what is interesting about a crowd of New Yorkers watching the wrong guy beating up the right guy is that nobody does a thing for you. Nobody says anything. And having a cop for an older brother isn't much help.

I don't know why it would be. But it sounds helpful, somehow.

Peter turned away from the bad guy. Peter got up. He just got up and started walking, hoping that this would close up the scene, pull that whole thing off, finished.

The bad guy followed him, shouting for him to fight.

Peter suddenly veered off in another direction, still walking. Just moving away there, moving fast.

"You want _more_ of the same?" the bad guy shouted. "You want some, now, _because?_"

It was pretty damn clear that Peter didn't want more of anything. He kept walking and finally the man stopped following him and Peter had turned that angle around the Flatiron Building to get away from the crowd watching him. Maybe they were breaking up by then, anyway. Mob coming apart. Only a very few stick around till the end is over. The pushy ones. Styleless. You're supposed to make your exit *before* the end. As if you didn't need it. In New York, you're only as big as what you don't need.

That's how you stay out of trouble: by looking as if you don't need it. Keep walking. Don't listen. Peter kept walking and didn't listen till he stopped shaking; and it was five or six blocks before he realized that he hadn't even noticed what direction he was walking in.

The next day, Peter had dinner with his brother. He told his brother what had happened in front of the Flatiron Building, knowing, as he outlined it, that things like this never happened to his brother—not because his brother was a cop but because they just didn't. Cary looked like the man goons didn't start up with.

"The thing I want to know," said Peter, "is did I handle it right?"

"Well . . ."

"I didn't fight him because I would have gotten creamed. So that was the smart thing, right?"

". . . sure . . ."

"No. *No*, no, *look*, no, no, *okay*, no, *look*. Look. I'm not asking you," Peter tells his brother, "what you would have done. So *no*, okay? I'm asking what you would have done if you were me."

There are times when you give a straight answer, the hell with it; and times when you give the right answer, to soothe someone's wrecked feelings. Cary awkwardly touched Peter's arm and said, "The right thing to do is not to let it eat at you. You made a good choice in a tough spot and it's over and out now. So you relax."

Peter shook his head. "It'll happen again on some other street, won't it? There's fights all over the world here. When you run out of your own, they make you take someone else's."

"Don't worry about it, Pete."

Peter started to speak, but he felt himself shaking, so he waited.

"Come on, Pete—"

"I don't want to be a coward."

"You did the right thing," Cary told him, confidently sturdy about it now that he understood that this was the right answer. Not the straight one, the true one. But the one he was supposed to give. "Stop worrying about it. You're not a fighter. So okay, that's it. Some guys are fighters and some guys are other things."

"What am I, then? What other thing?"

"What are you?" Cary asked, scowling, restless. He exhaled, real heavy; suddenly he smiled. "Just put me on the spot here, Pete, *okay*, well, thanks a lot."

Peter said nothing.

"Maybe what you are," said Cary, "is a good guy to know, how about that? The way you can always meet everybody."

"Huh?"

"Well . . . yeah. I don't know any guys knows as many people as you. Goes as many places. Every time I turn around, right? you been to a restaurant or a show. Dancing places, cameras going off everywhere you look. All those parties. You're a real New York Peter. Right?"

Peter made a face.

"Well, am I?" Cary asked. "Right?"

"What does that have to—"

"So fighting wouldn't do you much good at a party, would it?" Still smiling, because he had figured out the angle here, Cary nodded at Peter. "Some guys' talent is

pushing their weight around. Your talent is having friends
and getting around the block. You're a born New Yorker,
Pete."

Or, translated into uptown lingo: you know how to
Connect. How to finesse a look, be agreeable, available,
helpful, quick, knowledgeable. How to sell yourself, too.
This is getting inside, getting on the free list, getting to the
table of the persons with the expense accounts.

This is New York.

Look, people with money want company. They like
spirited youth. You don't have to give them anything but
attention; they do other things for sex.

Boise crossed paths with Peter in the course of his
getting inside. Boise at some party, posing, decreeing. You
know what she told Peter? She told him, "Just keep moving, kid. The concept is energy. You *make* it happen,
capish?"

Here's one way. Peter would wangle important
phone numbers and hit the near-great for an interview.
The great might easily turn him down, but those in sight
of fame yet not in full possession of it . . . well, they have
to do the hustle, don't they?

Peter would be vague as to his credentials — something about *Vanity Fair, Playbill,* or even something called
Show Biz Weekly that Peter simply invented; but then, who
knows? There probably is one at that. A lot of the energy
in this world is based on what you can get away with in
the space between the gamble and the swindle. Authen-
ticity is all visuals, and everybody hustles. They know
you're lying, but they'd rather believe you. Besides, a lot of
interviews do get written and published because a ven-
turesome kid bluffed his way in, cute and smart and just
raw enough to please. What do they have to lose? A little
time, a little hustle, a little New York sleek there. Peter
maybe felt guilty about coming on to the starlets, but they

all gave in to him so briskly, right there in the hotel room, that he began to view blackmail sex as part of the scene, like having your hair spiked every now and then or letting quiet, stiff, wealthy older men take you to the theatre.

Exactly what scene Peter was going to be in, he wasn't yet sure; they all seemed to be as Connected as he was. He seemed to be heading for Communications, because he knew when to be silent, and when to be aggressive, and when to shoot off a little flash. He knew how to be nice to women, too. You think that comes naturally? Most men could take courses and they'd still be thugs.

Peter was no thug. Peter was a nice kid with a slightly crooked smile. One of his starlets, a host on one of the music video shows, reflectively told Peter as she was buttoning up her blouse, "That was more fun that it's supposed to be." She called him up later that week, in a tone blending uncertain and spacey. There's a message in that, you know. There's a craft in hearing the words people aren't able to say. Peter has always been extremely observant of people. He got the starlet's message, and he laughed so she could remember his crooked smile, and he invited himself over, and they were both happy.

That was when to be aggressive.

They dated on and off for a season, mostly late-night dancing with a crowd of friends—he thought they were hers and she thought they were his.

Well, so what? It's not how you met, it's who you meet. Who you charm. Who you collect, who you impress. Peter wondered if he was making an impression on his starlet, till she suddenly announced she was leaving for the Coast. Something about agents and a small role in a big movie, which, you know, is like *really* better than the other way around.

"If I'm ever in L.A.," Peter told her, wondering if he

ever would be, because he was a born New Yorker but he was getting Connected in Communications, "I'll look you up, okay? Give it six or seven months. Maybe a year, outside."

"I'll be too famous then," she said, smiling as gently as the occasion allowed.

That was when to be silent, and Peter was.

He worked hard at being a true New Yorker; one has to. You make it happen. He was glad to be good at it. It gave him a turf, a sense of acceptance. As with so many others of his kind, so many other true New Yorkers in Communications, it was not the sight of the place he liked, but the scene itself, the houses of Connection. Peter knew what mattered: how to get in, how to dress, where the good cheap food was, where the streets were unsafe even in daylight. He was making it happen, sliding up in the agency from desk to desk, down the hall, up the department. He stopped writing interviews, partly because now he was Important enough to be pushing a conflict of interest between his job and his writing, and mainly because he didn't need to use the interview hustle to make Connections anymore. He was there.

He still had dinner with Cary from time to time — or wasn't it more like at regular intervals? Every three weeks or so. Peter wasn't clear on why two such different men had anything to say to each other, brothers or not. They usually met for a fast one, while Cary was on his break and Peter between the office and the city night: the new-wave dandy and the cop in his blues greasy-spooning in the West Fifties amid a storm of prostitutes and browsers, tourists and trash, residents and professional intruders. Peter would talk about his career and Cary would talk about his love life. Cary was bound to say, "You've come a long way now here, Pete," sometimes more than once.

And when some lost soul staggered past them, eyeing the slicker and the copper at their table together, Peter would look up, observant as always, and he would be tempted to say, "This nice man is my brother."

He *had* come a long way now here. And he had the chance to go considerably farther, for quite suddenly his boss dangled before him a high-concept promotion, hooked up to a transfer to L.A.

"It's tricky," says the boss, head of Peter's department and second in line from the agency's head man. "It's very tricky."

Peter toys with the possibility of saying, "I work real well with tricky" through his crooked smile. But this isn't when to shoot off a little flash; this is when to keep silent. Maybe just the smile? No. He does a thoughtful nod. Anyway, *what's* tricky? Getting the L.A. job? Keeping it? There's a lot of turnover in Peter's line of work. In other businesses, people leave one firm for another. In Peter's business, people leave the business.

"It's tricky," the man concludes, shaking his head with a rueful smile, as if the vanity of the world were only just striking him in all its graceless majesty, "because everybody we send to Angel City, they go crazy."

"Crazy like how?" Peter asks.

"Crazy like they're bored ditsy. They can't walk anywhere and everyone they know is stupid and the menu is very limited. No hot dogs, I hear."

"How can a city that big not have hot dogs?" Peter replies, thinking, This is a very sophisticated New York conversation. Right.

"They have the wrong kind of hot dogs. Not real New York hot dogs."

The man was sitting on the edge of Peter's desk, trying to seem friendly; but he wasn't a friendly man.

"Another problem with L.A.," he went on, "is every-

body's A-list or junkmail. There's nothing else. You're a
star or a bum in Angel City. New York, now, we got the
people in between. We have bum stars, star bums. All that
street bonkers. It's colorful. And we got friendly cops. You
know what the cops are like in Angel City there? Aliens.
Monsters in a monster movie. You're going along somewhere there, it's the world, it's a nice day, it's good to be
alive. Suddenly, out come the monsters, they want to kill
you. Aliens in shades, infiltrating the system there. Kill
you, shoot your blood out of the fucking veins there, Angel City. I'll prefer a New York cop anytime. Sure, they're
born junkmail. I mean, what cop ever got anywhere?
Street trash in a uniform. But at least they're human,
right? They're human guys, cops. New Yorkers. Where
does your family live, anyway?"

Peter shrugged.

"It's tricky."

Cary was impressed by the promotion.

"Even if you don't take it, Pete," he said, "it feels
good that they're looking you over, you know?"

They didn't say anything about Peter's going to L.A.,
leaving New York, getting out instead of getting in. Where
do you belong? What are you supposed to belong to?
What scene? It's tricky.

Peter had one close friend in the scene, a photographer named Brenda who free-lanced at parties, snapping
the famous and the sidekicks and the types. She was first
choice for these gigs because she took pictures that set off
the look of the town.

"Great composition," the honchos would announce,
eyeing the contact sheets. They meant: she celebrates style.

Peter couldn't get her into bed but he could talk to her.
Somehow, all the women he knew gave you sex or under-

standing; none gave both. But of what she did give, Brenda gave truly. She was a good listener. She'd sit and listen to you complain for hours. Cary was a good listener, too, in his way; but Cary couldn't understand anything he didn't already know. And he kept pulling that blood-relative thing, expecting miracles from you, like demonstrations of brotherhood without end. Brenda didn't expect anything. All you had to be was polite; she was tense about that. Peter found her a little affected. She seemed to see herself as Cinderella, walking through life with dainty steps to protect her glass slippers.

But she listened big. That's a rare gift. She had a good sense of organization, too, an ability to bind up the strands of your complaint. All Cary could do was pat you on the back. Brenda would declare a Tea with tiny spoons, put some escargots in the oven, and say, "Isn't there anyone you'd miss if you moved away?"

"Sure," Peter replied. What else can you say?

"I don't mean me," Brenda went on. "Don't you have . . . people to know you and . . . help you?"

"Why don't you mean you?"

"We New Yorkers need our friends."

"Friends?" said Peter. "All we need are partners. There's partners for dinner, partners you dance with, partners for sex—although that might be the same group."

"How very isolated that sounds. How private. Is that why you came to New York? To have nothing more than partners?"

"I didn't come to New York. I started here and stayed here."

"Won't you be lonely in Los Angeles?" she asked, cutting up the French bread.

"My brother says I meet people easily."

"I expect you do, Peter. Sometimes I wonder if you meet so many people to distance yourself from the people you know."

"No, I don't." Then Peter thought about it. "I don't," he repeated. "I just do a lot of networking. Comes with the business."

"Do you like networking?"

"You're supposed to partner as fast as you can. That's New York."

Brenda, busy with the plates and flatware, said nothing. She had her when to be silent, too.

The phone was ringing when Peter got home from Brenda's. He was tired, and didn't run for it, scarcely wanted to answer it. There was a time, not long before, when every ring was like a summons from an enchanted land, when any call might be Important. Even wrong numbers and phone peddlers couldn't exhaust Peter's enthusiasm for his present and wonder at his future. Like so many New Yorkers, like a real New York Peter, he would check for the red light on the tape machine the moment he entered the apartment. Mail was just bills and invitations to parties that needed you more than you needed them; but the telephone is people.

"There are no ideas today," someone told Peter at the Odeon, told him quite mildly. "There is no morality. There is only interpersonal interface."

Peter didn't disagree. But the telephone can only give you what you already have. It will not change your life; it affirms it.

So, at short length, he learned. When his tape machine began to make demented noises instead of recording his calls, Peter simply disconnected it. After all, anyone who had to speak to him could call his office, or at least message him there. He was the only one anybody knew who didn't have tape monitoring his phone; but being the only one who does something has its swank. New York Peter.

He was thinking about Brenda, about what she said, really; but about her, too. He decided to pass the call up. But the phone kept ringing. What was it now? Ten rings? Twelve? Peter stared at the phone, digging his heels in, willing it to stop. What kind of idiot just hangs on, ring after ring after ring like that? Do they do this in Cincinnati?

Maybe someone's in trouble, so desperate for his help that . . . sure, right. Who would be desperate for Peter's help?

Cary?

"Yo," Peter said into the receiver, cradling it under his chin as he loosened his tie.

"Fiasca and Miss Debutante want to have fun with you," said an odd, high-pitched voice.

A crank. Welcome to New York. Peter hung up.

The phone immediately rang again.

"Hello?"

"This is Miss Debutante," said the same voice. "I just want to know what you'll be wearing to the drag ball this Saturday because if we're both in the same dress I'm going to scream the place down."

Peter hung up, pulled off his tie, poured out a glass of juice, and stood looking out his back window at the debris in the yard below. The beer cans, brown paper bags, and vilely stained mattress did not surprise him. But where did they get the antique dressmaker's dummy?

The phone rang again.

Peter did not move.

In the brownstone across the yard, a young man, nude, stood gazing out of drug-blinded eyes. After a moment a young woman, nude, joined him. She put a monster mask on his face, and, as he slowly turned toward her, she hung a bathtowel in the window, blocking them from view.

The phone continued to ring.

Peter shoved the window open and leaned out to find the sky. Even the very west Forties have one, some-where. He shivered, closed the window, crossed the room, picked up the phone, and immediately hung it back up.

Twenty second later it rang again.

"Listen, you shitheads," Peter said, "if you don't get the hell off this phone—"

"Peter, it's Brenda," she said, briskly. "I just thought of something I should have—"

"Brenda! Gosh, I'm sorry. Some phone crazies have been after me and—"

"Yes, of course, it's just—"

"No, I honestly didn't—"

"I wanted to say this before—"

"I just—"

"No, *listen*, Peter. It's about your moving. About the certain city of Los Angeles as a place to live."

There she halted.

"Well, okay," said Peter, thinking about how Brenda looks when she's on the phone, all so tidily ensconced in her armchair in that way she has. She wears a lot of sweaters with nothing under them; and she has a beau-tiful pair, small but very, very round. And that is a rare thing. But of course if you tend to gaze at her nipples she gets peeved.

"Shoot," Peter told Brenda. "I can take it."

"My thought," she said, in that careful tone she rel-ished when she had to rate you off for Inconsiderate Be-havior, "is about 'partnering.'" She indicated the quote marks as Jane Austen might indicate the poetry of Muhammad Ali. "I wonder if that concept isn't coloring your mode of life in quite a perilous way. Perhaps even without your full knowledge. Peter. Have you . . . have you considered how much friendship *enriches* our days? We give up privacy for intimacy."

"Yeah, well, can't a guy do that in Angel City?"

"You're such a nice fellow, Peter, even if you don't particularly care to be. I hate to see you turning your deepest feelings into . . . buzzwords and flip cop-outs."

"You sound like a sixty-nine-cent violin," Peter told her, surprised at and immediately regretting the bite of his tone. "Christ, Brenda, I'm sorry."

"No, that's your feeling. But—"

"No, that's *not* my—"

"Surely I'd best ring off now," she said, quite gently, as she hung up.

Christ! Peter thought. Now I'd have to send her flowers, if I were the kind of person who sent flowers. Oh no. None of those flip cop-outs for me. Send you no flowers.

Restless.

So smooth it out. Tempo is everything.

Expand, as that fiercely rich old queen from Seventh Avenue told Peter from across the table when Peter was young and didn't know anything. "Expand, pretty boy," and Peter, bewildered and nervous, got as tight as you get.

Expand.

A pile of magazines signaled to him. Catch up on Trend, know what They're doing. But after snapping through three *People*s, two *Vogue*s, and a *Vanity Fair,* Peter bounced up, hit the phone, and tried to set up someone for a late dinner and hacking around—anything, he told himself, but the Odeon. After reaching five tape messages, which he hung up on, he got a fellow agent who regaled him for ten minutes with viciously intemperate shop talk and then said, "So what is this call about?"

"Maybe about dinner tonight," said Peter. "Drinks. A

little here and there and a subject on my mind, which is
the town of Angel City, a town, I believe, that you are
fatally well connected with. So no? So yes?"

After a moment, Peter's colleague replied, "There
may be those in this town who accept a bid for dinner at
seven o'clock on the night. There may well be those. But
I'm not one of them."

And he hung up.

Alone in his apartment, with night coming on and
the city roaring and laughing and sulking around him, Peter sat by the window waiting for a breeze, an idea, something cool to think. Funny: it used to be sexy to be cool;
now it's sexy to be hot.

The phone rang. Peter answered thinking that there
may be those in this town who reject good company at
seven o'clock on the night, but he wasn't one of them. He
gave an affable hello, and Miss Debutante said, "*Who*
have you been talking to all this time, your gynecologist?
Dear heart, we have to discuss that money you owe me.
Fiasca wants to wait outside your building with his pit
bull, Great White, and when you come out, Great White
will tear off your cockadoo and balls, your three-piece set.
That wicked Fiasca. I said no, let's give him a chance. He's
probably very nice, Fiasca, you don't know. He might be
young. With a sweet face and soft hair to brush back from
his forehead, and a lovely three-piece set. He could sit in
your lap, Fiasca, and you could play with him. Yes, I told
him that. But don't let Great White catch you."

Miss Debutante chuckled.

"Please," Peter began. "Please, will you stop? If I ask
you nicely?"

"I don't get enough nice," said Miss Debutante coyly.
"I could do anything for a nice young boy with a lovely
three-piece set. I could be beautiful to you."

"Please—"

"You owe me money and I want it," said Miss Debutante, suddenly hard, tight, slamming shut on the fun. "I'll call till you pay me. I'll call till I get what I want. Miss Debutante says it's good. Miss Debutante wants it all!"

Whispers, a struggle, then a different voice, screaming, "Give it up, you puppy-faced *burzhui*, or we'll come by there —"

Peter holstered the phone, unplugged it, wrote a note on his pad to get the tape machine fixed or replaced, put the Beatles' White Album on the stereo, poured himself a stiff Finlandia, straight up in the glass, and stretched out on the couch, listening to the music, and to nothing else, as carefully as possible.

There are many scenes in New York, many areas of Connection. Countless subsystems pester and dodge each other, all sharing space but contesting point of view. Walking to work the next morning, Peter ran into one of the abutting systems while crossing Forty-ninth Street at Ninth Avenue. He had just stepped off the curb when a policemen heading toward him shouted, "Drop it, man! Just *drop* it!"

Peter froze, bewildered, but the cop strode past him, still yelling, and Peter turned to see a crazed bum grinning with a rock in his hand. He threw it, at nothing, then turned to the Korean fruit market just behind him, its wares set forth in the open to jog the impulses of that essential New Yorker, the passerby. Prepackaged pineapple slices to the left. Mixed melonberry salad to the right, glistening in plastic bowls. Defenseless grapes in the center — and the bum went for them, running his filthy hands over them with savage giggles as the cop and a Korean wrestled him away.

Peter moved on, wondering how cops keep their temper with so many idiots on the loose and ready for jazz. He wondered how Cary kept his temper; nothing ever seemed to infuriate him. He could get tough with you but never angry. Peter wondered how anybody kept his temper around here.

His boss's boss — the real boss, head of the agency — asked Peter to lunch. *Told* him to lunch, rather. They went to O'Neal's on Fifty-seventh Street, a typical New York place to eat: the food is good, the servers are unemployed actors hot to charm, and you have to reject the first two tables they offer you to keep your self-esteem in place. At that, every table is too close to every other table; Peter and his boss ended up inches away from a couple mouthing evilly at each other in an undertone. Peter's boss, formally offering the L.A. job, talks as if the two of them were alone in a fairy bower, but Peter can scarcely concentrate on what he's hearing because of what he's hearing.

"You don't have to keep telling me what Stephen said, you shrew of death," the man next to them was hissing. "I know what Stephen said."

"It isn't Stephen, it's your hooligan face," the woman murmured. "It's your crass mentality of life and the way you smell like a mushroom in heat."

"Let me tell you what money we're talking," Peter's boss blithely went on.

". . . and if it weren't what Stephen said," the man pursued, "it would be what Andrew said, wouldn't it, you filth, you diagram of a ball-chomping cuntbrain? Or what Lloyd said?"

"Lloyd's a fag," said the woman.

"Good, because that's just about your speed!"

". . . this house on the water at Malibu for at least the first month," Peter's boss suavely continued, like a jeweler unpacking his case.

"Anyway, if you don't shut your mouth of gutter

slime, I'm going to fill it with that so very delicious salade niçoise and then—"

"You don't have the *balls!*"

"Your favorite word, roundheels. Why don't you go sniffing at Andrew's crotch, you Henry Miller catbitch?"

"Andrew's a fag."

Peter must have been staring at them, because suddenly the man and the woman were glaring at him and the man was saying, "Hey, would you *please?*"

"Tourists from Bayonne," the woman sneered, taking out a cigarette, and the man nodded, lighting her up.

"So what do you think?" Peter's boss asked.

"Have . . . have I been living like this all my life? Has this place always been—"

"Right," said his boss. "Take tomorrow off to think about it. We can sign it all up on Thursday."

The phone was ringing when Peter walked into his apartment, and he stood contemplating it for a moment before he picked up. Taking a deep breath, he said hello.

"Look, it's me." Cary, his usual salutation. "I was just wondering if you heard anything about that L.A. job."

"Yes, I . . . I just did. They offered it to me. I have to tell them the day after—"

"You want to talk about it?"

Peter realized that he was crying. "Yes," he told his brother. "I want to talk about privacy."

"Huh?"

"Where do you want to meet?"

"Is something wrong? You sound funny."

Peter wiped his eyes. "Nothing is wrong. Good news and good money. You know."

"What do you mean *privacy?*"

"Nothing. I mean . . . I don't know what I mean."

"Maybe I better come over there, huh?"

"Okay," said New York Peter, still crying.

There are certain things Peter won't let Cary talk about, and Cary brought them all up in Peter's apartment that evening. Peter had collected himself in the time it took Cary to arrive, and now he fluently outlined the positive aspects of the L.A. job as if taking over the suave salesmanship of his boss, as if peddling a piece of jewelry from his boss's case of samples.

Attractive to the eye, reassuring to the skin. Washable, removable, enviable; and it leaves no mark.

"It's a good career move," Peter concluded. "No one turns down a good career move."

"But . . . but you're all broken in here," Cary said. "You're a natural New York guy here."

So they tilted to and fro, Cary thinking of reasons against it and Peter calmly reasoning them aside.

"Just tell me one thing," Cary said. "Tell me the truth, and no matter what it is, I'll accept it and I won't try to talk you out of it, okay? No matter what the answer is."

"Fine."

"The truth, Pete. Even if you don't like it. Even if it hurts, like . . . like whatever was going on with you on the phone before. I swear I'll let you alone if you tell me the truth."

Peter stood up; but this seemed so absurd and unnecessary that he immediately plopped down again, and he laughed.

"What do you want to know?" he asked his brother.

"Tell me, on a scale of one to ten, how ready you are to go to L.A. Forget the job and the career move, all that stuff there. Just compare being here and being there. Here in a place you grew up and you're related to it. Whether or not that's good. Think about what you'll find in some

place you move to. I mean . . . *moving*, Pete. It's like . . .
like cutting yourself off from what you . . . what you are? I
mean, what is it, ten to nothing for L.A.? Eight to two,
maybe? So maybe even six to four, what?"

Peter said nothing, and Cary shifted his weight
slightly as if he were going to get up and do something
nice to Peter, and they were staring at each other, so Cary
saw how easily Peter could lose his confident pose, how
the facade of New York crumbles like a child's alphabet-
block castle. Cary stayed where he was.

Who are your partners? That's the thing. Not who
you dance with; who you give your word to.

"I just haven't been thinking of it in those terms,"
Peter finally said.

"How about thinking like so now? For me."

"Except I'm trying to. I really am." Peter was pleading.

"What is it, seven to three, five to five? You must
have some idea by now. You were crying before, weren't
you? On the phone? Don't you want to tell me why?"

"No."

"The hell you say no. Don't you want to tell someone?"

"I don't . . . maybe."

"Who would you tell in L.A. maybe, if you were there
now?"

Suddenly Cary was out of the chair, and he had Peter
on his feet, one brother's face right on the other's there,
scarcely enough room to breathe in, too many eyes in this
place, judging what you do.

"Just tell me, Pete," Cary insisted. "One to ten, come
on."

"I don't want to go," Peter blurted out. "I mean,
sometimes I don't. And sometimes —"

"Are you afraid they'll can you if you turn them down?"

"No. A couple of people turned it down already. They don't want to leave New York. They're all . . . they're all networked up."

Cary rubbed Peter's neck. "Come on, Pete," he said.

"Yeah, but I never do the right thing. Can't you see that?"

Peter started to pull away but Cary held him fast.

"Where the hell are *you* going?" Cary asked.

"That's the hundred-dollar question, right there."

"Yeah . . . well . . . okay." Cary tousled Peter's hair.

"Hey, quit it!"

They were laughing now, and Cary said, "Come on, why don't you make us some coffee?" The phone rang while Peter was grinding beans with one hand and positioning the filter with the other, so Cary answered.

"Hello . . . it's *huh*? . . . This is his brother . . . You want to run that by me again? . . . You *what*? . . . Listen, they got a nice spring night working outside. Why don't you take a walk and cool off?"

Peter was pouring boiling water over the ground beans as Cary hung up. Peter turned to face Cary, studied him. Cary smiled. Get tough, not angry—that's the style of Cary.

"Who was that?" Peter asked.

"A crank, I don't know. Some guy says he's a debutante. It wasn't for you."

"He's going to call right back."

"Bet you he won't."

Peter surveyed the half-filled mugs, got a carton of milk from the fridge, readied its spout.

"That's all there is to it," said Peter. "Right? The correct comeback."

Cary shrugged. "Hell, they're giving you bull, so you

bull them right back. Happens all the time, like a game guys play with each other. The guy with the best bull wins the game."

"Funny," said Peter. "I always thought I was the guy with the best bull."

"Come on," Cary told him: because Cary sees life, all too simply, as a series of contests that Cary wins because he's a together guy, and that Peter wins because he's Cary's brother.

Maybe I just need a vacation, Peter thought, a bit later, as he headed for the cash machine. Maybe it's just big-city jitters.

Maybe. But he was acutely, uncomfortably, wounded-to-the-heart impossibly conscious of every violation of the social contract that he encountered, as if he had seen so much of it that now he could not see anything else. Every doorway held an unpleasantly surprising tramp, every turn of corner produced a crazy who was raving out bombastic paranoia, every pedestrian enthusiastically covered the land with debris, as if garbage cans were tourist attractions, not for the natives. Radios bombarded him for the fun of it, con men accosted him, and suddenly every idiot in town couldn't bear to leave his apartment without a gigantic kit bag, whole crowds of them contentedly sideswiping everyone within a radius of twenty yards. What did they find to put in those bags? What do you need to carry besides a wallet and keys? What are they, a new class of the yuppie homeless, toting their Cuisinarts and fluted bud vases through the streets?

Lining up at the cash machine, Peter wondered if they get big-city jitters in Boston, New Orleans, Denver. He knew they don't in L.A. Angel City doesn't have jitters; Angel City has tofu and mañana. The angels there never ask each other, Did I do the right thing? because

there is no wrong thing in Angel City. It's the world capital of the no-fault life-style—no phone maniacs to challenge you to cope, no street trash to outwit, no penalties
for being a younger brother.

Maybe, Peter thinks, I should have been a cop.

The woman just ahead of Peter has been playing with
the cash machine, repeatedly sending her card through
the system and trying all the buttons, reading the screen,
nodding, considering. She believes everyone will think she
is Important because she has so much business to trans-
act. The line, stopped dead at the one machine under her
command, has been growing. People behind Peter are
fidgeting and muttering, but the woman blithely—more
grandly, even—pursues her fantasy of having a part in the
doings of the great world.

They're giving you bull, so you bull them right back.

"Do you need some help?" Peter asks the woman,
politely, with just a shade of irony.

She glares at him. She is nondescript but at least she
is there. "Do you *mind*?" she snarls.

"Hey, *I* mind," calls a man far down in the line.

The woman returns to the machine.

"Hey, *I* mind, lady!"

"Somebody call a cop."

"Will you just look at this?"

New York is bulling back, but "Hmm," the woman
tells her machine, sliding her card in again. She's a top
trader on the stock market, a vagabond executive checking
in on the boss computer, a spy decoding orders. She is a
deluded moron using your time to fill out a chapter in her
day.

Peter abruptly walks away, the shouts of the people
still in line echoing as he heads for the deli to scarf up
some dinner. Did he do the right thing? At the deli counter a black man with a gym bag bumps into Peter, stares

at him, then says, "You said excuse me, right?" Peter pretends the man does not exist. Did he do the right thing? Heading home with a corned beef sandwich, extra lean, Peter has to jump backward to avoid a Chinese take-out delivery boy speeding along the sidewalk on a bicycle. The delivery boy pulls to a halt, calmly chaining his bicycle to a parking meter.

Peter walks up to him and says, "Why don't you stay in the street where you belong?"

"Look where you're going, asshole," the delivery boy replies, shouldering his bags.

Peter stares after him. It does not feel like the right thing.

Then this happens:

Two blocks from his apartment, a young couple comes bumbling out of a doorway and down a stoop, both of them laden with luggage. The couple is ratty and their luggage is junk; they lay everything on the sidewalk, blocking the way. Peter has to step into the gutter to get around them, and the young woman matter-of-factly walks right in front of Peter and throws her hand up to signal a cab, socking Peter in the eye.

And Peter drops his sandwich, grabs the young man by the hair, and slams him flat on his back on the stairs of the stoop.

"Tell your girlfriend to keep her hands out of my face, you fucking jerk!" New York Peter roars, staring at the astonished young man to lock it all in before storming home.

All *right*, that's *it!* That's *buster up* and Peter has *had* it, raging in his pathetic walk-up closet, banging stuff around, making up his mind at last because *no one* has to live like this, and where's Miss Debutante now when you need him to do the right thing to, which is hit on *him* the

way everyone hits on everyone *else* here. Buster up, Angel
City, and give me some mellow. Peter's got some paper
out to write some letters, going to say good-bye to the
people who matter to him, partners and some others. This
is where you find out who they are, opening your address
book to count the names of emotional reverberation, and
Peter will write down how he feels. He's going to drench
himself in his sorrows and that's how he will dry out.

To Brenda Peter writes that he may have to go to a
place like Los Angeles in order to appreciate New York.

To Cary Peter writes that he won't be a New Yorker
till he feels bound to come back to it.

There is no third letter. To Peter's surprise, he really
has nothing at all to say to anyone else in his book.

He felt better the next day, because none of this mattered anymore. He left word at the office that he'd be in to
straighten out the L.A. job that afternoon and went out
into the breezy New York day for a nice long think walk. It
was real city out there, the center of the world, where
even the sunlight struts.

In the park in front of the Flatiron Building Peter sat
on a bench and looked out on the place where he was
bustered down onto the sidewalk while the city people
watched. Every New Yorker has his sites. Here you ran
into a former lover, staggering in a druggy daze; there you
gave a bum a quarter and he spat at you. Everyone's crazy
because there's so much street traffic, too much interac-
tion with strangers. In other cities, everyone lives in cars
and houses. In New York everyone lives in public.

A bag lady sitting on Peter's bench cackled quietly to
herself. "Look at all the candy," she said, gazing on the
lunch-hour crowd before them, shifting and laughing and
doing. "Ties, books, stockings. Some of them got hats and
they're gonna give each other presents later. And what are

they eating? Sandwiches, same as me. People's all the same. Everyone wants to talk. They want a little social visiting to break up the day. You need some of this?"

She offered Peter a sandwich that looked like Rumpelstilskin's vomit. Peter shook his head.

"Gotta eat some time," she said.

"I'm too worried to eat."

"A whippersnapper like you, worried?"

"I'm worried about privacy."

The bag lady nodded. "All the good things is hard to get," she observed, "and privacy's good. Look at all that candy there on benches with their sandwiches, how they eat such tiny bites. Like their food got something funny in it if they ain't careful. Worms in their caviar. Rats in the lunchbox."

About twenty-five people faced them, office workers taking the air dotted by grinning high-schoolers on hooky, free-lancers waiting for the next job, players in the game of getting bulled and bulling back.

"'Course, they're quiet now," the bag lady said. "They know we watching them. But they'll be fighting later on. Candy's always fighting. They come a thousand miles to fight, think no one knows 'cause they so special to themselves."

"What do you think they fight about?" Peter asked.

She cackled. "They don't need *about*. They live to fight and fight to live. That's candy."

She went on eating.

"It's quiet now," said Peter.

Even the dogs that romp unleashed in the center of the park were sitting one out, and the drug sellers who throng the entrances were playing it very cool. People sat, lunched, read, pondered.

"Maybe they waiting to spring on us," said the bag lady. "Candy move real sudden when they please to. Got

all that energy to work off. That's why they always fighting. One day you wake up, all your energy's gone and
your fighting's over. Know why? You're dead. That's why
they keep fighting, candy. It's how they know they're
alive."

"Anyway, it's quiet now," said Peter.

"Just wait," said the bag lady.

She seemed content.

THE WOMAN OF WEIMAR

*The old woman meets a
young student, and ancient
history and youthful art then
tenderly undertake a contest
for domination.*

IF I WERE A COWARD,
she thought, I would have a cat named Döblin or Brecht.
No. *Two* cats. Male and female. She would of course be
Jenny, for Lenya. And when I put on the records, the cats
would hum along and flaunt their tails and dance, and I
would sing for them of the cabarets and the books and the
cinema, of our beautiful lost Berlin that was already dead
when I was a child.

That was my fate, she thought: to be there for
Partisan Review and the McCarthy witch burnings and
Jerry Lewis, but to miss that amazing Weimar Germany of
the arts and the truth and the life, when for the first time

in their history those magnificent Germans stopped making trouble for the world and unleashed the best of themselves in the theatres, the concert halls, the opera houses, the art galleries, the bookstores.

Oh, I was there, she thought. Ja: till Hitler came in and we fled to Austria and I was nine years old, fit for schoolwork and dinners, not Weimar cabarets. That clumsy, ignorant, boring little hamlet of an Austria; but three years later we were in England, and two years after that in the United States, and even by then I was only fourteen, scarcely old enough to comprehend my parents' lamentations.

Ach! if you had seen it!

Ach! to have our Berlin back!

Ach! Otto Klemperer, Marlene Dietrich, George Grosz and Kandinsky, Fritz Lang, *Caligari* and "Moon of Alabama," Maria Nemeth, Piscator and Reinhardt, Claire Waldoff and her gritty, tuneless, marvelous songs of the working-class districts!

And wasn't I a sight for America, she thought, the fat girl with the braids and the accent, so ridiculous in a place like New Haven, Connecticut; and didn't everyone at school let me know it? Too smart I was, too. Too artistic, too intense. As serious at play as I was at serious things. Not smart enough to prepare the appropriate personal-cultural defenses, no. Yet not so fat that I could abandon every hope of being courted by some earnestly amiable young fellow with an intelligence. And not so ridiculous that no one would listen to what I had to say. Still, not artistic like an artist, to create. Artistic like a critic, to make my footnotes. Imperious. Candid. Sharp, with a cutting edge. Cultured, o *je*, relentlessly cultured, was I not? All the fine young boys from me ran, all the truest parties were given without. So what was I? Books and piano lessons all through high school. That is what I was.

"Germy," they called me.

So apt.

I was the germ of the dead Weimar, *inculcated, exhorted*. The all-wise priestess of history, put forth into being by parents whose belief in the future of the world ended quite, quite certainly in 1933. Everything before Weimar was *Vorspiel*. Weimar was paradise. After was hell.

So they died, the parents, and left behind a germy emigrée intellectual who made her present in the past, endlessly analyzing the possibilities and determinants and contradictions in the Weimar Republic. Three careers came of it: university professor, leftist periodical essayist, and lordly clothbound historian, tome after tome on totalitarianism and Germany and Jews, even leading to some promotional television appearances — to the accompaniment, she was certain, of millions of turning dials. Who is that fat foreigner? What is this longwhiling . . . *boring* . . . lecture on everyone who now is dead? As her students love to say, You had to be there.

She had been there, but only just. A child of Weimar, an infant then — and now here she was, delivering broadsides and interpretations on it. *Ausgezeichnet!* We can choose our own present. We select our homeplace. So mine is Weimar Berlin, in a gone Germany. Gone? Finished? Even now, four decades after she became American, her English slides into reminiscence. Copy editors queried her, at times, in shock. "*Very* antique usage." "Dubious choice of word." "This is not English." It isn't? But surely "longwhiling" is more evocative than "boring," yes?

Everything comes through better in German, thicker, broader, taller, grander, like a roast with dumplings and gravy. You do not only know it is meat. You *taste* it is meat, *nicht wahr?*

She was having dinner in the university cafeteria, alone of course, always alone. In a way—in a way that was very important and saddening and bitterly reasonable to the Woman of Weimar—she had been alone for decades, isolated from her surroundings, from this culture of football players and cheerleaders, even from her friends. Once she was only alien; now she was eminent and international, a professional emigrée. Her books had been translated into every major European language, into Russian, Hebrew, Afrikaans, Japanese, Finnish. Some might call her a world figure, and there were many, many things that world figures must not do, many places they cannot be seen in, many people they rather ought not know. The illustrious are not free.

Also. The *Grosssiegelbewahrer* sits in the university cafeteria as always, dining off a tray of slop the farmers of Jungbunzlau would not feed to their pigs, and the Woman of Weimar, the Greatsealbearer of the democracy that was too perfect to live, is about to laugh at the vanity of her glory when a student asks if he might join her.

The Woman of Weimar looked up, almost amazed, at a handsome blond boy, a strapping fellow, but with refinement, perhaps from a private school before the college. A prince's face on a peasant's body—this the Woman recognized as "the preppy look." Soft eyes and rude hands, standing before her with his tray and his request.

"Unless . . . I mean, if you're waiting for someone . . ." he tells her.

She gestures. "So sit."

He settles in with a shy look of gratitude, quick, like all Americans, always ready to talk. They will tell you anything that is on their minds, but why should they bother? You can read their thoughts in their faces. A land of overly mothered children, too much change in their pockets.

"It's just that I see you here almost every night," he was telling her. "You always seem to be alone. With all the distinguished professors on the campus, I'd have thought . . . you know. I would have expected a Germanic version of the Algonquin roundtable."

"What do I want from those grim old Solomons, or they from me, then? We've all heard everything we have to say. Leave me from those *hondlers* in peace, ja? Charm me instead," she told him, "with your youth and joy and energy. Tell me what is new in America."

He beamed at her. Not a word. He just beamed.

"Now that you have come to sit with me," she said, "I realize how foolish I am not to want this before. I should be more welcoming."

"Oh, it's not your fault. Everyone just assumes you're too . . . too important to bother with us."

"I teach you, no? So. Dinner is more teaching. I am too icy at the table. You must be brave to dare to ask to sit! Ah, such a pun: I feel like one of Goethe's mistresses — *eine Frau von Stein!*

He doesn't get it. *Eselkopf!* Americans read nothing but *Rolling Stone.*

"I'm German myself," he told her, "a few generations back." He paused. "My name is Gustave Fluten."

"How eloquent. You could be a character in one of Thomas Mann's tales," she replied, trying to forgive his not getting her *Wortspiel* on "Charlotte von Stein" and "woman of stone."

"It was von Fluten centuries ago," he said. "But we don't have that sort of thing here. Everyone's . . ."

If he says "equal in America," I throw my tray at his smug American privileged face.

". . . everyone's a little shy about owning up to our class system. The English people here say it really baffles them. And they ought to know."

He laughed, the mouth wide, sure of its noise. All Americans have Swedish teeth.

"And what ought you to know, my young Gustave von Fluten?"

"Everything, because I'm going to be a writer."

"Naive or sentimental? From the instinct or the doctrine?"

"From the late-night staying up and rewriting. Where I come from, you have to work to succeed."

"Ja. Work. But they have a saying in Chemnitz: You either got it or you don't."

He laughed and she nodded.

"So what do you write?" she asked him.

"Well . . ." Three beats, and the shy is over. Life in America. "This story I'm working on now? It's called 'The Last Jew in Berlin.' It's about this guy who hides out in an attic all through the war."

"What war?"

He was bewildered. "World War Two." Is there any other war? Like those people you meet at a party who say, "I so admire your book," as if your entire career should be whatever they were reading that week.

"The Second World War is one of many, many wars," she explained. "In this century alone, many wars. How is anyone to know what you would mean with this phrase, 'the war'? *The* war!" Her heavy accent and her scorn opulently combined, smashing from the left and smashing from the right. "Why do you not strive for precision? Make yourself clear, ja? And if you have to know of a single war, Herr von Fluten — why is it one that was over before you were even born? If there must be such a thing as 'the war' for you, it is America's involvement in Vietnam. Why not 'The Last American in Saigon,' while we're writing stories?"

He stared at her.

"Herr von Fluten is shocked," she said. "You didn't think I was going to be an old grouch, did you? You brought your tray over to me in your earnest young way. Chivalry in the college! You were hoping to meet whom? Mother Goose. So you got Mother Courage."

He looked hurt. "Do you want me to go?"

"No," she said. "No." His hands were clutching the rim of his tray, as if ready to make a run for it, and she touched one of them lightly. "No, Herr von Fluten, stay. Tell me of 'The Last Jew in Berlin.' Is it expressionistic? In the attic where your young man is hiding from the Nazis, is there a rat, amused and cynical, like a true Berliner? He steals food for the hero, and converses with him, seasoning his philosophy of life with sarcastic comments in Yiddish? No?"

Smiling, the boy asked, "Who said there was a young man?"

A wave of her hand at this piece of nonsense. "All young people write autobiographically. First fiction is about one's ideals. Middle-period fiction is about one's view of the world. Last fiction is about one's youth. The oldest people write the youngest books. Look at Goethe. He spent fifty years writing a play about a man who . . . what? What does Faust do, my young scholar?"

"He bargains with the devil for . . . to be able to comprehend beauty."

"What else?"

"He roves the world. He experiences everything."

Stubborn, stupid boy. "He becomes again a *young man*, my Gustave von Fluten. Faust is about how only age can appreciate youth." A glance at her watch. The illustrious are busy, above bourgeois protocols.

This much, at least, the boy understood. He even nodded, affirming his dismissal. But: "Professor," he asked, "can I come back again some evening if you're here? We can tell some Chenmitz jokes and you can poke some more fun at my absurdly inflated ambitions."

Self-satire from an American? Overwhelmed, truly charmed, the Woman of Weimar laughed. "*Chemnitz.* And yes. Yes, come back to me soon here, ja? You'll tell me more about some last Jews in Berlin. Then you'll push it away, ja?, and write about today, your world. The youth. The music. The age of what it is, which you will tell us. *This* is for you, not an attic halfway around the world in a city that never was. Never for you."

"We have to write," he told her, "about what moves us."

"I find Fräulein Lily Tomlin," she said, "very moving."

Is she joking, or what?

Which is more apt: to tell an invented story or keep secret a true one?

The young student Gustave Fluten returned with his tray and a bright smile to dine with the Woman of Weimar the very next night, and many nights after. The two spoke of a wide assortment of topics, truly a great vivacity of topics, from what we might be to what we were and thence to, hardest of all, what we are. An entire world lies therein.

What we might be is the last Jew in Berlin, conversing with a rat who yodels facetiae of the *Spreeatem,* the "Athens on the Spree," and undercuts the querulous solemnity of history with *en Stickl Jidisch*. What we are is a handsome youth trying to please.

Or we might be an empathic *Ewig-Weibliche*, symbol to some men, mystery to many, delight to all — for who has not read, somewhere, of the astonishing glow that her love can in a man build, and not wondered how it would feel to be that goddess for some Goethe, tall, strong, and true? What we are is the Greatsealbearer of a quaint old picture that has lost its color, something for books that have no matter. Democracy is a spoof and culture is whatever the tyrants of the day permit.

And what we were, going back far enough, is the Crusader and the ghetto Jewess in a dangerous encounter. Crusaders always win in the end — *their* cousins, not the Jewess's, wrote the histories then.

It was along these lines that the Woman of Weimar and the young American student laid down their perimeters and dug in for battle. For yes, he was back at her table in the cafeteria, and again and more and soon every night, and they fought because she was flinty and he was affable, and because she was brilliant and he was still looking for his knowledge, and because she has been to the world and he only wants to write about it.

And he wants her to read what he has written. Oh, so humbly he has asked, in truth! He is respectful of her time, her patience, her glory. He is fearful of her honesty — ja, he had better be, no? "The Last Jew in Berlin." The gall of him, to treat something so bitter and vast and so very beyond his dear American boyhood, with the rah-rah and flasks of forbidden tonic for the prom dance. They hop them up on kill! kill!, then they drug them stupid, then they send them to war. These smiling innocent young Lindberghs. Prairie faces, the Woman imagined, though she was glad to say she had never as much as glimpsed a prairie, even by stereopticon. Such likable faces, because such unwittingly naive faces. Look at those American eyes, so . . . untroubled. They don't deny what is real: they have never heard of it.

"I would just . . . I mean, I would be so interested to hear what you had to say," he was telling her. "I'm not a beginner. I've been writing seriously since I was fourteen. So this isn't—I'm not wasting your time with entry-level stuff. And, after all, you're the authority on Jews and Berlin and so on."

She sighed. One of the most profoundly conflicted eras in history, the most intensely informative time in the course of humankind since the Lisbon earthquake—and our Gustave von Fluten sums it up as "Jews and Berlin and so on." What a story he must have written, for truth.

"Then you could show me a story of yours," he was going on, with a conspirator's smile. "I'll bet you've got—"

"I have never written fiction! *Never!*"

Her energy shut him up *auf eins, zwei.*

"Are not volumes of social and cultural dissection enough to buy my credentials? Must I humiliate my memories like thus? Distort them then? Bend them into picturesque attitudes for strangers to gape at?" The illustrious are not invulnerable. "What is this for a presumption?"

"Fiction isn't humiliating, Professor. It's self-expression. It's the way we can leave something behind us, tell the world that we have been here! This fiction thing . . . I'm sorry if I offended you. I only meant it as a compliment. Really."

"There is enough writing about Nazis and Jews without it has to give fiction as well," she said, conciliating with a bit of shrug and an edgy smile. But then, they always fought and always caught their calm soon enough after. "Perhaps especially fiction from a descendant of *Edelleute* and *Junker,* my young American knight."

He blushed.

"*Also.* You give me this story about the last Jew, and I will read it and pronounce my critique. Bring it tomorrow here, ja? Or leave it in my office. You will tell me about that time, that famous time that all the world longs to know of, the time of Weimar and what came after. You will tell me and then I will tell you. *Richtig?*"

"*Jawohl,*" he uttered, prudently trying but half a grin.

"We Germans understand each other," she observed. "That was always true, even when some of us were Jewish and some were Nazis. Always true. It is the most unifying culture in Europe. Think of the English, how separate are the lords from their servants. Or the French, with their Parisian ways, and provincial capital ways, and village ways, and their bizarre Midi and Bretagne. Italy, too, with that jumble of city-states. But all Germans are always German. Always. Was it not Hitler's silliest mistake that he dragged the Austrians into his Reich? I believe so. Austria is so . . . Spanish . . ."

She was lost in thought.

Surrounded by artifacts of the past, the old woman considers a voice of the present.

Actually, it is not as laden with mementos and relics as one might think, her apartment on West End Avenue. Some first editions of the relevant books, a few 78s for color, a setting of old UFA stills on the wall—but none of this was snatched, smuggled, sent in fond sorrow out of the place and time, as the cynic would suppose. Such a picture of the refugees of culture, disseminating the objects of Weimar throughout the world! Such a picture there to see, frame-ready, no?, as the Americans would put it: the possessions of the dispossessed.

But no, my cynics. Sorry. All of the Woman's Weimariana was collected after the fact, almost all of it purchased right here in New York, some of it as recently as last year. The old is ever new, perhaps. Her readers sometimes mail her things. One of her steady correspondents, a man in Sacramento, sent her an LP of Berlin songs sung by Marlene Dietrich that he found in a flea market. He had made a tape of it himself but he wanted her to own it. He hoped she didn't already have it.

She loved it, but she tried to talk herself into sending it back. Letters, yes, it is appropriate, from reader to writer. She enjoyed her fan mail, even if some of her writers could not distinguish between the bondmaking of fit praise and the impudence of unsolicited critique. Some letters the Woman swept into the wastebasket. But these gifts that would come . . . this is unnerving. This is a personal act, *not* appropriate. It is funny how some people who read your books want to reach out to you in such a way. It is curious, no?

So, in her house of state, in the company of a good-sized but not absurdly militant assembly of historical souvenirs, the Woman read young Gustave Fluten's story, "The Last Jew in Berlin." She was constantly distracted by her own expressionistic rat, Maxine, the only rat in all the northeast who spoke the absolute American of the Southern California Valley.

"So ês it, like, *rīlly* good?" Maxine asked. "Does it, like, captüre the *flavor* of the *times?*"

"So far it is all in an attic in Charlottenberg," said the Woman. "So what is the flavor in an attic?"

"Not too coo-ool," said Maxine.

"The protagonist is trying to keep up his cheer," the Woman explained, "by thinking his way through the Wagner operas, note for note. That is how he keeps track of time in his solitary confinement. For intermissions, he reflects upon his past. He is a painter, ja?, or he *was* a painter before he went into hiding, and then of course the author compares the character's pictures to Wagner's pictures, Wagner's themes to Nazi tenets, Vaterland to independence . . . and all this entirely in the protagonist's mind, you see."

"Oooh," Maxine observed. "Intēriör mônologue *citty!*" She seemed impressed for once.

"No," said the Woman, putting down her spectacles. "No. It is not good. It is too imagined. It misses the bite of reality. It cannot be done by a youth of today. He knows some things. But he needs command. The culture is too large for him to put on just because he feels the need to, like a coat.

"Read me some," Maxine urged.

" 'In his mind, he drew a series of watercolors of the buildings, people, and street traffic of the Kurfürstendamm, each image so precisely detailed that, so he imagined, the eye would take them for black-and-white photographs that had been tinted. Yet there was in fact little color, for even this great central throughway of the city claimed little more than shades of gray and brown. Berlin is the color of rain.' "

"Oooh, añd, like, *wăs* it?"

The Woman of Weimar took off her glasses, crossed to a record player so old it had settings for all the speeds once in use — 78, 45, 33, even 16, the speed that never was, planned to inaugurate a consumer revolution that was not executed. Some ideas have a past, some a future, some not even a present. Switching to 78, needling in the past, the Woman placed Claire Waldoff on the turntable for a few minutes of bracing self-reinforcement in the cabaret of deadright honesty, ironies of the human condition set to simple melodies for the uniquely crabby voice that once held an entire culture in its grasp. Claire Waldoff sang:

So was ist ein Berliner?
Was braucht er, Art und Fach?
Und was wird der Berliner?
Da kräht kein Hahn danach!

"What's all that about?" asked Maxine, sniffing and creeping and not impressed. "I mean, that, like, *tot-tal-ly* cheeses me *out!*"

Ach, to have their Berlin back! "That is a singer of the yesteryear, on the question, What is a Berliner?" The two of them listened to the shaggy delivery over the dump-truck piano accompaniment, the artist's scathing insouciance probing, nudging—What does the Berliner want, what will he be?—till, all questions posed, the artist paused for air, then cried, "No rooster's doing any crowing over it!," an old German idiom roughly translatable as "Who gives a — — —?"

That was Weimar's way of taking a philosophical position.

"Rillly," said Maxine, at the record's end, "she's no Julie Andrews."

"Da kräht kein Hahn danach!" sang the Woman of Weimar. And she said, "The truth is not made to be pretty."

"Oooh, like, *crow* me into the *barn*yard?"

"The truth is for those who were there," the Woman went on. "The truth is for them to share with us. Others . . . cannot know." She was weighing her words with gravity and grandeur. She knew she was right. "Only those who were there can know," she insisted. "This is why history is written by the privileged. They are educated, pensive, remote. They treat not the experience, but the *results*. So fiction is written by the underprivileged, especially the ambitious bourgeoisie, for they treat nothing but their feelings about the experience. Together, history and fiction form a fair impression of human life."

"Yes," said Maxine. "But what are you, like, going to *say* to your *student* about his, uh, *story*?

The Woman nodded, left the record player, and put her glasses on. "Let us read forward," she said.

The Greatsealbearer breaks the seal entrusted to her, to make way for new history.

Gustave thought it so exciting that the Woman of Weimar had consented to read and tell, that he insisted on meeting her not at the university cafeteria but at Jasper's.

"For once," he told her, "we'll sit down at a real table in a real restaurant and eat real food."

The Woman of Weimar hesitated.

"My treat," he urged. And he can afford it, can't he?

In Europe, the students are penniless revolutionaries. In America, the students are all ready to be the President.

"Jasper's?" she asked. They were in her office, her domain. Yet the illustrious are at times uncertain, wary, complex, flustered.

"It's the real thing," he told her. "And look . . ." This part was difficult. Gustave pulled it out gently, like a doctor operating on his mother. Well. It seems that Gustave's Boston cousin was giving a party that night, an after-dinner get-together. Small. Plain. Very conversational. He gives these Boston-kind-of-parties, you see, where the emphasis is on intelligent talk, a thoughtful exchange of takes on the world. Not New York style at all. A New York party, now, well . . .

He wants to show me off, the Woman thought. The *Grosssiegelbewahrer.* As if any of these beautiful American children had heard of history, much less of a historian.

"I'd be in Harlan's best books for life if you came, I can tell you that," said Gustave. "He not only has your books, he annotates them. He puts photographs and articles right inside the book, too. I mean, he'll keep his cool and all—Harlan's nothing *but* cool. But—"

"Harlan?"

"My cousin. My family is sort of planted up and down the northeast. As if we had consulates in every city. So when each of us kids goes to college, the cousin living nearest him is expected to squire him around a bit. You know. Take you out to dinner, offer you a day trip to their weekend place, pass you their opera tickets if they can't use them."

Summer places and opera subscriptions, ja. The rich are always with us.

"Look, I know probably the last thing you want to do is blow an evening with my cousin's friends. Please don't be offended that I asked you." His *please* always seemed to plead with her, not just punctuate but petition. "I just thought, well . . . in case you would be amused to try something a little off the track . . . you know? I mean, if you wanted to come . . . well, they would make you feel very welcome."

"Your cousin is a patrician of Boston?" the Woman asked.

Gustave grinned. "The way we play it is: Yes, but you're not supposed to say so. In Boston you don't talk about anything. Everything just *is*, and all the insiders know it. The outsiders . . . well, that's Boston." He shrugged, but only with his eyes. "In New York, of course, everything is gossip and sizing up a guy's status. Boston is like a small town—it never changes. But New York is in a permanent state of redevelopment."

"So young," said the Woman, "and already he knows the world."

"Pieces of it, anyway. Pieces here and there."

The Woman of Weimar was smiling.

"You'll come, then? To Jasper's for dinner and Harlan's after that?"

Listen to the names of these yuppisch cavaliers.

"For dinner I come. We'll see about what is after."

"Great. And . . . are you going to tell me . . . about . . ."

" 'The Last Jew in Berlin.' "

He nodded, less confident now.

"At dinner," she said.

"You don't want to . . . maybe give me a preview?"

"No."

She glanced at the clock and picked up her pen, her signal to students that the meeting had ended.

"Oh boy," said Gustave. That curious American expression that stated any of a hundred things, depending on the inflection. The Woman of Weimar had never mas-

tered its nuances and always waited to hear what was said
directly following to read the meaning.

"See you later," said Gustave, leaving with a bounce
and a wave.

"Von Herzen gern," the Woman of Weimar murmured,
back in her books.

She had never heard of Jasper's, for this East Side
restaurant tries to be as little known as possible. The manager, fleet, effete Jasper Devon, never advertises, and he
discourages testimonials in the dish columns. Yet how can
he evade the scrutiny and curiosity of the town, with such
a splendid clientele? At least he does his best to make
strangers, no matter how well-spoken or nicely dressed,
as uncomfortable as he can — waving them over to the bar
with a taut smile and no promise of a table; seating them
at what is known as The Oubliette, back against the wall
between the kitchen and the men's room; and sometimes
not even bothering to attend to new arrivals at all,
blithely, keenly chatting up his regulars while some perfectly guiltless couple stands helpless at his door, waiting
for Godot, or Jasper.

Inexperienced though she was in such surroundings,
the Woman of Weimar instantly saw Jasper's for one of
those impenetrably exclusive clubs with which the rich
and powerful dot the city, the kind of place the Woman
had been avoiding — one might say fleeing — all her life.
She felt doom and anger. She felt her person insulted, her
feelings treated with contempt, and, worst of all, her intelligence rated as irrelevant. She scanned the room twice to
be sure . . . no, Gustave was not there. She hated him for
luring her into this trap — and now up to the Woman of
Weimar comes this excellent host of such a hospitable
café, and she braced herself, and cursed her miserable stab
at early-middle *Partisan Review* chic; but then, what do
clothes count for in a world of interrogations and torture

and genocide? The Woman of Weimar prepared to give this death's head of a doorman a good dusting up if he as much as lifted an eyebrow.

But he greeted her by name, and led her with what must be called ceremony to what was certainly a major table for those who care about such things, in the center of the room against the picture windows. Every eye was on her, and yes, she saw them whispering and wondering. But the Woman of Weimar is above tedious gaieties. She looked at no one. Even alone, waiting for her partner, she *presided* over her table. A waiter deferentially brought her the Manhattan she had ordered.

At least I know how to ask for the trendy drink, she told herself.

Keeping an eye on the door for a sign of Gustave, the Woman saw two smartly dressed businessmen enter Jasper's, full of confidence and aplomb. Good, there are the people for whom such a place made was. But Jasper led them to The Oubliette, airily leaving them to utter, "This is absurd" to each other as they sat.

It is hard to guess who is to be included, the Woman thought. It is not something visual. It is something secret, something written on a list in the minds of arbiters.

She watched with interest, trying to master the system, as two women who looked as if they might be legendary were given tables of honor, in the Woman's section; as a somewhat rowdy foursome were sent to the bar with a shake of Herr Jasper's head (and as he turned away he made a grimace); as an unbearably WASPisch family in blazers, from tall Father to little American Junior, were granted a limited visa, in the center of the room but away from the windows (and while Herr Jasper was polite, the waiter seemed hasty).

Where would they have seated Goethe? the Woman mused, and now here was Gustave, beaming at her, and the room was looking, and Herr Jasper himself was hovering nearby, doting, and the Woman, startled, realized that her worshipful student was a figure of prestige among these tycoons of *Vanity Fair*. No doubt it was his ancient family and their money. What else matters to these people? Such a gang as this to be among, she thought, fretting at Gustave's smile. How firm, how unquestionable he looked in his dark brown suit, so much older than he seems on campus. This is the present without past, taking its future for granted, a race that inherits the earth out of simple self-esteem.

But he was thoughtful enough, no?, to have warned Herr Jasper how to treat the Woman of Weimar.

"Are you going to tell me about my story?" Gustave asked, spoiling his coffee with vast quantities of milk and sugar.

"It is terrible to make human suffering glamorous," said the Woman of Weimar. "Fiction about the Holocaust does this. It exploits the victims by making them touching. It turns them into heroes of fate instead of puppets of history. Terror becomes a ballade. I believe this very strongly. Some objects are perhaps not suitable for story-telling."

"Oh boy," said Gustave, but he said nothing after.

"It is also perhaps terrible to discourage youth in anything. So I will say as well that your story is of strong craft for a beginner. At your age, a writer is far, far ahead of his great season. This is your maytime, your period of learning and folly, *nicht wahr*? Yes, *wahr*. One day you will come back to this story and see that it is an apprentice piece. You may also then see that such stories make myth and poetry out of human suffering when it would be better only to report on it, to reveal it as it was and may be again, and so reproach the world."

He was silent for a while, then asked, "Didn't you find my character sympathetic?"

"All victims of tyranny are sympathetic."

"But can one write about *all* victims?"

"I do," she said.

He nodded, stirring and stirring his coffee. Idiot habit. So unnecessary and irritating.

"What is real to you?" she said.

"I . . . everything, I guess. Everything that *is* real. Or . . . what do you —"

"What is fascinating? What is outraging? *These* are your subjects, not an attic in someone else's life."

He smiled. "Well," he said, "I don't know whether I passed or failed. Will you come to my cousin's party?"

"Yes." She was not apprehensive of these people now. She held a high table at Jasper's and felt majestic and a little tipsy.

"That means I passed," said Gustave.

On the way to his cousin's place he was thoughtful, quiet, no doubt digesting her challenge to him and his writing. Here is altogether New Yorkisch activity, she thought: riding in a taxicab next to someone you hardly know, or have just in a way quarreled with, or need something from. It is intimate, presumptuous, this intrusive American recklessness raised to its highest degree.

But the party, she could see at once, was almost European in its gentility. Mendelssohn in the background one heard, but background Mendelssohn, not major work, so this is suitable for party music. The cousin Harlan had the gravity of a Hanover merchant, his wife Kathleen the radiant clarity of a Scandinavian fairy princess. They were honored to receive the Woman of Weimar — they not only said so, they seemed so, granting her respect without insistence. She might have been in London.

It was British, too, she thought, to include a little boy among the guests, a very serious child who shook the Woman's hand and told her how late it was and then sat quietly on a couch with his father Cliff and Cliff's fine lady Ruth Ann. A Jewish-Gentile union, the Woman decided. They are very common in America, very rare in Europe. American racism is very, very inconsistent.

There were a few other couples at Harlan's. The evening was all couples, even, if one counted Gustave and the Woman of Weimar as a couple—if one counted the present and past as legitimately linked. But they have antagonistic needs, do they not? History moves so very, very quickly now. During World War II, the United States loved Russia and fought Germany to death. A generation later, Germany was the lover, Russia as evil as original sin. History has many stories.

The Woman of Weimar entertained at the piano. So physical a talent never falls away. You can become rusty, but not incompetent. She played Bach, some of the three-part Inventions and the poignantly delicate allemande from the Fourth Partita, noblest of the noble Six. Gustave played, too, some little poetries of Debussy. Impressive. But then the Woman was beginning to realize that Gustave was more than just another amiable college youth. He had perhaps promise. He looked very penetrating at the keyboard. Is it the word? Penetrating? As if he were *consuming* as much as making music. When he finished, to warm applause, he was motionless. Then he turned to his audience and was, for an almost imperceptible moment, blank and pure, his senses exhausted, his needs soothed to nothing. Then he looked at the Woman and was himself again.

They were all too kind, too fine, too *learned,* even, for the Woman. Their failure to offend offended her. It was un-American. She preferred to be annoyed; it kept her sharp. "How do I know what I think," she liked to say, "till I hear myself disagree with you?"

Even Gustave, her recently favorite sparring partner, appeared not to mind her refusal to pet his story.

What do they believe I am? Some ancient *Dame* who must be flattered and coaxed and lied to?

That was probably why she did it.

The illustrious are dangerous, too, remember, for they have more to defend than most people. The party waiter with a vigorous attitude problem is only an outrage to you; to the celebrity, he is a catastrophe, for he is mugging not only a morale but a career, a public persona, an importance.

That might explain her rudeness.

But then, is rudeness always explainable, reasonable? The Woman of Weimar's rudeness that night was avantgarde, a postmodernist tantrum perhaps answering an artistic need. She wrote no fiction. But like us all she needs, at times, to perform; and she was at the piano delivering Claire Waldoff's "Was ist ein Berliner?" when she suddenly broke off and said—to those aristocratic faces with their expressions of rapt delight, all of them leaning forward as if fearful of missing a single umlaut—that even the biting cabaret of social commentators left an incorrect history behind. For after all, the Nazis took power in the end, did they not? The cabarets did not stop them, did they?

"What stories you must know," said Kathleen. "About those times."

"I have many stories," said the Woman of Weimar, smarting. "But a story . . ." She shrugged.

"She doesn't believe in fiction," said that grinning Gustave.

"Do I not?"

"I mean, fiction about the Nazi era."

"Isn't fiction endless?" said one of the guests.

The little boy was asleep in Ruth Ann's lap, curled up, still, holding on and held. The Woman of Weimar saw this.

"A novel . . ." said another guest, apparently in awe of something.

"Life," said the Woman of Weimar. "Life and the record of life. The truth. What happened. Who to whom. This is what to pursue. How can art describe?"

"Art is not description, though, is it?" said Harlan. With his arm around his wife. "Art is . . . what? projection."

"How would you project a story about the rise of Nazism, or the Second World War of so many millions dead, or the Holocaust?" asked the Woman of Weimar.

"Well, I'm not an artist," Harlan replied. "But I believe art can do anything. In the proper hands—"

"Yes, I am certain, yes," said the Woman of Weimar. "Perhaps even a song about the Hitler death camp, ja?" In the Claire Waldoff style. What was that song about . . . ja! So!: "In Steglitz," Waldoff's dig at a Berlin suburb populated by train conductors and zoo keepers, each verse closing with the ironic refrain, "In Steglitz, in Steglitz."

"In Dachau, in Dachau," the Woman of Weimar began, touching a few chords to support the typical Waldoffisch *Sprechgesang*. "Now, it is one of my favorite numbers," she told the party, enjoying their bewilderment and their attempts not to show it, "and I hope it's yours. I would like to dedicate this number to my manager, my agent, my PR lackey who grovels, and also my favorite table at . . ." She forgot the name.

"Jasper's," said Gustave, with a smile.

"Ja. They loved this number in Las Vegas, and you will, too." And she sang:

There is a guard at Dachau
Who has a giant dog.
They march among the work details,
Killing Jews for fun.
In Dachau!
In Dachau!

The little boy woke up, looking around at everyone, and everyone also looking around. Good. I show them art and history.

The guard, his name is Heinrich.
The dog, his name is Wolf.
And Heinrich sees a Jew and points
And Wolf bites off his eggs.
In Dachau!
In Dachau!

The Woman of Weimar was smiling knowingly, as befits the omniscient cabaret *Sprecher,* as sure of herself in improvisation as in old repertory. She nodded at Harlan when he stole a glance at Gustave. Ja, now you see. She waved languorously at Ruth Ann, stroking the little boy's hair. I show you, I show you.

Another guard is Ilse,
Who tends the pregnant Jew girls.
She binds their legs together
And laughs as they give birth.
In Dachau!
In Dachau!

Kathleen, who had stood the first verse with a look of benign inquiry, was staring at the floor. Cliff

was concentrating on his family. Gustave was still grinning.

The Woman of Weimar abruptly halted, then laid
both her arms from fingers to elbow upon the keys and
banged out truculent nonchords.

"That is the Weimar cabaret," she said.

There was no applause. So! But immediately one of
the guests, a well-meaning fool, suggested a parallel between the Woman of Weimar's "simple cabaret of truth"
and "horror rock" (are these terms in general use?) and
someone else took that up, as if they were Norns spinning
out the web of the world's future.

*"If I had a drink of something in my hand, I would
throw it in your stupid faces!"* the Woman of Weimar cried.
"You hear nothing! You know nothing! What has softened
you Americans? It cannot be art—you have no art! You
have no intelligence to see the world! You have no patience to listen!"

She felt such anger that she began to choke on it, and
a sudden agitation of helping and worrying hands bil-
lowed through the room at her. Harlan, behind her, forced
her arms straight up in the air, and this made her even
angrier; but the action apparently opened up her clogged
esophagus, and the coughing stopped. She felt a redden-
ing of the face, saw them all peering at her.

Genug. I go home.

Somehow she managed the extremes of acid tact and
self-possession needed to pull off thank-yous and
farewells after her extraordinary performance, and Gustave merrily led her downstairs to share a cab.

"That was amazing," he told her.

"Of course it was not. I embarrassed everyone and
taught nothing. I was a scene at a party. No more than
this."

"You were direct and powerful," he said. "Just as I believe the best art is. I wish we had taped it."

"What will your cousin think?"

Gustave laughed. "No one ever knows what Harlan thinks. He's such a deadpan about everything."

"Will you be in trouble with him? Lose your spare opera tickets?"

"Oh, nothing of the sort. I imagine you shocked Kathleen somewhat. But that's like saying you shocked Squirrel Nutkin."

"So I failed to shock you. That makes me sad."

Riding up Eighth Avenue in the darkness, past neighborhoods of no importance, he looked at her, wondering.

"I wanted to shock you," she said.

"But why?"

"Why," she said, sighing. Why, how to say this why. At first, she said nothing. Then: "Because you are so handsome, my Gustave, such a fine fellow. So bright and well-behaving. And your story was much, much better than I wanted to admit. Even to myself. So I would now seem to have misled you as to its value, and does *that* at least shock you? I have been selfish. Very, very self-protective. I wanted to spare myself . . . It is an exquisite story. So imaginative and lyrical and vivacious. It is not realistic but it is true. You have done this. And you see what effect it had on me, that it has made me to be dishonest."

The cab had stopped in front of the Woman's building.

Without looking at him, she said, "Thank you for dinner."

"Wait —"

"No." She was weeping. She held her hands up between them, half shielding herself and half pleading with him.

"I cannot look at you anymore," she told him. "Who asked you to be so kind? It breaks my heart."

The illustrious are human, whether naive or sentimental; and the Woman of Weimar went upstairs to her apartment and sat in the old Wesenbar armchair and thought. The subject of her consideration was: if I had been born in *this* country twenty years ago, what would I have been like?

At that moment, Harlan and Kathleen were loading the dishwasher, wrapping up the cheese and crackers, and discussing the possibility of switching to Bridgehampton for their summer rental.

Ruth Ann and Cliff were making love with the density and abandon of two who have everything to lose any day now.

Maxine was terrorizing the family in 7-B, next door to the Woman's apartment, because their fourteen-year-old was a stereo bully who kept the Woman awake at night.

And Gustave Fluten, who could be a character in one of Thomas Mann's tales, virtually barged into his own apartment, rushed to his desk, snapped on the light, thrust open his notebook, and began a new story, on the advice of the Woman of Weimar.

"If I were a coward, she thought," he wrote, "I would have a cat named Döblin or Brecht. No. *Two* cats. Male and female . . ."

HIS FAMILY: A FAIRY TALE OF THE CITY

THIS IS A SHORT ONE: because there lived in New York a couple who were deliriously happy in each other's company. Theirs would not be a long story, for happiness has no plot, no quest, no beginning, middle, and end. Happiness is.

In fact, the happy couple would have had no story at all but for one tiny problem.

Her in-laws.

You see, she was the fairest maiden in all of Staten Island. When she rode the ferry to work each day, men were enchanted and women sighed.

And he was the handsomest man in all the Bronx. So maybe that isn't saying much. But he was dashing and intrepid, and honest and understanding, and gentle and tolerant. This is why the fairest maiden in all of Staten Island (whose name was Lucy) loved the handsomest man in the

Bronx (whose name was Brian). She was glad that he was comely. She did not mind in the least that, when they were first dating and he would see her home on the ferry, women were enchanted and men got thorny. But what Lucy really liked about Brian was his good qualities.

Girls she knew always seemed to have troubles with their beaux because of a deficiency of good qualities: they were not punctual, or they were thoughtless about birthdays and anniversaries, or they sneered at people who were different from them, or they were selfish and tyrannical and mean drunks.

But Lucy had no troubles with Brian. He was not only punctual, he tended to arrive early: because he was so intent upon seeing her.

He was thoughtful about birthdays and anniversaries, especially her birthday and their anniversary; and instead of giving her troublesome gifts like flowers that wither so soon you feel sad, or candy that does violence to a girl's figure, he took her to romantic yet delightfully dietetic dinners.

He did not sneer at anyone, and he was selfless and easygoing and never drank more than a mug of beer after work, or a glass of wine at their romantic dinners.

Maybe Brian could have been just the littlest bit more flexible. Just the eeniest, miniest bit. Because once Brian made his mind up about a thing, he *never, never, never* backed down. However, as Brian was easygoing and life a breeze, he almost never had to make up his mind about anything. So he and Lucy got on beautifully.

There was just this one tiny problem: because Brian was so nice, he loved his family no matter how they treated him.

And they treated him like sludge beneath their feet.

Brian's father kept belittling Brian, telling him he should be more like his brother Don, who made a lot of money as an elevator technician, or like his brother Joe, who was a man's man and got into high-concept brawls in taverns.

Brian's mother complained that he didn't visit often enough. But when he did visit she hammered away at him with advice and orders and nagging; and when Brian's mother was exhausted from hammering at Brian, Brian's sister Darleen took over.

Brian's brother Joe always borrowed money from Brian and never paid any of it back, and Joe's wife Claire used Brian as a baby-sitter every time she and Joe went out. Brian had to take his four nephews and nieces to the zoo or the movies, and they were unsavory little punks.

Brian's brother Don was the only one who treated Brian fairly, but Don was so vexed with his awful family that he was never around.

Brian's family got on Lucy's nerves, so that was the problem.

Brian's family got on Brian's nerves, too, but he wouldn't admit it. "They don't mean any harm," he would say. Or "That's just the way they give one attention." Even "They must have had a tough week and don't know what they're saying."

But whenever Brian and Lucy came back from a visit with Brian's family, Brian would be very drained and quiet and not at all the vivid and joyful man Lucy loved. It would take Brian a good two days to recover his spirits, and a week or two later his brother Joe would borrow some money, and some days after that his sister-in-law would recruit him for a zoo trip so she could take in a matinee and the following weekend his mother would order him home for a dinner—"and make sure you bring plenty of wine and soda, and the beer for your brother! I'm not made of money, you know!"—and no sooner would Brian step inside the door than his father would say, "Did you see the Porsche Joe drives? And what do you run, a Volvo?"

Brian's family treated Lucy the way they treated Brian. Joe laughed at her. Darleen ridiculed her. Brian's father ignored her. Brian's mother openly hated her, and savaged her clothes, her job, her opinions. Brian's mother pretended she could never remember Lucy's name, and would make a game of calling her something different every time she referred to her, such as Corinna, or Lumbaga, or Princess Grace.

The first time Lucy met Brian's family, she could scarcely credit her senses. How could a man as fine as Brian come from people so vile? Throughout their engagement, Lucy found ways to avoid seeing Brian's family more than every now and then. But once they were married, she was bound to join him at the dinners. It was like going to war, only Brian refused to fight.

Lucy fought.

First she tried treating them the way they treated her. She ruthlessly corrected Brian's father's praises of everyone but Brian, called Brian's mother Mrs. Ragmop, imitated Darleen's dowdy B and T ways, and kept asking Joe when he was planning to repay Brian the money he owed. But after one night of this, appalled at her rash conduct, she wept all the way home.

Then she tried boycotting the family dinners. But this hurt Brian so punishingly she could not bear it.

"You are handsome and nice and good," she told Brian. "Why do you let them push you around?"

"Family is family," Brian told Lucy, and he tried to smile, but he could feel it dissolving even as he put it on. So instead he put his arms around her, and held her so long and tight they both ached with love and sorrow.

So Lucy determined to get advice from her guardian

fairy. Well, really this drag queen named Walter who lived down the hall from Brian and Lucy.

Lucy's guardian fairy was very wise, especially about the ways of the human heart. Indeed, he knew everything there was to know about love except how to be in it.

"What will you give me," asked Lucy's guardian fairy Walter, "if I tell you how to solve your problem, so you and Brian can live happily ever after?"

"My eternal gratitude," said Lucy.

The fairy had no need of this.

"My profound respect."

The fairy had no need of this, either.

"Well, what would you like?" said Lucy.

"Hc v about your black velvet number with the lace sash and the matching bag?"

"It's yours," said Lucy.

"Then I shall tell you how to solve your problem: from now on, when you and Brian visit his family, agree with everything they say. Back them up all the way *no matter what.*"

"What good will that do?" Lucy wailed.

"Trust me," said Walter.

"You want me to side *against* Brian with his atrocious relations?"

"Exactly that."

"What else am I supposed to do?" Lucy asked. "Get home by midnight and climb a beanstalk?"

"Don't be a smartass," said Walter.

Despite her misgivings, Lucy obeyed her guardian fairy's command the next time she and Brian had dinner with his family. At first blandly and calmly, then playfully, and at length with a furious, wanton intensity, Lucy seconded every assault on Brian, flattered her various in-laws' self-image, and turned the world upside down.

Brian's family was flabbergasted. Brian was horrified. The more Lucy supported her in-laws' attacks, the more discouraged Brian became and the more avid his family waxed in their sorties. They earnestly sought to outdo all their previous efforts, auditioning new material as they harassed and grouched at and disparaged Brian.

They were like a pack of hounds pursuing a stag— and none was keener on the scent than Lucy. Or none *seemed* keener: for inside, Lucy was dying at the look of bewildered hurt in Brian's eyes. But she steeled herself and persevered, for she trusted her guardian fairy's counsel, and knew that following it *no matter what* was essential if she was ever to free her beloved Brian from the thralls of his scoundrelly family.

Yet even so Lucy almost broke down before the evening was over, for by dessert Brian's family, rapt with the sport, had left their seats to surround Brian—yea, even as the baying hounds close in on the fallen stag—and devour him from up close, Brian's father and mother and brother and sister-in-law and nieces and nephews all chiming in with litanies of Brian's failings and reviews of his mistakes and comic routines highlighting his eccentric personality. So complete was this last assault that finally they all dropped back into their chairs, spent and dreamy-eyed and utterly in bliss.

"That's enough for one night," said Lucy, regarding them all tenderly as she rose from the table. "We must save something for next time. Come, Brian. Lend your brother some money and let's be on our way. What a lovely dinner this has been!"

Brian and Lucy drove home to East Eighty-fourth Street in silence, Brian disconsolate and Lucy feigning contentment.

Finally Brian said, "It was worse than usual tonight."

"They don't mean any harm," Lucy crisply replied.

"I felt as if they hated me," said Brian.

"That's just the way they give one attention," Lucy told him.

"But they were so *mean* to me," said Brian.

"They must have had a bad week and don't know what they're saying," Lucy responded.

There was a pause, and then, as they stopped for a red light, Brian turned to Lucy and said, "How could you do that to me, Lucy?"

There were tears in his eyes, and Lucy had to control her every decent instinct in order to tell him, "Family is family."

In the apartment, they went their several ways, Brian to bed and Lucy to park herself at the television to VCR an old Joan Crawford movie, because that night she felt like Joan Crawford. Poor Brian, for the first time since they had met, did not seem dashing, and also for the first time he did not give Lucy a hug when they got inside, as he habitually did. His hug was a symbol of the unique penetration of their love, a celebration of their immaculate world of two as one, two into one, two is one. Brian always hugged Lucy the moment they got inside the apartment. It was their game and their truth. But they did not hug tonight.

"Poor, poor Brian," Lucy thought.

But a few days later, when the effect of the family dinner had just about begun to wear off, Lucy told Brian that his brother had called to borrow some money and his sister-in-law wanted him to take the kids to a movie and his parents expected them for dinner the very next Sunday.

"No," said Brian quietly.

"No?" Lucy asked.

Brian started to speak, but only shook his head. He

sat on the couch, facing away from Lucy. She stood where she was and patiently awaited developments.

"I'm not going through that again," Brian finally said.

"Ever?" Lucy asked hopefully, coming around to face him.

"I mean, I know you don't enjoy visiting my family. I should have been more understanding. From now on, you don't have to go. I'll go by myself."

Lucy wasn't sure what to do next, but she hesitated for no more than a moment.

"I'll be right back," she told Brian. Then she raced down the hall to ask Walter what to do.

"You're going, too," Walter told her. *"No matter what."*

"You got it," said Lucy.

"And don't forget about the dress."

"I'm having it cleaned for you," said Lucy, slipping out to return to Brian.

"I'm going, too," she told him as she came in.

"No, Lucy," he said with a near-shattering finality. "You are not."

"Oh yes, I am!"

"Oh no, you're *not!*"

It was their first quarrel. Lucy was amazed, and a little thrilled, at how angry Brian could get.

"Not only am I going," said Lucy, "but I'm going to videotape it."

"Then *I'm* not going at all!"

"Oh *yes,* you are!"

"Oh no, I *won't!*"

"Is that final?" asked Lucy, her heart racing.

"Yes!" cried Brian. "Yes, that is *final!"*

"What about Joe and the money he wants?"

"Let him borrow it from *Don!*" Brian shouted.

"What about taking Joe and Claire's kids to the movies?"

"Let *Joe* and *Claire* take them!" Brian bellowed.

Lucy turned away, shaking—Brian imagined—with fury. No: with joy.

"Well," said Lucy calmly, "I expect I shall have to accept your decision." She turned back to Brian. "But if you ever change your mind . . ."

"Don't worry," said Brian. "Because I have *made* my mind *up*. And once I *make* my mind *up* about a thing, I *never, never, never* back down."

"Now," said Lucy, "can I have my hug?"

Well, Brian's relatives were absolutely furious, and Walter simply adored the dress, and Brian and Lucy lived happily ever after.

All of which demonstrates that, every now and then, even in New York, everybody gets what he deserves.

THE LIFE OF
MAGGIE
DILLINGER

"YOU COULDN'T CALL
her a good soul."

"Nor a bad one, neither."

"No . . ."

Two old friends come to pay last call at the funeral
home.

"But she was a hard one, wasn't she? Didn't care
what anyone thought of her."

"Almost like a man in that, she was, wasn't she? It
takes a real woman to care what her neighbors think of
her. And be proud of their respect."

"That it does. But she *was* proud, anyway."

"She was that, wasn't she?"

A scattering of people, mostly alone, as Maggie so
often was, and each a stranger to the others. She habitu-

ally kept her friends separate, and now they furtively eye each other like detainees in a police roundup, wondering what they're all guilty of.

One of the two women nods at two men in their late twenties sitting together down front, out of place among the widows and old single gentlemen. "Her boys." The women shake their heads in wonder that Maggie Dillinger had children at all, hard and proud as she was. Could there have been a time when Maggie held infants in her arms, fretted at their helplessness, rocked and soothed them? Had Maggie ever loved?

"Her heart's no colder now," says one of the old friends, "than it was when she lived." Then, "Poor thing," she adds. It sounds like a question.

"She was a woman of stone," answers the other.

No one is born hard. Hard living turns one so: lacking amenities in a culture of profusion, or needing a sense of purpose in the busiest city in the world, or missing love in a family. Martha Dillinger's parents were alcoholics, but her father worked nights and her mother worked days, so they never drank together, seldom even met. One night they passed in their tenement hallway, she coming home and he starting out; he was already drunk, and followed her back into the apartment and made love to her for the first time in years. Thus was Maggie conceived, on a playful bender in the New York slums.

"I shouldn'a let you," Maggie's mother would tell Maggie's father ever after. "I shouldn'a let him," she told Maggie.

It was always dark, always late; it was icy or stifling; it was messy, noisy, unhappy. It was hard living. The Dillingers did not again dishonor their mutual contempt and had no more children; they scarcely had Maggie. Had their tiny two-room flat been a fancy soirée, a social column might have listed Maggie as Among Those Present, admitted but not especially welcome. As early as she could, she took to staying out till evening, playing with the friends she hadn't yet quarreled with, having dinner at their homes, returning to her parents' place only when someone else's parents told her to. She called her parents "the people I live with." They let her run wild, though she was not wild, only impetuous. She was bold around the boys and scornful with girls; sometimes, accidentally, she was most tense with those she most liked. No one taught her how to behave, and when she lay on her couch under Army Surplus blankets, waiting to fall asleep, she counted all the social blunders she had made that day — at least, they appeared to be blunders, from the way everyone would look at her. She decided, early on, that she had better not mind what others thought of her, as it didn't look as if they were going to think much.

There are some, come to this decision, who become rambunctious, as if daring their gang's reproaches. But Maggie grew less bold and scornful, almost pensive. She hardly bothered quarreling anymore. Peaceful, she seemed uninteresting, and so lost her friends anyway, and grew solitary. The boys still liked her, and she let them date her; why not? But none of this came to anything, and at seventeen she left school to work full-time behind a bakery counter. She would have preferred a hardware store, but they weren't hiring women.

The boss of the bakery liked her right off. It was he who named her Maggie, said Martha didn't suit her. He grew physically familiar without making it seem like advances. Or he would whistle snatches of songs, twisting the lyrics into a joke — like the time a fat couple with nine fat children bought a huge box of pastries, and the kids tore into the box squealing before the couple could get out of the store. The boss whistled the music to "Just Molly and me, and baby makes three." Then he tilted his head at Maggie and winked.

He could make Maggie laugh; she liked him for that. And there was that night, as occasionally occurs, when they were alone together, closing the store, and he doused the lights, and rather than move toward the door they both stood there, and one thing followed another. But instead of dragging her off to some dire corner like the boys she had known, he gracefully asked her if he could take her to a place he knew of. She liked him for that, too. He was old for her, and somewhat overweight, but he was a good guy. A good married guy: which was fine with Maggie till she found herself thinking about him when she wasn't at the bakery. Fondly dwelling on his eccentricities, his whistling. Missing him. The next day, she found a job in a bakery on the other side of town. Her boss was a woman and all her coworkers were women, and Maggie thought that was a good deal.

Some of the male customers sometimes made a play for her; she didn't lack for company. But she didn't particularly need it, either. Once she moved out on her people, she realized that she liked living by herself. She liked having time to kill and a bed all her own. She would look out of her window on a busy street and watch the strangers pass and make up funny stories about them.

People moved in and out of her brownstone at a dancey rate, but she stayed put. She was friendly in the halls because it meant nothing. They'd be gone before she as much as got the name down. But there was a guy on the top floor who was so nice and easy that he made her nervous. She preferred her men edgy, easier to handle.

And this guy kept on living there, kept on with the nice and easy till Maggie thought maybe she should move. It's a big city, always somewhere else to go. At least he didn't whistle.

But finally there came one of those nights again, and one thing following another; and soon Maggie didn't know which apartment the two of them were living in. And finally he knocked her up. She knew it that night, even before she missed her Friend and went to the doctor. She just knew it, that's all. And she came right back from the doctor and told the guy on the top floor, and because he was nice and easy he said, "Okay, so we can get married."

"It's that simple, huh?" she said.

"Sure," he said, and smiled, so okay. But nothing's that simple, Maggie thought, standing there, considering what to do. Nothing's that simple.

"So when?" she asked him.

He shrugged. "You want a church? Or downtown?"

She said, "I don't know a church."

"Downtown, then. Saturday." Then he whistled "Here Comes the Bride."

"I didn't know you whistled," she said.

"So what if I whistle?"

"Nothing."

They named the child Cary after Cary Grant, Maggie's idea. She thought maybe it would be good luck for him, so he could grow up handsome and debonair, not run a bakery or have a night job or waltz in and out of jail like the men Maggie knew.

It was a nice-and-easy marriage, without a lot of questions asked—just as well, because no one ever likes the answers. Maggie was annoyed at having to give up her own place, even more annoyed at having to park the baby with a bakery customer who ran an informal daytime sitting service. But Maggie was not annoyed that her husband expected her to keep the baby out of his way. She didn't especially want to share it with him, come to that.

"Women's what I like, anyway," he told her. "Not babies. So let this one be the last, huh?"

Score up another hard life, Maggie thought, watching her baby sleeping in his thrift-shop crib. She stroked its little head when it cried, and played with its tiny fingers, but she feared to pick it up, afraid it would like the feel of that and want more, more than there usually was for babies like this one, in this world of the hard life. Maggie was smart enough to know that her husband wasn't going to hang around nice and easy forever, and she wasn't sure what would happen when he left.

He's lazy, she thought. That's why he's stayed so far. I do everything for him and I don't say nothing when he goes out for a walk that lasts all night. I keep the baby out of his way. So he'll stick. At least till it gets hard.

A year later she was pregnant again. This time it surprised her, and at first she worried about what her husband would think. After a while, she stopped worrying; she was almost lighthearted when she picked Cary up at his day care, and when she told her husband, she smiled to see the anger flicker in his eyes.

She thought, After all this time, he's not so much. He immediately took a walk that lasted three days. Maggie had a locksmith see to the door, and she didn't answer when her husband finally came knocking. She was holding Cary in her lap as a special treat for them both and had just been telling him that he shouldn't get used to it because it was going to be a hard life. Cary thought this over, gurgled, and nodded. Her husband was calling her name, angrily pleading, and Maggie put her finger to her lips. Cary smiled at her, because they had a secret, and she had to force herself to put him down, let him be alone. Her children would have to be strong, not nice and easy. Not whistlers and pastry eaters. Strong and hard, like Maggie.

The new baby was a boy, too, and Maggie named him Peter after nobody, the last name Dillinger, her name, and Cary became Dillinger too, and Maggie herself decided to be the Widow Dillinger, because if you said you were divorced people asked nosy questions. Death made them quiet.

Somewhere Maggie heard that life passes faster for a mother than for other people, but Maggie's life slowed to a gentle drag as she raised her two sons. She would not play with them and make them soft, but she taught them to keep each other busy, and sat on the bed watching them together. When they asked where their father was, she warned them that it would only be the three of them forever, and that the two of them must share everything and be kind to each other. Who else would? she asked them; they weren't sure. When they fell into giggles, she said they must be serious, must prepare. She lied about their age to get them into school early, reasoning that the sooner they got smart, the better. Smart people didn't have hard lives.

"Smart and strong," she said, "is what you're going to be."

And that's how they turned out—separately. Cary was strong and Peter was smart: but Cary was slow, a merry oaf, and Peter was soft and quirky. Maggie fretted. She'd better instruct Cary, toughen Peter up. She scolded them when they failed to improve, and they looked so hurt she had to turn away from them, feigning rage. But she must not back off, or they'd end up no better than their mother. "How've you been?" her friends would ask, and Maggie would reply, "Overworked and underpaid." Yes, she had her friends, her dates, her life. She was there still. But going out and doing things made her impatient; she wanted to get back and check on her boys' progress, see if Cary showed some new quiver of understanding or Peter some backbone. She had the younger boy read to them all from library books — Dickens, Stevenson, and, when these made little effect, tales of robots and atomic blasters. She made Cary teach Peter self-defense, and insisted they pursue it even when Peter, constantly bested, wept with shame. He needed comforting; Maggie let Cary handle it. The look Peter shot her when she sent them to bed almost made her repent. But almost in a mother is failure. Almost is nice and easy, not strong and smart. Maggie had been bold and scornful once, and tense with her friends, and she had it in her yet.

If I have to, she told herself, I will. It was never dark there in her apartment, never icy or stifling, never messy or noisy. It was not warm, either. But what do you want in a hard life?

There were times when it felt terribly bad to be so strict, bad as a bite that won't heal. But at other times it seemed to run along on its own power, the way wisdom teeth stop hurting after a while if you ignore them long enough. And they had nice days, laughing family days, when she took them on trips to the zoo or the beach. They didn't even have to go somewhere to laugh, for Maggie taught them her game of looking down through their big front window at the street and thinking up stories about the people who passed. Peter was the best of them at it. He seemed to come out of himself there at the window, connecting one stranger to another as if he might put them all into a show. Even Cary, the worst of them at the game, took fire from Peter's energy.

"Now, that one," Peter would say, as a man in a suit rushed along chattering furiously to himself. "That one got yelled at the office because his boss is mean. And now he's telling his boss off but good."

"Where's his boss?" asked Cary. "That one?" Another man in a suit, ambling along on an elegant smile as if he owned a percentage on the sale of subway tokens.

"No," said Peter, weighing it. "The boss is drinking champagne with a movie star."

"I wouldn't let a boss push me around," said Cary.

"You couldn't help it," Peter told him. "You'd be married and have kids and who would feed them if you got fired? Then you'd see them standing around all hungry and afraid to cry."

"I'd punch the boss's lights out for him," said Cary, "is what."

"Let's see who else is here today," Peter would continue, surveying his stage.

So one was born strong and one was born smart and that's how they stayed, no matter what Maggie tried. Yet she could not bring herself to accept it, and the effort told on them all, especially once the two boys got into high school, where strength will get you *these* attentions and smarts will get you *those*. From the start, Maggie laid down a rule: Cary had to stand up for Peter if anybody tried to bully him, and Peter had to help Cary with his homework. Among the three of them, she could hammer at Cary for not knowing enough or try to stampede Peter into fighting harder. But outside in the world of the other life that was not hard, you were probably supposed to have allies.

One day, when Cary had had to stay late for football practice, Peter was watching Maggie as she cooked dinner. She sensed he was about to say something, something strong perhaps, like a little man, and she waited, stirring the chili—watched him back, really, without having to look.

Finally he asked her, "Why do you like Cary more than me?"

"I don't," she said, surprised.

In the silence, she turned to face him.

"I don't," she repeated, and she *knew* that was true. But there was that bad look of his again, because he didn't believe her.

"Give me one example," she said. "Just one, even."

"There's too many to give."

"There's none."

It was late fall, in that crackly New York weather stirred by an angry wind that makes New Yorkers extra cross or extra clever. Peter became both at once; maybe clever was his way of being strong. How much he looks like his father, Maggie thought. Cary favors me.

"Cary thinks so, too," Peter went on. "That's why he's protective all the time. Of me. From you."

"He's protective because I taught him how," Maggie explained, trying to be gentle. "He's bigger than—"

"You never say my name. You only say his."

Was it true? "I say both," Maggie told him. "Both names." If I hug him now, he'll never be strong. He'll hunger for love. She stared him down, praying he wouldn't cry. If they see you cry, they'll take advantage. Maggie never cried. Overworked and underpaid.

Peter turned away and Cary came home, and after dinner she was at them with literature and self-defense till they fell asleep on the couch in front of the television.

Maggie made certain they were asleep before she kissed them.

She was not feeling well; something in her system, obscure and crotchety, was drilling at her. It hurt her to stand behind the counter, a bit more each day. Finally, she had to visit a doctor — her first trip since she carried Peter. It was cancer, he said, in fancy words about choice of treatment and second opinions, big doctor words. Something in the bone.

I shouldn't have gone, Maggie thought. If you don't go, you aren't sick. If you go, they kill you.

The doctor told her it would be very gradual, slow, years yet. Maybe three, maybe six.

"I'm covered," Maggie told him, thinking it probably depends on how much insurance you have. She had so much, they'd give her the six easy, maybe up her to eight, maybe let her live. It costs money to die.

Cary was seventeen, Peter nearly sixteen, and Maggie calculated how much time it would take to see them off proper, make Cary smart and Peter strong. They can't grow up at their own speed now. She told them she had medical trouble, and it was nothing to worry about, but even with the insurance they needed money to pay for things. One of them would have to quit school and go to work.

"That's okay by me," said Cary. "I hate school anyway."

"You're not the one," said Maggie.

Peter began to shout horrible things and Maggie let him, because it was better so, everyone letting out feelings so they could know where they all stood. Maybe, at a time like this, the fewer secrets the better.

"Why can't we both quit school?" asked Cary.

"Because you need to graduate," Maggie answered. "So you can get good work."

"Peter likes it more than me, anyway," said Cary. "Let him do the graduating."

Peter has to fight for his work. I'll make him fight, put the fight in him. He'll have to show me. He'll need to, then. Revenge on his mother, if that's how it has to be. If that'll make him strong.

"Peter will work and you will graduate," said Maggie, bolder than she'd ever been. I have no choice. Something in the bone. Get them settled, lock up the future. "Then you will go to the police academy and become a cop."

At this startling prediction, phrased as invincible truth, both boys stared at her.

"And what will Peter be?" Cary finally said.

Maggie looked at Peter; his head was bowed, but as he felt her gaze he raised it, glaring. Good, she thought. *Fight.*

"Who says I even want to be a cop?" said Cary.

Another clerk at the bakery had a nephew who had gone through the police academy. Maggie had arranged for him to meet her son and tell him what the tests were like, what sort of questions. Then Peter could coach him.

"No one says," Maggie replied. "Just do it." It was a good job for a merry oaf, give him a chance to work off his steam without getting into trouble. He can be worth something. Twenty years later he'll get his pension and he can open a bar somewhere, or a sporting goods store. Might as well, with everyone walking around in sneakers nowadays.

"What are you going to be?" Cary asked Peter.

"Please don't do this," Peter said to Maggie.

"Oh, get out of here, the both, and leave me be!" Maggie stormed. "Didn't I say I got medical trouble? Can't you think of someone else just once?"

Cary led Peter out; and not a second too quick, for, as the door closed, Maggie cried, too. Just this once, she thought. I'll let myself. Something in the bone, in the hard life. Something in Maggie.

Cary fell into the plan easily enough, as it happened, but it was trouble with Peter from then on. He stayed out a lot, and took up with the worst sort of friends, the kind that lead you into trouble with drugs and idle vandalism, the kind that never got into the other life that is not hard. Once, when Maggie was over at a friend's, watching an evening of television, there was a show about a model child, hero of the wrestling team and an honor student, who was secretly getting into trouble with the kind of friends that Peter was running with. And it turned out that the model child was not feeling loved by his parents, and had got into trouble to get their attention.

"Oh yeah?" Maggie snapped at the screen. "They didn't give him enough attention feeding him and giving him clothes to wear? What are they supposed to do now, tell jokes and do a funny dance?"

"They always blame the parents," her friend agreed.

"Such a *nerve* of these people!"

Maggie disengaged Peter from his bad companions by having Cary threaten to beat them up unless they left Peter alone. So now Peter was alone — and bellicose and sour. He lost each job as soon as he got it, and spoke to Maggie as seldom as possible. He was mad at the world.

Like me, once, Maggie thought.

She held firm to her plans, and stood by as the brothers grew closer; and Cary grew smarter, cramming for his tests under Peter's guidance; and Peter grew stronger, as if willing himself to defy his humiliation and succeed, as if his success would astonish Maggie, and annoy her, and hurt her.

Sometimes Maggie worried about what Peter might become, as he seemed to have no idea himself. But as long as he had ambition, she told herself, it doesn't matter. He'll be something soon enough.

Maggie wasn't there to see it, though she had news of it here and there. She was present when Cary got his academy diploma, and when he joined the force, and when he married. The day Cary and his wife brought their first child home, Maggie opened the door for them, and took the baby, and carried it inside so gently that Cary thought she might be losing her mind. No, it was simply that Maggie did not have to train this new one to escape the hard life. The family was prospering, and these children would be raised for the joy of it, for the love of children, without worry.

Peter had moved to Los Angeles some time before, to get into the film industry. He had never made peace with Maggie. Perhaps she should have told him, after all this, about taking him out of school to make him strong. Grabbed and told him, forced him to listen. Tough Maggie; she could have done it. But she was never good at explaining, and anyway if she *had* told him while it was happening, it wouldn't have worked. Later, he was gone. He and Cary traded letters once a month, so Maggie had reports of him. But he wouldn't write to her, or even speak on the telephone.

All right, Maggie told herself. It's the strength working. But one time she wrote a little note and had Cary enclose it in his next letter to Peter. Peter never acknowledged it.

Now, listen to what he was, because this is important. He had begun to succeed as a talent agent. It seemed he had a gift for picking parts for actors that caught them at their richest, their direst, their most confidential. In Hollywood, they said he could take one fast look at anyone and immediately tell him what he ought to be—Cinderella, Cowboy Bill, Granny Mystic, Uncle Fool. Sitcom, prestige feature, miniseries, genre. Peter always knew. Peter could make you.

Maggie had begun to fail at last, and had to quit work and lie down all day. She worried about Peter.

"Did he grow up?" she asked Cary. "Is he strong?"

Cary shrugged. "With the kind of money he's going to make, Ma, it won't matter. Guy is really doing well out there. He really is."

Maggie was quiet for a while. "I don't mind it for me, after all there's been. But it isn't right for two close brothers to be a whole country apart."

Cary held her hands. "It's all right, Ma. We can't be brothers forever."

"You'll always be."

"I mean, not like we were. Little kids doing homework together." He smiled at her and she touched his forehead, such a rare gesture that he forgot what he was saying.

"I wanted you always brothers."

"It's a little hard to be brothers when you're a husband and father, too, Ma." He laughed. "And a cop. I'm everybody's brother now. The big brother of the whole city."

Maggie shook her head. "Tell me about him. Tell me what he does." She wept. "I don't know what he does now."

"Ma, be—"

"No, I'll dry my own eyes. It's *my* eyes, aren't they?"

He waited as she composed herself, searching his memory

for a time when she was like this. He could not recall one.
"Now, tell me," she said.

"I *keep* telling you, Ma . . ."

"Well, keep *on,* will you?" Dangerous Maggie,
now.

"He's an agent. You know, movies and television."

"He hires the actors for the shows?"

"No, he's bigger than that. He guides their careers.
He figures out what they should play. He . . . he puts
them into stories, like."

Maggie was thinking.

"Okay now, Ma?"

Maggie reached for Cary's arm.

"I want you to tell him something for me," she said.
"Tell him—" Maggie scarcely knew how to put it into
words. "Tell him about the window. The game at the window."

"Tell him what about it?"

"I taught him the game. Remember?"

"Ma . . ."

Maggie was nearly frantic. "You'll tell about it? I
taught him . . . at the window! Stories about people, like
you said before."

"Okay, Ma, okay."

"You'll tell him?"

"You can tell him yourself, Ma. He's coming east.
Ma?"

Now Maggie was quiet. "He's coming," she finally
said. "Why? Why now?"

"Yeah. So, listen—"

"I can tell him, then."

"Sure. That's the whole point of what I'm saying."

"Tell him about the window, after all."

"Now get some rest, will you?"

As he started to rise, Maggie grabbed his arm again.
"If I don't get the chance," she said evenly, slowly, weary
in the bone. "If for some reason . . . You'll tell him about
the window for me. Making up stories about the people
that came by us. Will you remember?"

"Sure, Ma. I'll tell him, I promise."

She fell back on the pillow and closed her eyes. He
didn't understand; but Peter would. Peter always understood things.

Peter had not been planning to come east; Cary had
thrown that out on impulse and now had to talk his
brother into the trip, getting angrier at every sentence because Peter kept saying no.

"Can you imagine how she feels?" Cary said. "Can
you? Because—"

"It's because of how I feel!" Peter cried, hurt and rage
spilling out because his brother was on the right side, but
not Peter's side. "Isn't it?"

"It's her last thing!" Cary shouted into the phone.
"Her last thing on earth!"

There had been a number of nervous silences in this
conversation, and here was another, the two of them
thinking how children without a quarrel will fight because
of their parents.

"If you can't do it for her," Cary pleaded, "do it for
me. Please."

"Anything," said Peter, "but this."

"Do you want me to hate you for life?"

"I already have one of those," said Peter.

"Jesus, do you have to make Hollywood jokes when
Ma is dying?"

"I'm sorry. You know it's not you."

"I don't care who it is. You're coming back here and
see her before she dies or I'll come out there and bring
you here in handcuffs, and Peter—I mean it!"

Peter could tell that from the way Cary spoke; and he agreed to come out on the next reservation. It took less than a day, but Maggie could not wait for him. She was very, very tired, ancient, never-get-well tired, too tired even to speak anymore. And so she died silent, though her eyes lay open.

Thus Peter came east for a funeral attended mostly by strangers, and Peter, like Maggie, was silent, as well he might be. In the great long empty space before the service began, Cary leaned over and said, "Ma asked me to tell you something about the window."

"What window?"

Cary put his arm around Peter, his way of covering up a sensory overload. "She said she taught you at the window. She made a big thing about it, like it was a secret you two had."

"*Us* two? That's really some joke, I hate to tell you."

Cary looked at Peter for some little bit. "It was important to her, Pete. Please. Please."

Peter looked back. "So okay. You told me. Don't make it worse."

The two women at the rear of the hall note this exchange and nod at each other.

"The boys turned out fine, anyway," says one. "Her boys."

"One a policeman," says the other. "And the youngest is someone in the movies."

Her friend clucks her tongue. "Where does it come from? Such a mother — not a thought in her head for anything or anyone."

"Stingy with her feelings."

"I'm telling you, the children have to make themselves up from nothing."

"Oh, the woman of stone."

"From nothing."

And that was the life of Maggie Dillinger.

A DATE WITH
A HUSTLER

NOW, THIS IS THE CITY: Irene Dare is stiff as a crash in the office of the most influential fashion magazine in the world. Irene Dare is its most influential editor and she is in an influential mood, because this all but virtually *perfectly unknown model* has just walked into the room ready for a cover shoot and some assistants are noodling in the doorway and Irene is just looking at this model and then she breathes out, "Oh, that is . . . just . . . so . . . *body!*" and suddenly she *snaps* into system like the lights blasting on in the first moments of a Twyla Tharp dance symphony such as you would attend at the Brooklyn Academy of Music, *absolutely* sold out, fabulous fashion crowd with a *lot* of *take* and that *up to the second* contempo that tells you it's the City of Cities forever, never stops getting newer, and Irene says, "I am going *right* to the *accessories table!*" and everyone's running down the hall

after her except the model (who stands there as cool as a
jade princess waiting for them to do it to her) and Boise
(who sits at a desk, smoking and taking in this . . . what is
she? a fourteen-year-old who looks like an order of seven
deadly sins to go; hell, if she were my daughter, I would
never let her . . . would I?), and Boise remembers what it
was like to be a young woman, a very attractive one, with
that radiant aura, that freshness, smoothness. Youth is
cream. Nothing gets old quite so fundamentally as skin,
does it? Thirty, and you're already past it. Forty. Forty-five.
Boise thought forty was scary but, ladies, fifty is the true
killer. Even worse: fifty-six. Forty may be over the hill but
fifty-six is Dead and Over.

Charging through her domains on her way back to
her new discovery, her hands glittering with sideshow
trinkets, Irene Dare is shouting, reminding, inspiring,
shaping opinion. She is like a swarm. She calls out possible cover lines, topics for articles, subjects for photo
spreads.

"Get on it!" she cries, leaning into offices, startling
meetings, surrounding her staff. Back in the office where
the meltingly ice-cold young model stands, still passive
and absolutely in control, Irene takes another look at this
girl, lets out a cry, and begins to distribute the accessories.

"This is a *beautiful* cover *dream*girl, isn't she?" Irene
croons. The model does not respond. "*Isn't* she?" Irene
asks, widening her focus to take in her employees.

"But yes," an assistant agrees. "Very nipples."

"A sort of quality," Irene dares, "I don't know, bam-
boo, starlet, jazz, sexy, haughty, wishes."

She stares at the girl.

"What are you telling me?" Irene asks her.

"Huh?"

"You're telling me, '*Stare. Need* me. *Buy* me. *Buy* me
on the *cover!*'"

Kathleen, in the doorway, peeped in looking for Boise.

"I'm all finished," Kathleen announced.

She had been down the hall modeling for a spread entitled "The Belles of Manhattan." Kathleen did not act anymore. She merely appeared, strictly a visual, inviolable.

"Teresa and Ruth Ann are meeting us here," Boise told her.

"What *schematic* names," Irene muttered, stepping back from the teenage model to survey her.

"The *glow*!" Irene cried.

The model beamed.

"The *turn*!" Irene ordered.

The model revolved, rapt.

"The *look*!" Irene whispered.

The model put one hand on her hip, turned her face slightly to the right, and froze.

"Needs more *green*!" Irene shouted as her assistants surged around with swatches and tiny bottles, hustling the model out. "Go to the setup and start with the Polaroids," Irene told them. "I'll be there in a morsel."

"I was that young once," Boise said to Kathleen.

"We're calling her Dream," said Irene. "She's *intensely* contempo. Now *you*"—she told Kathleen—"excuse us for a state-of-the-heart address."

"I'll see if Ruth Ann and Teresa are here yet," said Kathleen, closing the door after her to leave Boise and Irene alone.

"Whatever it is," said Boise, "don't you dare."

"I'm your oldest friend, and I *will*. Yes, I *must*. I know that look—the poor old lady sliding deeper and deeper into it. *Yes*."

"Don't treat me like one of your letters to the editor. 'Signed, Has-Been.'"

"As I see life," Irene intoned, with the authority of a

pixie in an enchanted glade, "everything is Before and After. What you need is a quick-me-up date."

"None of your behind-the-scenes solutions," Boise warned her.

"To quicken you up, and recenter your cover art."

"Irene —"

"You haven't looked savvy in months. Boise . . . face it."

Boise and the most influential woman in New York fashion eyed each other like gunfighters.

"Am I not your closest friend?" Irene asked. "Brisk and wise? Yes."

"Oh, pook."

"I know what you need."

"What I need?" said Boise. "What I need, my old friend, is to be seventeen again."

"*Adventure* you need. A little mistos on the side."

"Your cure for everything is adultery."

"My cure," Irene was certain, "is the Italian Riviera, with a Campari in one hand and a gondolier in the other. What a cover you'd make!"

"For what? *Cronemapolitan?*"

Irene pawed through her rat's nest of a desk top for her address book, big as heaven's files on Judgment Day. "Why did you come here if not for my *tips for happiness?*"

"I came to meet Kathleen and the rest of my brunch club."

Irene found a number, tore off a sheet of her cream-brown Tiffany's notepaper, wrote down the data, and handed it to Boise.

A name and a phone number. "John?" said Boise.

"He's unbelievably expensive, but that's partly to screen out the health risks, and, besides —"

"John who? John why? What is he?"

"A gigolo, of course. *Very* body, but too tall to model,

and he can't act. So what else is there? Make sure you leave my name on the tape as your reference. He's absolutely—"

"Just what does he do, this unbelievably expensive gigolo?"

"Sometimes everything. Sometimes . . . It depends on what he thinks you need to get quick again. To get back on your cover. Sometimes, I have heard—yes, I have heard this—he mostly . . . talks . . ."

A knock, and two assistants burst into the room, crying, *"There's not enough green!"* and Irene runs off with them.

Boise comes out to the reception area, a strangely humble circle of Scandinavian modern couches, to find Ruth Ann telling Kathleen and Teresa about Colin's latest caper, the Hot Dog Shop. The four friends have decided to try taking their brunch out for once, and, as they walk the two blocks to the Russian Tea Room—Boise wanted to treat, or else—Ruth Ann says, "You help him set out the franks, the rolls, the mustard, the ketchup, the sauerkraut, the relish, and the chopped onions, and of course each item goes in a special bowl that fits it *exactly*. Colin is very determined about that."

"Good materials," said Teresa, "yield good work."

"How much does he charge?" Kathleen asked.

"No money changes hands," Ruth Ann answered. "Colin doesn't sell his hot dogs. He *honors* you with them. No, ladies, this is a very serious matter with Colin. Very serious. But he's willing to joke about it. His father does that, too."

Ruth Ann paused, as if wanting to register that perception along with her friends. As if needing to hold on to the picture of a man who brings a graceful touch to the defiance of his troubles.

"Colin takes the orders," Ruth Ann finally went on.

"You can have a hot dog any way you want it, from just plain on a roll to the works. Colin is very liberal about that, as long as he gets his . . . his little condiments into the appropriate bowls. And of course, sooner or later he announces his slogan, designed to appeal to the consumer's best instincts — 'You can get anything you want at the Hot Dog Shop.' Then his father always says, 'Especially hot dogs.'"

She and Teresa and Kathleen laughed. Boise was distracted — by the name and phone number Irene had given her (*assigned* her, really, because Irene could be very pushy; but Irene was so often right about a lot of things), but also by her dissatisfactions in general, and even by two children she had seen on the other side of Fifty-seventh Street, running their parents into pieces with a game that consisted of circling around every sign or lamppost they passed, singing some odd little tune. Boise couldn't catch the words. First the little girl, about three, would do it; then her slightly older brother would follow her as she rushed up to the next metal tree to dance around it, dance and sing. Their parents kept trying to get them away from the edge of the sidewalk, glancing nervously at the traffic in the street. But they were smiling even as the kids broke away and ran for another lamppost.

"Sometimes," said Ruth Ann, nearly joking, "I don't know if it's Cliff I'm in love with or Colin."

She and Cliff were going to be married in a month. "It is not necessary to marry," Boise had said when she first heard of this. But Cliff wanted Colin to have a "positive mother." Those were his words. It is necessary to marry, to define a state of being for Colin. His natural mother had moved to California during the divorce. Cliff loved Ruth Ann and wanted her to be his wife.

"He doesn't want to date me anymore," Ruth Ann explained to Boise. "He wants to live with me."

You are marrying a tragedy, Boise thought. This she did not say. Unnecessary. Ruth Ann reads her contracts. She knows the terms. Besides, Boise thinks it inspiring that Ruth Ann is willing to share fate with a man whose son may be terminally ill. It is inspiring and terrifying. But one faces terror with greater energy when one is young. Nowadays, Boise thinks, all I can bear is a cigarette and Martinson's decaf and Irene's reproaches.

Six months ago, Boise told Irene she was going to divorce Jack, my rich husband. Irene had said, "Boise, you don't want a divorce. You want a fling. *Yes.*"

Irene and Boise went back a good twenty years. And if Irene's coffeepot could talk, they'd both be ruined.

Not enough green, Boise thought. Not enough youth. Not enough realization.

As Ruth Ann, green and young, told her three friends at the Russian Tea Room all about that dear little boy and his terribly nice, terribly devoted father. As they wondered, one by one, what must come of this. As the brunch club meets.

Boise would have made a disastrous parent. She always knew that.

"I don't have the energy," she would say, meaning: I don't know that style.

Irene had been threatening to give her the hustler's phone number for some weeks now. Yes, it's done, now and again. These are the great women of New York; you think they can't do as well as men? You see Boise in a babushka, perhaps, measuring prices on oven cleaners in D'Agostino's? You believe Irene Dare puts the world's most influential fashion magazine to bed and then sleeps alone?

You think Boise just walked into her wealth, Irene has been faking her smarts?

No. They went for it, worked at it. Irene is a woman

professional. She can do what a man can't or, believe me, a man would be doing it. And Boise is a professional woman—yes, that's a career. She started as an amateur, a daughter, Anna Maria Boisante. Her family were puppeteers in Little Italy, running one of the last of the ancient fairground troupes that gave adaptations of medieval classics, most of the year in the little family theatre on Carmine Street but twice a year on tour to cities from Boston and New Haven to Chicago and, once, to San Francisco. All the men in Boise's family took up the profession, with a self-importance tempered by resignation. It was hard work manipulating the giant marionettes, and it got so hot backstage that even in their skimpy undershirts Boise's uncles and brothers would feel just this side of fainting. But it was significant work, a final tender vestige of the Old Days—and when someone in Boise's family said "the Old Days," he meant old as Columbus is old, old as the Leaning Tower of Pisa when it was just the Tower of Pisa.

There was history in this work, culture in it, something sacred and even desperate. Yet, Boise felt, her family didn't appreciate it in any real sense. They were unique, so they felt special. But they saw these tales of knights and sorcerers, of damsels and traitors, of Crusaders and infidels as little more than westerns in rhyme. Boise, sitting with her mother at the end of the front row of their theatre— *their* theatre!—responded to the strenuous passions behind the action, the love of maiden for hero that would grow even stronger after his death, or the ferocious sense of honor that would lead even the wisest knight to his doom, knowing he was destroying himself but unable to betray his behavioral code. Boise's favorite character was the knight Rinaldo, so furiously honorable that he went mad, literally mad, when his ethics were threatened. As it happens, one of Boise's brothers was named Rinaldo after

the character, and he was the brother Boise loved the
most.

Listening to Ruth Ann's tales of Colin, Boise wondered how much passion there was in her young friend,
how strong her love would prove if death interfered in the
new life she had laid out for herself.

It takes great strength to live well, Boise thought.
Look at Irene — almost as mad as Rinaldo in the field, as
true to her code as a princess of the realm, as absolute, as
final as poison.

Look at me. I didn't make it all the way from Carmine Street on good intentions.

It was just as well Boise decided to reinvent herself,
for the Old Days had been long over before her family
faced up to it, sold the theatre, and dispersed. Boise's parents had actually gone back to Italy. Perhaps this was why
Boise was so fond of Teresa; she reminded Boise of her
simpler, purer, undecorated self. Teresa accepted her role
in life; Boise always longed for promotions, more lines,
sharper scenes.

Everyone was looking at her.

"Sorry," Boise told them. "My mind was drifting.
Who said what?"

"We're making five-year plans," Kathleen told her.

"We're outlining major projects," Ruth Ann put in.

"My major project," said Boise, "is to get a divorce
from Jack, my rich husband."

She said it seriously, and no one laughed.

"I shall divorce him," Boise went on, "so we can
spare each other the cruelty of seeing ourselves dissolve
into a pair of cheesy goblins, all gums and cocoa. The
trouble with marriage is, it doesn't know when to quit."

Ruth Ann and Kathleen looked at each other. Unpredictable, alarming Boise.

"You'll see," she told them. New York is impetuous,

whimsical; but it can bear grudges for decades, get hot at you for no reason. "You'll see if I don't."

And Boise, I assure you, had every intention of calling John the gigolo. There can be a deflating abundance of routine in a life, not too much security but too little surprise. How is Boise to remain unpredictable if she doesn't veer off whimsically now and again? Routine, and more routine, and more and more routine, day after day, and a date with a hustler isn't all that avant-garde.

Now, divorce: divorce would be avant-garde. Divorce is very difficult for a woman. Men don't realize that. They think of divorce as a no doubt regrettable but occasionally necessary step. To a woman it's like having all your vital organs replaced at once.

But Boise is in one of her go-to-hell moods, and they can last for months at a stretch. Heaven only knows who will be well when the smoke clears.

Oh, Jack, my rich husband, will be well. There's a survivor, goes his own way, probably will feel a little relieved, even, though it will disrupt his routine and cost him the moon.

Not to mention, she thought as she dialed John's number, disrupting the moon and costing him his routine. It makes sense if you think about it.

John's voice, on his tape, was deep, his tone smooth enough for television news. A touch of Texas or thereabouts in the accent. He sounded—so Boise decided, in her usual hit-and-run critique—six-feet-two, light-haired, green-eyed, with wide shoulders and a long waist, the kind of man who has to keep reminding himself not to overwhelm his women with his looks, and so overwhelms them with his feelings.

His tape is a screen, and he was at home, and he called her back after a respectable ten minutes. Attentive but not desperate. Well, at *these* rates he's probably in the vault counting his money. Two thousand dollars for a date, Irene had warned Boise. What could any man possibly do for you in a single afternoon that would be worth two thousand dollars?

John (the irony of that name!) did not say what he does, though he and Boise spoke at length. I'm really doing this! she marveled, amused at her own flaunting of the Boise image. How would Irene put it?: "A sort of quality, I don't know, steel eyes, mercurial, dragon lady, presiding, needing, New York."

John didn't make out-calls. "Well, Boise, I have everything set up very nicely here," he explained. "And my friends appreciate the notion of a secret trysting place, a place of rendezvous. That's so much more romantic than having me come to them, like a carpet cleaner or a piano tuner making his rounds. Don't you agree, Boise?"

He was pointedly using her name a lot, like a salesman. Oh please, she thought. Let's get serious.

"Why do you do this?" she asked him.

"It's a beautiful way to meet women," he replied.

The more he spoke, the taller he got, the wider and longer, lighter and greener. And his feelings simmered in full view, butter in the pan. Boise was fascinated. She wondered where she would stack up in the ranks of his customers (his *friends*, did you hear that one?)—better-looking than most? But older? Certainly smarter and livelier. Boise was not a one to let her depressions show.

They set the date for the following afternoon at an address in the West Seventies. Boise asked Elsie for a cup of tea and went out onto the terrace to watch the boats float down the East River. Jack, my rich husband, would be home soon. Sweet foolish Jack, though on the other hand he's nobody's fool. He probably thinks Boise has been playing cheat-for-hire on him for years—just as he, surely, *surely*, has spent many an afternoon on a divan with some seventeen-year-old Ann-Margret, someone who could do a cover for Irene. Youth is always the theme, always there. When you have it yourself, you want it in others. When you don't have it yourself, you want it in others. Youth is all there is.

Strong tea with a spurt of lemon, no sugar. Everyone probably thinks I sit out here all day sipping gin. Pook! One shot of Tanqueray is for show. Glass after glass of it is for old soaks.

Tomorrow, she thought, I will wear the black and red tailored suit, the fashion-to-die, no-joke, slightly dykey look, like Patricia Neal in *Breakfast at Tiffany's.* Then: needs more green, Boise thought, and this is a jest, so she laughs out loud on her terrace.

She was fluttering a bit in the cab the next day, and shook her head at her anxiety. Two thousand dollars, and *I'm* nervous? That hotshot with his beautiful way to meet women is the one whose performance is on audition, let me tell you! The address was one of those medium-sized piles of junk between Broadway and Columbus, lacking the charm of a brownstone and the power of a high-rise. Well, who cares what his building looks like, do you know what I mean? Another flutter as she pressed the buzzer, a larger one as she heard his "Yes?," even deeper than before, on the intercom.

"Boise has arrived," she said.

"Welcome," he told her, releasing the door.

Elevator to the third floor, 3D. Door closed. She knocked. He opened.

Now, this is a loaded moment, one of great feeling and wonder. Boise's blind-date coucher avec moi: and now she has eyes. Steel eyes of the mercurial New York dragon lady. By now John had become a host of people in

Boise's mind; he could have been anyone from Superman to a little dip of a guy with a deep voice. The blazer and striped tie surprised her, little-boy clothes on a male hooker, dressing against type to throw her off base; and she didn't expect him to shake her hand—kiss it maybe, like some leftover Valentino, so cinema; and now that she has to see it for herself through her steel eyes, six-two is an absurd height for a man, what is he, a house?; but she had guessed right about the soft yellow hair falling into his eyes, you boyish thing, you farmboy just in from the gridiron of glorious Saturday afternoons of football and touchdowns, and about the eyes, definitely enough green, green sweetness to make the cheerleaders fall over their pom-poms when you pass by, and the Li'l Abner shoulders and the Sean Penn waist, what is this, a one-man gallery of American heroes?

And what about his feelings? But in America we start from the visual. We see what's on the cover.

And Boise sees. It's *almost* perfect, *almost* incredible, *almost* too much to bear, as Boise walks into John's apartment—one room, with the kitchen along a wall, and I can't wait to look over the early-middle pissoir elegance of the bathroom, tiled in decorator shades of landlord maroon and Upper West Side pink.

To be fair, the room itself is beautiful, almost no furniture—succinct, you might say, in its lightness and space and air. Arresting photos on the walls, one of Venice brooding in her canals in grays and blues no guidebook knows, an antique shot of some prep-school track team, and one of a world-famous celebrity half-smiling at a window overlooking Central Park that Boise recognizes as a Brenda Briand. The man has taste.

There is only one odd note in it all, the one notch less than perfect, incredible, and too much to bear:

"How old are you, Lochinvar?" Boise asks.

"Forty-eight," he says.

Boise laughs. "No kidding."

John shrugs pleasantly. "Does this matter, Boise?"

"No." Somewhere in it is the feeling that it should matter. "But I'm surprised."

"Anyone can be young," John observes. "Experience is harder to come by—and in my line of work, experience is the fundamental component. You must admit, I haven't lost my looks."

"You're a dazzle boy, all right," says Boise, trying the room's one chair, a sturdy-looking piece with a straight back that turns out to be soft and giving. Its solidity deceives.

"Boise, would you like a glass of wine?"

"Sure," says Boise. "Let's go fancy." The bravado of uncertainty.

As he opens a bottle of something white and, Boise guesses, important, he measures out chatter—the rap melodies of the put-the-lady-at-ease cabaret. No, go more gently, Boise. It's his job to soothe. This is your holiday.

As he hands her her glass he says, "My friends usually like to ask me about my line of work. This is understandable. It is an esoteric profession, and they are curious. I think they are trying to reassure themselves about me. This is fair. Is there something you'd like to ask?"

His friends. "What are the most popular questions? I'll run along with those."

He thought for a moment. "Well, they often ask if I'm gay. Obviously, I'm not, or I would be doing this with men. Another question: Do men ever call me? Yes. Yes, they do. They call—on behalf of their wives or lovers. I guess some people would find that shocking. I find it touching. I really do. These men obviously care a great deal about their women, and don't want them risking harm at the hands of some psychopath. And they are big enough to accept the idea that their women might want to try a date with another man. It is a natural urge. The men have it. Why not the women? So they call me up and talk awhile, to test me out. Another question that I hear: What health precautions do I take?" He smiled. "All of them. I've been in this line of work for quite some time now, even before anyone had heard of herpes. If I didn't exercise the most extreme prudence, I would be out of work. Or something worse."

Boise nodded as he rattled away. This is script to him.

"Now I'll tell you the question I always ask. I can seldom get a straight answer, though. What would you like me to be?"

Boise eyed him from top to toe, thinking all this over. Care a great deal, natural urge, precautions, the blazer and the wine and the divorce. And the green eyes. But how can you evaluate eyes until you know what they see?

"I'll tell you, Boise. A few of my friends . . . they come here to me with the hope of experiencing something special. Something they've had in mind for some time. They have saved up for me—not their money, I mean. Their fantasies. They have ideas. Ideas about something that no other man they have access to can give them. I am not speaking to you about elaborate pantomimes or psychodrama or questionable rituals. My friends have too much class for that."

He smiled again, now a touch boyishly. Isn't life silly? he seemed to say. Aren't we rash buffoons, acting out our daydreams with strangers?

"One friend did admit to me that she wanted me to seduce her against her will, so to speak. That is, to *persuade* her into bed very gently . . . very, very gently, she insisted . . . but firmly, no matter how much she begged me to stop. I think she wanted to see what it was like to

be with a man who was so engrossed in pleasuring himself, and in pleasuring her at the same time, that he would
seem utterly swept away by her."

He paused, recalling it.

"I think that's what she had in mind," he said.

He smiled again, lighting candles.

"Many of my friends are too shy to tell me what they
want me to be. I hope you won't be shy, Boise. I really
enjoy my work. I like to feel that I can give my friends
something very wonderful and unique, that they will always . . . well, what are the words for this? . . . they will
always be a little happier to have met me."

He was pulling the curtains closed, heavy linen scrap-
ing the half-open Levolor blinds. Candles and coax me
amid the afternoon scurry of upper west midtown. Our
little secret, do you love it? His *friends*. And when do I
start taking off my . . . oh, I see, you first? Casanova by
candlelight. Flickering shadows against his skin, that's a
nice touch. He's slow, not showy. Confident, as all men
are, no matter what they say. Why shouldn't he be? He's a
professional expert. He does this for two thousand dollars.
John and his friends. Running his hand through his hair,
rubbing his neck, a little stiffness there, poor thing. Brings
out the mother in a lady. Boise's adultery preceding her
divorce, with a youth (only) eight years her junior.

Down with the pants, and I see where the two thousand dollars comes in. Well, John, you're a wonder. A pro-
digy. A rainbow bridge. Poor old Boise was so strung out
Before, and look what's happening After. Wise Irene. Always ahead of you, always down there in the dead center
of the city, finding out and understanding. Well, this is
going to have me, for the first time in my life, gasping at
the dangerous bliss of being well and truly and ultimately
possessed, I suppose. I wonder what the protocol de-
mands of me in the stroking of such a beast, and the tast-

ing of it. One thing men can never get enough of: absolute worship. Or shall I stay put and quietly admire? Gee, but it's good to be here.

"Boise, so much of love intensely relies on the visual. Yet what is love but feeling? I've heard love called many things." He was loosening her clothing, kissing her around the ears and neck. "Some people say love is simply a need not to feel lonely, or a way of making up for something lost. Something *lost* . . . But to me, love is nothing more than a very wonderful way for two people to share an emotion." He guided her hand to him, helped her arouse him. "Love is . . . love is not an escape, as some people might think. Love . . . is . . . the most central . . . thing . . . in the world. Everything else is an escape from *love*." Holding her, slowly spinning her around, with this wild low-rent grin on his face. "An escape from sharing. We can share as friends or as strangers. I've noticed that." Slow now, close, kissing, and the hand there again. Well. "I've noticed it, but . . . Boise . . . strangers can be friends . . . can't they? Oh, I'm going to slowstroke you now, very gently, and I want you to tell me how it feels." Steering her to the bed, expertly moving, holding, delighting, and stripping her. Laughing a little. Earning his fee.

"I want you to tell me how it feels," he repeated as he tongued her, moving up on her like a quilt on a winter night, on a rhythm all his own, first puppying and then igniting her—yet all of this was tender—and arranging her and idling with her, and "I want you to tell me how it feels" again, but Boise tells him nothing, so he concentrates on his work for a while. Still, just before he sets to quickening her up, he says, "Tell me, at least, what you want me to be," and Boise says, "Kind."

It's a cliché. But that doesn't make the wish any the less worthy.

At home, Tanqueray in hand on the terrace (tea seemed rather too facetious for her state of mind just then), Boise toyed with the idea of telling Jack, my rich husband, about her date.

Absurd fantasy! Don't hurt him. Just divorce him.

No complications. For an ideal life, the older you get, the slimmer your schedule becomes. No complications. Worry is for the young.

Impulsively, Boise called Ruth Ann. Just to say hello, just to chance a few minutes in the real world where women love and work instead of going on two-thousand-dollar dates. Just to share some of Ruth Ann's burden, the chores of commiseration and custody that she had taken on. What is love but feeling?

Everyone is fine, Ruth Ann told her. She sounded brisk and content. Is something wrong over at Boise's? She seems nervy or something.

No, Boise is fine. She's always nervy. What about the little boy and his hot dog shop?

Oh, Ruth Ann starts in. Oh, and Boise hears her weeping as she tells a smiling story. Oh, so much feeling to be shared in the world. So much family all over the place — Ruth Ann, already, a wife and mother. Boise can remember when Ruth Ann was only a niece.

Back with the gin on the terrace, Boise recalls her own family. She left all that behind her — the culture that fills and binds you, elates and chokes you, with its ever-erupting passions of manly jealousy and insecurity, its whore-or-saint gender mentality, its worship of ignorance and intolerance simply because they are traditional.

What an impudent little number I must have been. Whatever offended me, I got rid of.

Life is too short, she likes to say; she was saying it at seventeen, as she waved behind to her neighborhood accent and inner-city manners and loser-class notions, like so many minor devils. Magazines, television, the movies, and streets of uptown—all this was her college, her finishing school. How easy it is to learn if you only trouble to observe. Don't just inhabit the world: watch how it works. Somewhere on the way to here, Boise crossed paths with Irene, two slickers negotiating their rises to glory. Each recognized the other as a kind of double. They became confidential, collaborative. They gave advice. Irene did, anyway.

And Boise took it: such as Irene's suggestion that marrying a rather pleasant and implausibly wealthy man "makes everything so much *swifter* in the long view of it all." True enough; and Boise prided herself on making sudden and very crucial decisions simply because they felt right at the time. She liked to live on the blade of possibility, to snatch at a chance and deal what it got her, good or poor.

That way, she felt, one could never be diminished.

She wondered what her life would have been like if she had married someone like Cliff, married not in order to make the scene but out of compassion.

Or Harlan, Kathleen's husband, whom one would marry, Boise supposed, out of need for supervision and protection.

Or John, whom one would marry for ecstasy. But one did not marry John, as a rule.

She wondered a great deal that evening: for instance, how much sharing of feeling was one entitled to, especially at the age of fifty-six? We are nearing the end of an epic, you know; one takes a last full look at one's cover. This is Review City. How quick are we? How sharable?

"Aren't you cold?" Jack asked her, coming out onto the terrace. "It was rather pleasant on the street. But there's always a wind up out here."

He looked at her smiling, waiting for an answer. Boise shrugged.

"Well, anyway," he said, loosening his tie. Elsie brought him his nightly drink, Jack Daniels on the rocks, so routine, so corny, so like a husband. So like mine, anyway. When I met him he had a boyish streak, remember that?, something about the way his eyes blinked, the way he would turn suddenly at a noise, a laugh, the opening of a door, like a child who wants to be on intimate terms with the entire world. Now he is gray, soft, slow, and happy.

"I brought you something," he said. "A present. It's so big and strange, I don't know where we'll put it, but . . . well, come on and see it. I left it in the living room."

As she passes him, he stops her, one hand light on her waist, still smiling, and, gray and happy as he is, he kisses her softly on the forehead. What is he, now, my father? Yet she accepts the gesture, then grabs for him, holds on tight, squeezes him, even, tries to squeeze some boyish out of the old man, and he says "Hey!" with appreciation, in a teddy bear's growl.

She steps back and he holds her by the shoulders. "Well," he says, after a bit. "You're in a unique mood."

Wrong, she is always unique and always moody. She is Boise the Great, a New York character seeking a resolution of some kind—whether she likes it or not—in the city whose stories never end. But I'll tell you what she likes. She likes a man who is generous and sweet. She is pretty damn sure of that now.

"They were tearing down another building and selling off everything they found inside," he explains, steering her into the living room. "The usual city jazz around here, you know . . . getting rid of everything that was, replacing it with a new version. Anyway, I saw all these huge dolls lying there, laid out on the street like corpses after a military raid. I thought if I bought one, it would be like . . . bringing it back to life, saving it somehow —"

Sitting on the sofa, almost as big as a man, was a marionette dressed as a medieval knight, his strings tangled and one hand shattered.

"Nobody seemed to want them, any of them at all, and I figured . . . well, we've got so much room here. Couldn't we give it a home?" He was laughing. "Maybe he'll entertain at your next party."

It was Rinaldo.

"It just seemed criminal to let him be thrown out, this warrior, this . . . gallant. I mean, who knows what tales he could tell, eh?"

Rinaldo. Something *lost.* Hello to all that.

"Did I do right, sweetheart?" His arm around her, giving her a little shake. "How come you're so quiet?"

He stared at her, his eyes all bunched up and his lower lip thrust out to mimic her.

"Boise's in a grump," he says.

Precisely in tune after all these years, they reached for each other, held on close, and kissed, and made love — for the first time in several months — in the living room, mostly on the couch next to Rinaldo. It takes great strength to love well, great strength and a sharp sense of timing. Afterward, they lay together motionless for a few minutes, a tangle of open clothing and wet hair.

"What would you like me to be?" Boise murmurs.

"Immortal," he says.

Off in the kitchen, Elsie does a bungle and drops something crashing to the floor. Jack turns at the sound, the way he used to turn to look and find out when Boise first knew him. Suddenly, he seems to be something, well, sacred and even desperate. I don't think she'll divorce him after all. Maybe next year, two years, ten years later. Maybe never.

Because too much resolution is not a good thing.

Because the routine, in people we love, is a blessing, especially if they are generous and sweet.

And because life is too short.

Don't you think so, too?

Have a nice day.